Baked In Seattle

a novel
by

Shaw Sander

For my children, always

"Flapping your arms can be flying."
---Robert K. Hall
1966

"'There are going to be times,' says Kesey, 'when we can't wait for somebody.
Now, you're either on the bus or you're off the bus. If you're on the bus, and you
get left behind, then you'll find it again. If you're off the bus in the first place---
then it won't make a damn.'"
---Ken Kesey
"The Electric Kool-Aid Acid Test"
Tom Wolfe

"I do my thing and you do your thing. I am not in this world to live up to your
expectations. And you are not in this world to live up to mine. You are you, and I
am I, and if by chance we find each other, it's beautiful. If not, it can't be helped."
---Fritz Perls
1969

Chapter One

"Jesus, Liza and Cher, he's cuter than a basket of babies!" Drake trilled, waving at a blond hunk on the Pride Foundation float.

We picnicked on the curb in front of the Broadway Funeral Home watching dancing truckloads of queens gyrate to blaring disco. Drake shook his head.

"This parade is always such a *hayride*. I remember San Francisco…"

He wistfully trailed off, his palm against his unshaven cheek, having this well-worn conversation with himself. I watched him do the entire loop, get it out of his system.

He blinked a few times and waved his hand back and forth, brushing it off.

"Well, there's just no comparison. Why do I stay in Seattle? Please tell me one more time, darling."

"Because I'm here, for one," I replied, beginning our shared shorthand against recurring restlessness. "Because Top Pot Donuts is within walking distance of your Queen Anne one-bedroom and because this is the year you will find true love right under your nose. Shall I go on?"

"No. I think he *saw* me. Look, is he waving at me?"

Malcolm had once told me men believe strippers were looking at *them* and Drake seemed to think so in this case. The blond guy might be a sex-worker for all the clothing he didn't have on, grinding and thrusting in front of us.

"Of *course,* he is, Drake. Hey, there's Shelly!" I cried, calling my NA friend over to join us.

Drake sounded like a perfect husband, my straight friend Birgitta insisted, "except for the gay thing," which seemed to her a minor detail worth the sacrifice. I kept telling her he was a snappy dresser, a great conversationalist and understood my neuroses. I could tell him about being afraid of ending up living under a bridge, fatalistic like my elderly mother who worried volcanic Mount Rainier would tsunami Zenith Marina and swallow my house. Drake knew I kept an open bag of cat food on the floor, accessible in case I never made it home so the cats didn't starve to death before anyone realized I was missing. But I didn't want to marry him.

Actually, *both* Drake and I longed for Saturdays at Home Depot with our own tall tower of testosterone. We, Drake and I, would imagine dawdling over new appliances while our heroes found repair effluvia for handyman projects. Our job would be to hold the flashlight, keep the butch company, obligated to hang around "in case." Implicit was the other job: keep the kids away. The alpha's role was to know the right repair gizmo's name and application; the beta's was to hover nearby, offering beer and a big sandwich. Afterward, utter gratitude was expressed. I was tired of being superwoman, struggling to make my 1920's cottage and previous-decade Subaru chug along. I wanted to be the "girl," as my friend Malcolm said, and phrased differently, so did Drake.

Drake wasn't the yin to my yang but he was hella fun to hang around with until Mr. Right came along.

"S'up, chiquita," Shelly hollered, suddenly all over me, pumped for Pride Day with five strands of multi-colored beads around her neck. She kissed a surprised Drake on the cheek. They had never met but what the hell, it was a big gay holiday.

"You're the office guy Al talks about from the Ban Roll-On Building, right?" Shell boomed, a big voice in a tiny little body.

Drake nodded, his eyes stuck on Shelly's abundant cleavage even after she'd plunged back into the crowd.

"Excuse me for being so blunt, darling," Drake managed as Shelly flounced away, "but her bosom looks like a double-pack of sourdough rounds. Now, does size matter in this case? Do those make her more *popular* with the girls?"

Born Mishellina Maria Annarosa de la Cruz in Michoacan, Mexico, Shelly grokked my deeper secrets from the flip side. Like me, Shelly fell just as easily for men and women.

Finding similars was a rare experience. As members of this secretive breed, our Chimera personalities were never fully comfortable in either world. We got shit from both sides. Dykes obsessed you'd leave them for a man and most men made the switch miserable by bragging about their own virility at satisfying a dyke.

I met Shell in Narcotics Anonymous, me there to placate my decade-sober girlfriend Angel. Shell was lovers with Angel's friend Brady. Both love relationships ended but Shelly and me, we stayed tight. She was my heart.

She'd come up to me after my first meeting.

"You said in your share that you need a place to store some stuff," she'd said, shaking my hand. "I'm Shelly, got two years clean. I've got a small storage space in my apartment building that I don't use. You're welcome to it."

I said I'd take her up on that, being new in town and not knowing anyone but my girlfriend Angel.

Tears suddenly glistened in Shelly's eyes.

"Really? Just like that? Holy cow," she coughed, trying to cover her emotional response. "Gimme a sec."

I had no idea what she could be choked up about.

"Want some water or something?" I asked.

I felt uncomfortable, wondering if I'd made a mistake having anything to do with her.

"No, no, I'm fine," she said, touching my arm in a warm gesture that made me relax. Her oiled dark hair and the tears in her eyes were glittering in the buzzing sodium vapor streetlight.

"It's just....just that no one ever trusted me with their stuff before. I'm a junkie, recovering of course, but you know? To say you'd leave your stuff with me and trust that it would still be there next day, next month, I mean...wow. Keep coming back, it works, huh?"

Her pretty brown face dissolved in laughter.

"C'mon," I said, taking her tiny, delicate elbow. "Let's go get some coffee before they throw it out."

"Better, how about we go out." It was a statement, not a question. She gently steered me away from the meeting and we began walking I could use a new friend and you're just the right kind of chiquita."

Her eyes, no longer teary, were dancing with what she suspected about me.

"Both ways, no? Kiki. I could tell. Let's get some chocolate cake, too. I've been starving for sugar all day."

I'd always been a lipstick lesbian, too femme for the Chicago butches where I came out. There weren't many of us in the early 80's, Midwestern butch and femme morphed rigidly into short-haired separatist butch. Other kiki women were a rare find for friendships, especially outside of the Sunshine people I used to know.

I wanted to shop for feminine shoes, eager to shed the clunky Nikes of lesbianism. I didn't care that the running shoe craze began after a memorable Fire Island summer decades ago, I felt like a clod hopper in them. I was drawn to flip flips with spangles, Keds, sling backs with bows. I wanted alligator pumps and a partner who appreciated my great legs in them. Was that too much to ask?

Soon after I met Shelly, my final yelling match with Angel left me angrily buying a spite house.

"Fuck you," I'd yelled, enraged with vindictive competitiveness. "I'll get my *own* place!"

12-step programs taught me not to make huge commitments in the heat of a flaming breakup but the moment I bought the little house in Zenith the property values climbed. Leaving Angel was the best thing that ever happened to me.

Best besides my two kids, of course, my perfect storms of swirling DNA, Dupree and Penelope. My Dew and Peanut grew to become sleek, daring people, showing we had *all* survived the horror of separation when they were very small. It had been my only hope and it came true. We'd endured the chasm of distance and time and come scathed out the other side. Is there such a word without 'un' in front of it, like franchised without 'dis'?

We were scathed but alive, still love-strong.

Almost everyone feels the same thing, ironically proving us all very similar but I was *different* as a kid, never fit in. I never thought kid stuff was funny---clowns, people in character costumes, games, books. My face never cracked a smile, puzzled by why this was considered amusing or appropriate for anyone at all and disappointed that other kids fell for it.

I stayed a loner, writing in a spiral notebook, reading novels and women's liberation critiques. My loosely-grouped family called me a writer though they never read a thing. I kept my words under lock and key.

In my 20's, hair stiff with Tenax, I danced at the Swan Club on Chicago's Clark Street, wearing myself thin with lesbian heartbreak and dysfunction.

The big fist fight with Cora's butch crumbled my foundation, my energy flaming out after that. Losing Cora had almost killed me. I'd loved her with an ache for years, since Fawn Camp.

Then I met Joe.

I mistook Joe's quiet for independent strength, his calm demeanor for rationality. I was hungry for babies, for love, for social strokes. Joe came with a huge Catholic rosy-cheeked huggie family with Sunday dinner and family pictures that wanted to include me.

Me! How lucky was that!

By the time our first child came along, the in-laws' tentacled culture required dinner *every* Sunday, daily drop-in visits mandatory with lavish gifts a bartering wedge. A new washer-dryer set meant a month of being grateful. Cash pushed into my palm "on the QT" forced me to curtsey in proper wolf pack belly-show.

They were a closed system, clannish as Gypsies or Mafioso. No apartment, job, car, appliance, furniture or real estate could possibly be exchanged without a relative involved in the transaction. Life plans, relocation, vacations, leisure time and employment were all discussed as an extended family. Considering the whole was more important than individual need.

The promise of West Coast relocation after he finished school evaporated. Turned out he couldn't move away from this family, the beast too big to buck. Joe graduated college and took a local job, deciding we would stay within visiting range of his parents, dashing my Left Coast hopes.

I had not miraculously regained my figure after two pregnancies in three years. The exhaustion made me broody, the second child's miserable discomfort complicating childcare so I stopped working.

Joe stayed up nights doing the housework I hadn't finished and took the children to his parents for days at a time overnight, staying there himself as well. He took Peanut for her first baby shoes without me and played video games for hours with Dew.

Dew felt every nuance of his parents' simmering discontent and being the good boy and eldest, he took on the weight of our issues, trying to cheer us both out of it, forcing us together. He'd pull both our hands and place them on top one another, hoping we'd touch in earnest. He learned to quiet his sister so Mommy and Daddy wouldn't be mad, telling her "See, Peanut, the squash is good, yummy, eat it all up, then we'll help Mommy with the dishes." It broke my heart, poor three-year-old little man.

I dressed Dew as a little Superman for Halloween, his red and blue pajamas emblazoned with the big S logo. We were going trick-or-treating in his first Halloween ever, the red wagon ready to pull him around our own block.

Joe got furious.

"No way is he going to ride around *this* neighborhood! There's perverts in the inner city. What if someone gives him a razor blade? It's too close to Irving Park Road. You're packing him into the car and taking him to my parents' house this minute."

Tears of rage filled my eyes, my hormones racing with huge natural enhancement. I alone knew I was three weeks pregnant with our second child. I hated Joe at that moment for ruining my first Mommy Halloween experience.

Dew looked frightened as the emotional climate shifted. He really just wanted to get ready for bed. He was in his pajamas but we were going outside. It confused him, and now Daddy was mad and Mommy was crying.

I'd seduced Joe, hoping for another baby. In the surprise ambush, my urgent animal desire to procreate shoved his dick inside me before he could think and I'd ridden hard and fast.

"You need to find a good method of birth control," he'd growled next day. "We can't take any more chances. We can't afford another baby right now."

A moot point, I thought to myself.

Joe stayed angry at me until the pregnancy took a serious turn, suddenly high risk with dehydration, early labor, blood pressure worries. I spent months on bedrest. The six-month ultrasound I went to alone showed a girl and when I brought the long shiny paper sleeve of grainy utero pictures home, Joe tenderly made love to me.

I was giving him a perfect little matched set of children.

Maybe he'd really love me this time.

The Pee Wee Herman show helped us get through the scalding August Penelope was born. Peanut's uneasy demeanor reflected our own marriage as she screamed for hours, her body rigid against car seat straps, Snugglis, carriers. To get her in her bucket seat, I waited until her screaming paused for an intake of breath, then bent her rigid body at the hips. Little socks, then specially made mitts, went on her hands to keep her from clawing her own face. I'd nurse her on the couch while Dew sat in his fuzzy blue baby-sized Chairie, a buppie in each hand and one in his mouth.

Sometimes Dew would yank Peanut's buppie out of her little rosebud lips and plop it in his own mouth. I'd look imploringly at him as Peanut would begin to wail, but Dew would hiss "Mine!" through teeth clenched around the buppie.

I couldn't really blame him. The dynamic had shifted from solo ruler to shared kingdom. He was only a year and a half old.

Peanut learned to talk watching "The Wizard of Oz," which she insisted on doing at least once a day, her little mouth moving along with every bit of dialogue, her voice singing every song. Sitting on her knees, her legs would splay out impossibly double-jointed behind and beside her, each foot pointed outward, her ass on the floor. A buppie stayed ready, massaged between her thumb and forefinger, waiting for a dialogue lull so she could pop it back into her mouth.

Joe insisted my spending habits---diapers by the carload, formula, baby clothes---were breaking us so I got a receptionist job, arranging daycare in a flurry and paying the babysitter three quarters of my salary. Dinner was thrown together with cranky, overtired children hanging on my nylon-ed legs, the silence deafening between Joe and me.

I had to leave before I drowned, suffocating in the anaerobic environment. I got in my Subaru and started driving. As the family sucked my babies away, threatening legal action, I felt all the stuffing just taken right out of me.

The Sun-Times Building disappearing in my rear view had made leaving Chicago real. Six travel days later I'd seen The Seattle Post-Intelligencer's neon-eagle globe and it gave me new hope: E.B. White, my writing hero, had (badly) worked there.

Searching the newspaper classifieds for employment, I howled in grief for my children and my sanity down on the waterfront, watching the huge neon P-I globe revolve, the setting sun turning the Olympic Mountains and Mount Rainer pink, then, peach then orange before dark.

I took a job at Wildrose on Pike, cooking weekend nights for $3.50 an hour plus tips until I could find something more substantial.

My new life *had* to begin regardless of how shattered I felt. I had to make a second home for the children and bravely carry on. We would live through this, dammit, and remain intact.

Seattle and my dear friends saved my life.

A good therapist put me on Prozac immediately and let me weep for my children, lost to a wave of Midwestern wagon-circling. A feminist pro bono lawyer got me shared custody with big chunks of time and liberal visitation. But it was my friends who knew that though less than optimal, Far-away Mommy was way better than Suicide Mommy. They kept me on the planet each in their own way, Angel, Drake, Shelly Birgitta and Malcolm. When I met Angel, she soon became alarmed at my plunging depression and stuck me in her NA meetings for free therapy. Shelly appeared, an apparition of laughter and skinny-junkie joy, thrilled to meet me, another "byke" like herself. That alone gave me reason to go on. Through work I found Drake, Birgitta appeared soon after at daycare and Malcolm's restaurant was on my route.

Despite his vocalized abhorrence of minors, Drake listened to me weep over my long-distance babes, comforted me often and said the right thing. Drake bought his particular refrigerator because magnets would not stick to it, thus politely escaping the display of friends' baby and pet pictures. So as to travel on a moment's notice, Drake wouldn't be responsible for even a plant but he'd sent Dew a tee-shirt from the Oscar Wilde Memorial Bookstore in Manhattan. He'd given fashion advice to both children ("ascots *never* go out of style"), encouraged their wide reading lists, recommended Broadway shows and MoMA exhibits and acted as bon vivant uncle.

I didn't believe he disliked children as much as he claimed after he dressed up one year as Santa when the kids were little and came to my house.

I'd twisted Joe's arm to let me have Dew and Peanut for the holiday, borrowed the airfare and flew both of them to Seattle on Christmas Day, the moment peak season at my FedEx job ended. That night Drake walked down our lane ringing loud Christmas bells, yelling "Ho Ho ho! Mer-ry Christmas!" Single-digit Peanut and Dew stood stock-still, their eyes as big as dinner plates.

Drake looked every inch the Jolly Fellow, though perhaps getting too much into the dress-up spirit. While the outfit met all the requirements, I'd never realized Santa was so *fashionable*.

His cheeks bore angled slashes of two-tone glitter rouge highlights while his eyes were darkly mascara-ed, lined and shadowed behind multi-colored Bartell's reading glasses. I had to admit Drake's lace up Doc Martens made perfect Santa footwear. Beneath the crimson crushed velvet suit were the premium Capitol Hill-made Pac-Feather goose-down pillows usually encased in embroidered silk on his Bon Marche pillow-top mattress. Santa's thick black belt looked suspiciously like Drake's antique leather razor strop decorative bathroom wall-hanging while his gloves were the softest charcoal cashmere-lined kid-skin from Nordstrom. I recognized them as retail therapy after his dating disaster with the former porn star.

The cape was a bit over the top but the children loved it. Santa swirled in a red blaze, Peanut's eyes envious of the twirling radius.

"You like it?" Santa cooed, bending down to let them touch the satin lining. "Many tiny elves no bigger than Disney mice worked on this velvety beauty all night long, their little feet running in circles to make the stitches. I *wish* you could have seen it."

Both kids were entranced as he dragged a huge sack of pre-arranged presents to my comfiest chair. Dew's face was a wonder of conflict, certain this must be an imposter but sure he ought to keep quiet for his little sister's benefit. Peanut stayed mute and finally after much poking Dew became their spokesperson, their Santa liaison, translating his sister to Santa.

The whole scene was priceless and he swirled out as fast as he'd come in. Drake arrived as himself for dinner 10 minutes later in street clothes. I never forgot Drake's kindness at going so far out of his way.

Drake was truly a gorgeous man but he thought he was too fat, ceaselessly going to the gym and referred to himself as Shamu. An overeducated receptionist at a downtown law firm, he was the company pampered pet, their mascot, the spoke around which the entire water-cooler company culture hub revolved, the planning committee for every luncheon, shower, birthday, event and award ceremony. His bowties were as legendary as his witty group emails. Forgetting to CC everyone firm-wide once resulted in a paralegal sobbing in the bathroom, fearing she had been dropped from the inner circle.

When I wanted to remember a gay icon's name, when "Cabaret" was on t.v. or I'd see a reference to Topo Gigio, Neely O'Hara or Barnabas Collins, I'd call Drake.

Shelly pulled me through many times as well.

Glomming on to me at that first NA meeting, she showed me where the coffee was and said that if one hypothetically took home just a few extra packets of SweetNLow per meeting, one might hypothetically stock one's pantry for free. Coffee was the only reason she was there, she said, as we chain-smoked outside, waiting for the meeting to be over.

If I wanted to remember how insane lesbian love triangles were, I'd get Shell to tell me one of her stories of back-alley fights with butches going at it over her. Or how she got flowers from two lovers, one of each gender, for Valentine's Day. I told her about the butch in Chicago who had haunted my relationship with Cora, flattened my tires, stolen my license plate, calling and hanging up fifty times a day, the restraining order on file.

Shelly distracted me when I was sobbing over my children so far away, howling with primal grief that was endless, trying to get my mind off Peanut angry or miserable or lonely on the phone, a five-year-old's raw pain undeniable. Shelly told me I'd be alright after Dew explained his new favorite song: "It's about a little boy whose mother is leaving on a jet plane and she doesn't know when she's coming back again."

She'd stroke my hair and tell me of the flowers in her Mexican childhood, the blind fawn that ate out of her hand or her mother's hot flour tortillas so smooth they'd melt buttery into the tongue. If I was still inert with paralyzing sorrow, she'd move on to her using escapades.

Heroin had fogged her world for a long time. She'd hitch-hiked backwards, naked, on the Aurora Bridge one night, getting picked up by Seattle's most famous rap icon who appreciated her big butt. After much sexual romping, he'd helped her get clean the first time.

There was a series of stories where she'd drink until she blacked out and had woken up in parts unknown, far from the apple orchards of Wenatchee where her family picked fruit or her adopted Seattle. The tipping point was the time she found herself one bright morning in a hotel room alone with three hundred dollars cash on the nightstand. She had no clue what the fuck she'd done to "earn" those crisp hundreds and from looking out the window she couldn't tell where she was. Picking up the hotel phone, Shelly asked the front desk what bus line she needed to get down town. When she didn't recognize the names of the streets the operator was mentioning, Shelly swore in Spanish and stopped her.

"No, no, mamacita, listen to me, how do I get downtown Seattle on the *bus*?" she insisted, sure the operator misunderstood her.

There was a very long pause.

"Ma'am, you'd have to call Greyhound," said the concierge.

"What? Where the hell am I?" Shelly demanded, the black-out getting even more alarming.

"Why, you're in Houston, ma'am."

That was the last time Shelly had a drink or drug.

" 'Flashdance' was on last night," I told Drake as I unloaded FedEx boxes in front of his desk. "Did you know that Phil Ramone directed the music and Jerry Bruckheimer produced that thing?"

Drake knew I was a complete "Law&Order" fiend, loving all things Bruckheimer.

"Omigod, I haven't seen that in years. 'Going on a manhunt, indeed'. That little thing with the big eyes? Jennifer somebody…" Drake trailed off.

"Beals. Jennifer Beals. She went to Francis Parker, the rich kid school in Chicago."

"What are you doing this weekend, darling? You and Shell going to that 12-step lesbian rodeo?"

"Round-Up, Drake, they're called AA Round-Ups. And no. I'm sitting this one out. I have a date with a nice biker butch from the Madison Beach meeting. She's taking me for a Sunday ride on her Harley."

"I'm thinking about trying the tea dance at the Timberline Sunday afternoon. Does that make me an old queen?" He sighed and made a face.

"If you were an old queen, you'd go to The Eagle."

"Thank you, Al. I feel much better."

"I'm working tomorrow. Forced labor. Mandatory overtime. Sometimes I hate this job. I should have gone to college."

"Yes, darling, you *should* have because then you'd have a degree and get *ahead* in life," Drake said, spreading his arms like Carol Merrill, gesturing at his front desk area. "Like *me*. My English degree from the UW got me this glamorous receptionist job. At least with FedEx you get flight benefits and a free on-the-job workout."

FedEx had given me flight benefits to see the children, a 401K, a down payment on my house, a strong sense of self and a high-paying job, even if it was back-breaking and fraught with time-definite terror. I drove a diesel-spewing Grumman through downtown Seattle and though my bones hurt, Fred Smith's big company had factored into the equation anchoring my life. I was grateful.

That had been one of the therapist's ideas: find a job to enable me to see my children, despite geographic distance. I hadn't wanted to be a flight attendant and cargo handling and customer service paid crap. FedEx was the way to go. I used those flight benefits to see Peanut and Dew at least every two months.

Working a blue-collar job gave me access to the belly of every downtown Seattle building. My work-world was loading docks with huge screaming trash compactors, beeping trucks backing into precariously tight spots, men hollering and jousting for position. There were a few women but testosterone still reigned supreme in this world of four-wheel dollies, pallets full of shrink-wrapped freight, grimy dark cinder-block walls, diamond-plate freight elevators wearing quilted interior jackets and unceasing ear-splitting noise. Every surface was dotted with tobacco spit, footprints, crude graffiti, and hand-printed Magic Marker signs on torn cardboard ("NO holding frieght elavator").

But once inside the quiet building interiors, I'd find people like Drake, his position requiring him to sign for my deliveries. He'd brightened the first time we met when I'd commented that his fountain pen matched his bowtie.

"Well, sweetie, your eyes match your entire uniform."

"Which is why I chose FedEx over UPS. Gotta look good."

"What else *matters*, darling? I'm Drake, and you are…?"

He'd held out his manicured hand.

"I'm AnnaLee," I'd said, "but my friends call me Al for short."

"Al. Pity. AnnaLee is such a lovely old-fashioned name. Wasn't that the name of …?"

I was used to this.

"The woman in The Band's song 'The Weight'?"

"I was going for a more literary approach," Drake had smiled. "The original nymphet that Humbert Humbert fixated on as a child."

"Ah, Nabokov. Haven't read him in years. I think you might be right. Or maybe her name was like the Poe poem."

"That's Anna*belle* Lee. Not the same at *all.*"

"And nothing like that magic land where Puff went."

"Right. That was Honalee."

"And then there's the French movie."

"No," I smiled, "I'm nothing like Amalie."

"You're the new courier on my route?"

He pronounced it "root."

"Roger that. Every day, oh lucky man, you get to see me."

"Well, this will be *much* better than that enormous gal we used to have or the one who looked like she'd just escaped from Purdy."

"The heavy gal just got fired. Teresa does have the post-prison look, doesn't she?"

"She needs a better support garment."

"Drake, this is going to be the highlight of my day from now on," I said, grinning at his witty assessments. I couldn't imagine how he'd sum me up in a few words to someone else.

"Then honey, you need more excitement in your life."

A gift from the Norse gods, Birgitte got nudged into my reality by her twins. They both fixated on Peanut at Nursery Rhymes Daycare the first summer the children spent with me in Seattle. Birgitte's boys Sam and Adam had insisted on a playdate outside of day school.

By the end of the first hour at Shilshole Beach, Birgitte and I were already penciling in our next get-together, a friendship fast forming over our small children. Dew was instructing the younger children in making a rocky sand castle and we'd seen a few Herschels in the water, the pesky sea lions heading for the Ballard fish ladder to eat spawning salmon.

"Here I'm totally straight and I've never been married. The kids' dad was…nobody. Just some guy. I never even told him I was pregnant. It's not fair that you've been married and you're a lesbian," she'd snorted after we'd exchanged abbreviated biographies in the upfront Seattle way.

Birgitta's Scandinavian father gave her white-blond hair while her brown eyes smoldered with her Italian mother's looks.

"I'm not a card-carrying dyke. They took away my toaster and rescinded my membership since I'm on that slippery bisexual slope. I don't get the emails anymore," I grinned. "I'm more of a byke. Kinda both at the same time. Identified with the girls but still capable of loving everyone."

"Lucky you. It doubles your chance of a date on Saturday night. I'm hoping this guy Kyle starts to get serious. He drinks a little but nothing to worry about. He's good to the boys. I'm tired of all the polite dating and being *on*."

"That's much easier with women, I admit. But the break-ups are harder. More emotional."

"Having kids, though, that's the real focus. I give the boys all my energy. When does that end, do you think?"

"Maybe when they're….thirty," I laughed, trying to envision a time when DuPree and Penelope, patiently gathering stones for the sandy structure, wouldn't be my total center.

"Mom, play that song again about the boy," Dew asked. "please?"

He smiled at me when I looked in the rearview mirror. Dew and Peanut took up the entire back, double car seats crowding the Subaru.

It was the first summer they came to Seattle, Peanut in diapers and Dew still prone to sneaking his sister's buppies away then sucking the pacifier himself for a while

"What boy?"

"The one she's in love with."

"Okay," I said, pushing in the cassette of Trisha Yearwood. Dew began tapping the tops of his little Superman sneakers together and singing along. Peanut was looking out the window, buppie firmly in her mouth. Her pale skin showed eyes ringed with dark red circles, her tell-tale sign of being tired.

"Now play the other one."

"Which one?" I asked, already knowing the answer. This was our new ritual, our new joke.

" 'About The Weather.'" Dew's face grinned at me as we waited at Denny and John for the light to change. It was the first word pun Dew understood, loving 10,000 Maniacs' hit, 'About The Weather' and turning it into a Who's-On-First routine.

"Okay, that's what it's about but what's its name?"

"It's 'About The Weather.'"

"I know what it's about but what's its name?"

"Mom!"

I smiled back at him in the mirror and reached back to pat both their chubby legs.

"Hey look, Mom, there's the Space Needle!" Dew yelled as we started down the steep hill toward my first apartment with Angel.

"Pace Neo!" Peanut shouted through her pacifier, pointing her sticky finger.

"When's it gonna take off, Mom?" Dew asked thoughtfully. I explained again that it wasn't an alien ship but a building built for the World's Fair.

"Just around the riverbend…" Peanut began to sing to herself, her brain a rotating file of Disney animated movie soundtracks plus the entire Wizard of Oz dialogue and score.

"What should we make for dinner?" I asked, relieved the day was over, happy to be trundling them home from Nursery Rhymes.

"Dick's!" Dew shouted and Peanut chorused in.

"Fine with me," I smiled, turning around and heading back to Broadway. We'd take something home for Angel.

I was raised a stoner in the Sunshine Tribe. It was part of the rituals at vespers, holy days, festivals and daily life rhythm. When I retired from FedEx, I told myself, I'd light up a doobie on my front porch. I just felt better when I'm high, everything suddenly taking a deep breath and then smiling out a contented sigh. Got the creative juice flowing, too, interior wheels within wheels, information flooding in Leroy Niemann-color swirls to the surface, layered with sensation and deep longing. Add music and time turned inward, remembering the trippy foggy day I first heard "Love, Reign O'er Me" or that time I felt like I was floating in my '75 Corolla to "Solsbury Hill."

The Fabulous Furry Freak Brothers were right: dope will get you through times of no money better than money will get you through times of no dope.

Malcolm always said cruise control was an impaired driver's friend but on weed I'd never felt stupid or dull at the wheel. And I sure liked doing housework when I was high---smoke a bowl, put on some tunes, start washing the dishes and next thing I'd be scrubbing the wax off the bathroom floor on my hands and knees, happy as a lark. The few times I'd been stoned around my kids I was exceptionally patient, more relaxed and a helluva lot more fun.

But all that 12-stepping gave me the other slant and because of my job I had to "think the drink through." It wouldn't be worth losing my job over weed. Work now, reefer later.

Drake and Birgitte had both fled Bible-thumping hinterlands in Eastern Washington, Birgitte to work the fishing boats in Alaska and Drake to quietly find other gays at Seattle's UW. They had had dope in their high schools but never pursued it as seriously as I did.

Drake's family was a centuries-old Spokane-founding name and he lived quietly so as not to sully the family reputation. Buying a Janis Joplin album at 15 nearly got him thrown out of his mother's house. Birgitte was a good girl until she went to Alaska for a few years then showed up in Seattle six months gone and tight-lipped about paternity.

Malcolm, he smoked up whenever he liked, stepping into the restaurant's walk-in cooler for a hit. Everyone just attributed his aloof gaze to innate cool since he's a six-foot ripped black man.

But weed would have to wait.

Chapter Two

"How about we cruise down Madison and then wind our way around Lake Washington for a while?" Diane suggested, handing me the black spare helmet.

We'd kissed hello, my heart pounding enough to frighten me a little. Solid-built with a husky voice, Diane was a hot butch who'd just gotten out of a long relationship and I wanted a crack at her. Shelly had called me with the inside dope, Diane's partner weeping copiously in the Capital Hill Thursday night meeting that it was over, that their commitment ceremony plans had put so much pressure on them they'd caved.

Now the warm August breeze was perfect for a bike ride and here I was with this prize. Pick me, pick me, my heart kept leaping up.

I wanted sex, frankly, since a relationship with Diane might be a bit much to bear. Diane was a women's community pillar as owner of the lesbian totem store, Lavendar Labrys. Lesbian-in-a-box, I called it. Whatever lesbianism required was for sale there. One stop shopping for Everydyke, there were wide leather belts, dream-catchers, Melody Beattie books, key chain dangles, sage smudge sticks, decorative flashlights, Swiss Army Knives, signed Cris Williamson CD's, temporary tattoos, "Dykes To Watch Out For" and "Life In Hell" comic books, "Off Our Backs" and "On Our Backs," tool kits, camping gear, vibrators, dildo harnesses, dog collars, pocket combs, bumper stickers ("I've Seen You Naked At Michigan"), political lapel buttons ("Kate Millet for President"), Pat Califia porn, the free weekly with Dan Savage's column "Hey Faggot!," messenger bags and fanny packs. Enter simply curious and emerge an hour later on the street as---ta dah!---Power Lesbian.

Being a trailblazer seemed a heavy burden for Diane to bear. She always carried an expression of extreme concentration even as we got ready for the ride.

"Anything you want," I demurred, swinging onto the big cruising bike behind her, hoping I didn't weigh too much.

I held her waist, burying my nose in the leather smell of her shoulder as we zig-zagged around the park. She put her left hand back on my leg, holding my knee, driving me to distraction.

When we'd stopped down by the water, she shoved me against a big tree, her knee between my legs, leaning into my whole body, nearly making me come right there. She didn't touch me, just looked deep into my eyes.

"I want you," she whispered, holding my shirt tightly by the lapels. I swooned into her hard body in reply. "But I'm not ready. It's too soon. I promised my sponsor I wouldn't use sex to medicate my process. I've got a lot going on I'm trying to deal with."

Her lips were inches from mine.

"But...but...it wouldn't be, really." I had to think fast, sorting through AA-speak to tap into the right nerve. It wasn't 13th-stepping since I was no newbie. "It would be an emotional release with a trusted friend."

"*I'd* know, though, and I hate secrets. Maybe later we can connect. Like Holly Near says: maybe if it happens once, it can happen twice. C'mon," she said, pulling my shirt front down and smoothing it gently into place. "Let's take you home, pretty girl, before I change my mind."

"How was the date with Motorcycle Irene?" Drake asked over nachos at Jalisco on Queen Anne. I still missed the one off 15th on Capitol Hill. The waiter there had remembered what I liked every time.

"Her name's Diane. It certainly didn't go far enough for my taste. She makes my knees weak."

"Is it the power, Al? I mean, she does own Lavendar Labrys. Or is it the bike?"

"Both. And her long fingers."

"Tomorrow is my second date with Thai Guy."

"Doesn't he have a name?"

"That's his screen name—ThaiGuy. His real name's Eddy."

"What are the knowns?"

"That he's slender and too young for me. He owns apricot labradoodles and he seems to have money. Not firm on that yet." "Here's hoping, darling," I cooed, "maybe by next year you'll be lavishly taken care of and have a chocolate cocka-poo of your own, and you can go out on walks together in coordinated outfits. He'll make Thai noodles and you'll bask adoringly at him. That will be your entire job." "Sounds ideal. The law firm grates on me sometimes. Honestly, it's like herding cats." Drake sighed and swirled his gin and tonic. "We'll have a little winter place in Fort Lauderdale, too, with his mother. He talks about his mother rather a lot. She'll adjust her nipples poking through her skimpy halter top so they're even. God, the old women down there with the leather tans and the white shorts. Ugh. Oh, did I tell you? I'm going to Mexico in the spring. I'm taking a week's vacation and I'm going to Mexico City to see the art museums and swaddle myself in a glamorous hotel. There's a little resort place I found in Queer Adventures where they do a wrap in heated grape leaves for weight loss, then it's a hot stone massage while your fortune is told with chicken bones or something."

"Sounds ideal for you. And it's near the gay bars, of course?"

I knew the answer to this, since Drake traveled to be gay. Never a joiner, bar hound, dancer or theatre volunteer, he was the most isolated faggot I'd ever met. Independent of anything remotely "gay," he was satisfied with foreign film, books, and his Judy Garland records, gay all by himself in his little apartment. Twice a year he ventured out, flying thousands of miles to Paris, London, Athens, Rome or Rio to be gay, gay, gay in a two-week flurry of friendly or rented indigenous peoples. He hadn't had a steady lover since AIDS was called GRID.

"Well, there are three within a four miles radius. It's all in the central downtown area, very walk-able. I'll bring you a little Mexican tchotchke, Al."

"I have Mishellina so she's all the Mexican tchotchke I need. Spend your money on a cab. I worry about you walking around down there looking like an easy mark."

"You, Miss Jean Brodie, worry too much."

"How was the date with Thai Guy?"

"I'm not seeing him anymore. Now it's a trust-fund baby named Fred who has a place on Lake Washington or so his emails say. I haven't met him yet. Very hairy-chested too, which you know makes me crazy."

"What happened with Thai Guy?"

"Well, we had dinner at Wild Ginger and he was…less than fascinating after fifteen minutes. And do you remember I said he talks about his mother a lot?"

"And his labradoodles."

"The dogs I could tolerate. But when he said his mother makes his *underwear*, well, that was it for me."

"His underwear? Holy shit, how do you even *make* underwear, and what the hell is his mother doing making it for him? He's what, thirty-five?"

"Precisely. Something wrong there. *Next.*"

The Timberline country gay bar was a Lincoln-log lodge on the corner of Denny and Westlake, a scruffy industrial neighborhood of run-down warehouses. The area was fast becoming a glittering, upscale area with condos and a Whole Foods under construction.

An adequate dancer, I only got by at two-stepping because Angel had patiently taught me for months. Others were sensationally versatile, able to lead or follow while I was strictly a femme, following whoever held my hand.

Longing to be on the floor with the tough, smooth dancers like Diane, I'd ache, seeing them completely in control. I liked watching the dangerous-looking butches who had a little meanness in them.

One of them was Babs, a prominent AA lesbian, who had announced at the Madison Beach meeting that she was moving out of state. A huge going-away party was declared, the Timberline was rented out, a DJ chosen, and the log cabin was decorated with streamers and a huge sign wishing Babs well. Because she had entered the program so long ago she'd been underage, she knew everyone who was anyone, making the party the social event of the season.

I decided to give her *myself* as my going-away gift, figuratively speaking, dressing just for her that night. I thought about bringing Drake but I decided I didn't want to go with anyone just in case Babs *really* liked my ensemble.

Since dressing up to a Seattle lesbian is to iron one's jeans, I risked extreme couture to get her attention. A good femme comes complete with sewing machine so black velvet was cut and fitted with 18-inch corset stays. When finished, my mini-dress zippered on in skintight, strapless, sweetheart-neckline perfection. The hem was eight inches above my knee, the décolletage eight inches below my shoulders. I looked like a black hourglass, cleavage poppin' fresh to bursting.

I found black over-the-elbow gloves, seamed black thigh-high stockings and since it was a cowboy bar, wore my black cowboy boots. Around my neck was a string of innocent white pearls while smoky dark eye makeup made my intentions clear. Grabbing a little metallic clutch, I was ready to go.

A shock wave fluttered through the plaid-shirt crowd as I paid my cover and walked to the dance floor rail. My cheeks burned with the shameful excitement of being so openly provocative, but I acted regal, bestowing my greetings on wide-eyed friends.

Slowly I made my way to the guest of honor, her back to me seated at a table of laughing women. I stood still beside her, mentally willing her to notice me.

"Wow!" Babs exclaimed, leaping from her stool and knocking it into the railing, her eyes all over me. Her fair skin turned brilliant pink.

"This is for you," I whispered, leaning in, my lips inches from her studded ear. "This is my gift to you."

"I'm honored," she huskily replied, pulling me close in a sudden, tight embrace so strong I ached to bed her. We then awkwardly stood apart while balled lightning, I was sure, crackled visibly between us.

Babs' lover moved in closer, her jaw locked tight. Sensing danger, I moved along to the bar.

Nursing cranberry juice, I found a table at the dance floor's periphery just before the lights went down. A spotlight appeared on the bare wood floor, and the dj stopped the music, wishing Babs a happy journey and saying this was her day, her moment. Someone pushed her into the searching spotlight and we all applauded her for taking this big step to move away.

"This next dance is for Babs," the DJ said, "so she and the dance partner of her choice will be the only ones on the floor for this number."

Without the slightest hesitation Babs and the spotlight moved purposefully toward me.

Her boots echoed on the polished wood as the buzz of the crowd in the cavernous bar fell silent. Stopping directly in front of me, her open palm beckoned me onto the floor with her, her lover be damned.

My legs shakily raised my ass off the stool and as I reached for her hand, the entire bar went wild with applause. She had completely bitten my double-dare.

Her strong arm locked onto my waist, pulling closer as we stood waiting for the music before she gently but firmly sailed me through three of the most glorious minutes of my life, colored spotlights swirling us along, couple number one alone on the huge polished dance floor. I never took my eyes off hers, wishing only for Babs to kiss me. Left arm held horizontal and high in classic two-step pose, her other warm hand gripped me as firmly as our steady gaze. Behind my waist her fingers ventured lower on my ass every time she reeled me in, pushing her fingers into my tailbone, pressing me tight to her pelvis. In that sliver of time there was more urgent insistent sex between us than I could have imagined possible while our feet double-timed in a glow of twirling light. Tongues of fire should have burst from the top of our heads, visible flame to our passion.

Maybe Babs could tell you the song but the blood was pounding so loudly in my ears I didn't hear a thing.

Music over, the place whooped, stomped and hollered. I curtsey-ed and she bowed in the middle of the open dance floor. Babs courteously walked me back to my table then let go of my hand with a little head nod.

The DJ announced the floor was open.

I sat the next few out, waiting for my legs to stop shaking, wishing I'd brought Drake after all.

Babs' lover never spoke to me again.

.

"Kyle just called," Birgitte was sobbing into the phone. "That fucker skipped his court date and was warning me that the cops might come by looking for him. He listed this as his address, that asshole. Al, he hasn't lived here since the boys were young."

They'd had a quiet wedding when the kids were six, and Kyle had been an upstanding husband for a while, working hard, adopting the kids, worshipping Birgitte. Something had shifted in the family dynamic and Kyle started drinking in earnest, staying out all night, wrecking a few cars. His easy-going manner slid away and he became instead a sneering, cynical master of manipulation, keeping Birgitte in a state of panic and self-doubt, trying desperately to change him. She'd had no interest in drinking with him; he had no interest in AA or therapy.

Kyle lost his job, then another, then another. Home alone all day, he began to sit in the basement and drink. Birgitte got a second job then divorced him when he back-handed her into the china cabinet in a drunken rage, purpling her left eye and requiring four stitches through her pale eyebrow.

His bouts with the police still haunted her, as did his terrible credit rating and her self-blame. She'd scraped together the impossible sum it took to buy him out of their house and he'd squandered it on a Harley and a year of drinking in Wenatchee with new skinhead friends.

"Don't get sucked into his bullshit, Gitta-girl. He just wants you to notice him. He wants attention. Don't give it to him by falling apart and letting him have the emotional power. Did you suggest AA again?"

"He's not ready to stop drinking," she sniffed, blowing her nose. "I'm about ready to go myself just to have people to talk to about it."

"Not a bad idea," I said, as it suddenly occurred to me. "But you'd probably do better in Al-anon, for friends and family of alkies. I know there's meeting by you in some Ballard church. I went to an NA meeting up there once. Want some info? I'll get it from Shelly. She knows everything. It might be helpful to settle some of the screaming voices in your head."

"Yeah, sure, get me specifics. That fucker. I *hate* it when he does this to me."

"I need to date men again," I told Malcolm over a hot-bacon dressing spinach salad at his restaurant, the Blue Canoe.

The croutons were garlic and thyme, fresh from the oven, while the greasy spinach leaves warmed my insides after slogging packages in the rain all morning. Lunchtime for FedEx drivers was around two, after deliveries were done and before pickups started. Malcolm was free to talk by then, too, his lunch rush over and managerial duties relaxed.

Today he looked stunning in a deep green Peter Max tie and black shirt with jade cufflinks. His hair was freshly shaved, the almost imperceptible fade perfect.

I'd had no idea I wanted to date men again but when the words just came falling out, I realized it was exactly true.

"Little girl," he said gently, rolling his toothpick to the right corner of his mouth, "if you want to date the fellas maybe we should have a talk. I could give you some advice, help grease the wheel, know what I'm sayin'? I mean, I don't wanna hurt your feelings and all but you might need some *schooling* on the subject."

"Talk on, brother. I'm open."

He smiled large and took a sip of his Jack and coffee. I envied the restaurant lifestyle, the drinking and drugs. I couldn't wait until I was done with FedEx and the fear of random testing.

"When's the last time you had a man?"

"Fucked one or had a relationship with one?"

He smiled again.

"*That's* why I like you," Malcolm said, patting my hand. "You all right, you know that? You just tell it like it is. I wish all women were like that. It'd make life a lot easier."

"That part of me you like? The up-front, brutally honest part? That's the part that's a dyke," I smiled back at him.

"Okay, well, keep that part, for sure, just…kinda….tuck it in for a while. Ease back, go gentle for a little bit. You want lessons? I mean, I could give you some, snag you a captain of industry. You could quit that fucking awful job…"

"This fucking awful job pays my mortgage," I stiffened. "And for this goddamn spinach salad at *your* restaurant."

"See? Right there. That look on your face when I said that? That hard edge you just got. Lesson number one. *Lose that shit.* Defensive and angry in a flash is completely non-productive. No second date after *that* comes roaring out. That shit shrinks my *balls,* girl."

"Okay, okay. I'm listening. I'll eat. You talk."

"Well, wouldn't you like to coast for a while? You've been a humping beast of burden for what…the kids are in college, right? And you got to Seattle when Miss Baby…what do you call her again?"

"Peanut."

"…you got here when Peanut was still in diapers? I'd say fifteen or so years now you've been schlepping freight around, and didn't you tell me last time we had lunch how much your knees hurt? And the rotator cuff thing, too. Your body could use a break. And I'm not even gonna start on how much you want to write. Wouldn't it be the *shit,* girl, to have a man bringing down the chump change while you sit your pretty ass on the couch and finish that Great American Novel?"

"But…"

Malcolm put up his hands, palms facing me.

"Hold up on the I Am Woman, Hear Me Roar speech. Don't you always talk about being a femme, how all you wanted was to stay home and have babies, make organic whole wheat bread and love your family? Is that bullshit or are you for true? Can you just relax and let someone else carry the ball for a while? You bitch about how you want off the treadmill, to finally have time to create, do your art without worrying about the bills. Why not let a man *in*, sister-girl? We can find you a good man who would worship the cloud we're gonna have you walking on, pay your bills, fuck you silly, meet your family and maybe even marry your ass. I can help." He paused, twinkling eyes flashing. "You game?"

Wrestling with my id, I stayed quiet, digesting.

Malcolm watched my wheels turning, rubbing his thumb against the tips of his fingers, eyebrows raised, challenging me to walk my talk.

Feminism and independent strength had taken me this far. Yet an arts sponsor to feather my nest while I create sounded great....while getting laid, too? Having a Saturday night date with a sharp-dressed man who loves me?

Oh, hell yes. Sign me up.

I smiled, giving him his answer.

"Lesson one, as I said. Put the claws away. No one's fighting you anymore. This isn't the streets of Chicago, this is The Love Boat, baby. You need to purr a little bit, pussycat. We're all on the same side. No more turf war."

I rolled my eyes but I was listening. He had a point. I was a little defensive. I remembered the AA definition of fear and realized it fit far too often: being afraid I will not get something I want or something I have will be taken away. Time to put that aside, feel the fear and walk right toward it, chin up.

But believing everything would be alright was not my strong suit. Drake and I called it "Our Bridge Syndrome," since we both had huge chasms of fear, open maws calling our name around every corner, the bottom surely about to drop out, leaving us destitute, homeless and living under a bridge.

"I had a bad weekend with OBS," he'd tell me on a Monday morning and I'd know he'd wrestled the devil fears, feeling fat, worthless, broke, floundering rootless and going nowhere but down.

"Change the thought direction," Malcolm continued, reading my mind. "Drop the serious, the fearful, and project nothing but zip-i-dee-doo-dah sunshine. Lemme tell you something, Al, when you walk into a room and smile, you light the whole place up, I swear. When you first came in here you were sunny as hell and smiled at me and I was hooked *instantly*. You do know how to work a room so concentrate on that part of AnnaLee. You are beautiful when you *feel* beautiful. Like Gil Scott-Heron said, baby girl: 'You can be so very beautiful when you are who you are.'"

"Okay. I'll try that."

"Put an ad on the internet. Then you can weed them out, pre-screen, pick and choose."

"No fucking *way*."

"Honey, I'll show you how to do it so it's completely safe. Lots of…what do you gals call them?…boundaries, like it's the wild fucking west. Safeguards. No one's going to hurt you. I'll be on speed dial, that's part of the safety plan, the 'Big Brother Watching.' No one's going to fuck with you if you're careful. It's not all Green River Killer out there. I met my wife online years ago and my cousin met her husband online, too. It's really an efficient way to date. I'll help you, girl."

I'd had a hippie childhood with the Sunshine People, full of androgynous role-switching. In the 70's we'd dismantled the hierarchy so my training had stressed Our Bodies, Our Selves, carpentry, auto shop and overthrowing oppressive patriarchal gender roles rather than deportment and feminine charms. Sex was a given in our world, without any of the bothersome courtship ritual. I'd never dated, been given flowers, played hard to get. I understood none of the unspoken rules others seemed to innately use to join the romantic slipstream.

Sometimes that had gotten me into dangerous situations. As a teen I had packed a pearl-handle knife to level the playing field.

In my next life I wanted to come back as a tall black man like Malcolm, I thought, watching him talk. Women's fears were embedded, ingrained. We remained ever vigilant, our eyes furtively scanning the scene for predators, walking at night in protective groups, nervous antelope at the twilit watering hole. We kept keys between fingers, ready at any moment for imminent danger. Malcolm never had to feel like gender-based prey.

He was telling me something, his face earnest. I hadn't really heard him.

"Did you hear me? I said grow your hair."

"Okay," I answered. "I'll grow my hair."

"You want…what is it you tell me they say in therapy? You want your outsides to match your insides."

"In other words, grow my mullet out so I don't look so much like a dyke anymore?"

"That, too," he smiled, and moved the toothpick with his tongue to the other side of his luscious mouth. "Men like long hair. They want to touch it, smell it, hang onto it when…" he leaned in closer "…when they're riding y'all from behind."

I blushed deep pink and set my fork down.

"Okay, I'll grow it out."

"And get some dresses. I'm gonna guess how many dresses you own: none."

"Wrong. I have one."

"One. And you bought it in 19…?"

"Okay, okay, I'll get a dress. Some dresses."

"Get one and see if it feels comfortable to you. You might like it. Might not. You shave your legs now? Armpits? Christ, I feel like a sleazy gym teacher or something. But seriously, I don't want to assume shit. Men like smooth these days, is all I'm sayin'. Smooth *everywhere*. Get me?"

"I'm picking up what you're putting down, brother," I smiled, not so shocked this time. Maybe men and women *could* be friends and speak directly.

"And you're gonna have to learn to play a little hard to get. Men like the challenge. Fucked up, I know, but it's true. Give them everything and they don't want it. They want to fight uphill like fucking salmon to spawn. Put them off for a while."

"But I want sex, too. They want it, I want it, what's the big deal?" I didn't see the benefit in not getting right to the point.

"But if you want sex with dinner and conversation and the promise of more dates in the future, you have to wait. No sex until the third or fourth date."

"Jesus. This sucks."

"The good news is they buy every time. Pay for everything."

"What? Why?"

It didn't sound fair to me.

"Because," he said, very seriously, "...they are paying for the pleasure of your company. That's jessa way it is. Always been, always will. The man pays, period."

I stayed quiet, not sure men would pay for my company without an immediate payback. The bar phone began to ring but he ignored it. Malcolm went on.

"You have to choose really carefully to even get to the first dinner date. Then you have to choose all over again, whether you really want to have a long-term interest in the guy. It's a *given* that he wants you. Let that be your baseline. Don't *even* sweat that. Everybody loves a big-titty woman, like Chris Rock says. And you're good-looking, interesting and very sexy. So from jump street they like you, you hear me?"

This warmed my insides. Having a handsome straight black man tell me I was attractive was wonderfully uplifting.

After downing the rest of his liquid lunch, he went on, lowering his voice even further.

"You, know AnnaLee, if I wasn't married, you and me, we'd be....we'd have taken care of business a long time ago, know what I'm sayin'? You have that It, that Something, so just use it. You'll do fine."

"You'll help me write the ad, too?"

"*You* the writer. You do that part. But I'll help with all the rest. And," he smiled and winked as he got up to answer the phone. "...the man always pays so I'ma be the first man to buy your lunch. I'm comping that salad."

The writer. Right.

If you counted long letters, unfinished stories, unspeakably personal narratives and unpublished manuscripts, I was a writer, sure. No one ever saw my work, they simply *believed* me, while I squirreled myself away for long periods, a full ashtray beside my right hand, caffeine glaze over my eyes, phone unanswered, the hour unimportant. I never let anyone I knew read my stuff. I had ended relationships over unauthorized reading of my work.

My road to hell was paved with rejection letters from magazines, agents, and free weeklies, all of whom sent the most ingratiating notes while turning me down. It felt after a while that they must think their recipients were on edge and potentially suicidal as their tone was magnificently, even tenderly apologetic, careful not to crush the writer's spirit. I could think of no other professional circumstance where such care was taken with rejection.

So a few-line personal ad? I could do that.

Strong 40-ish single woman desires playmate

No, too…butch.

Elegant woman of mystery needs daredevil companion

Way too over the top.

Seeking charm, wit and quality banter in a black 40-ish male

Too direct.

Billie Dee, where are you?

Idiotic on paper but I did wonder where his clone might be.

Silver fox looking for salt-n-pepper match

That sounded like Steve Martin.

I finally settled on describing myself a bit, asking for what I wanted, and threw in a political reference to snag a smart one. Adding three recent pictures of me smiling in my gladiola garden with a purple silk scarf around my neck, I carefully reviewed the snapshots. The new black silk dress clung close to show my assets and my hair had looked great that day, the silver Bonnie Raitt streak off to the left shining through my growing dyed-auburn hair. The wording was short, to the point, and had some brain-teaser value.

Marilyn's stats, Poundstone's humor and a hunger for man appreciative of both. Fin.sec. SWF seeks fin.sec. SBM for endless exploration. Old enough to know the revolution will not be televised.

I pushed Send, paid my monthly dating site fee and called Malcolm at the restaurant.

"I'm ready for my close-up, Mr. DeMille," I said when he answered.

"What?"

Drake would have gotten the reference.

"The personal ad. I submitted it. What the hell do I do now?"

"Sit back and watch the responses stack up, baby. Come in to the restaurant tomorrow and we'll talk safety and strategy."

"Deal."

"Proud of you, Al."

After the Capital Hill meeting, I asked Shell out for coffee, alone, so I could tell her I was going to start dating men again. She whooped with glee.

"Girl, that's great!"

"Why does this make you so happy, might I ask?"

"So I can live vicariously through you! I've been bogged down with Blake now for a while and I'm restless. I've been noticing men again and they're noticing me but I'm too comfortable to change anything."

"Still having sex?" Lesbian bed-death was a common occurrence, the domestic scene as sexless as the twin beds in "Eating Raoul."

"We…kinda do. Once in a while. But she turns me off."

Shelly looked away.

"Honey? What does that mean? Kinda?"

"It means I do her and then I fake it right away because I get so turned off…"

"What turns you off?"

Shelly's voice got low, and she looked down, swirling her wet cappuccino.

"She…Blake yells like a banshee when she comes. Like yippie-ki-yay! Whooping. The neighbors look at us funny."

"What?"

"I know. It's weird."

"No, no, I mean…."

"C'mon. I've slept with lots of girls and I've never heard it like this. Like kd lang. It turns me completely off," she frowned, steering me into a Tully's that had been a Seattle's Best Coffee. In Chicago SBC had been Stewart Brothers Coffee, confusing me when I moved to the coast. All Seattle coffee was great but I was partial to Tully's since the founder was starting a new business on my Twin Toasters West building route. He was always friendly and warm, not something many folks were to blue-collar folk, had the whitest teeth of anyone I'd ever seen and signed for his packages personally with a huge smile, telling me to just walk right into his office. So I liked Tully's.

I wasn't sure how I'd deal with it, either.

"Well, it doesn't matter all that much since it's rare we even have sex. I'll just listen to your stories and fantasize," she said.

"Are you sure this internet dating is a good idea, darling?" Drake worried, mentally running through every axe-murderer scenario possible.

"I'm tired of being alone. I'm tired of lesbians after Angel fucked me over. I want companionship and a date with dinner. Black men appeal to me, and I'd like to get serious with a fine upstanding black man if it's in the cards. I'll never know til I try. I'm not gonna date anyone from work and I'm not gonna go stand at 23rd and Cherry. Plus Malcolm's coaching me on safety."

"Why would you need coaching?"

"So I don't have to be scared. Because I never dated before, real dating, like everyone else did in high school but I skipped completely. He set up a whole array of safeguards so I can feel comfortable meeting these complete strangers. The man is a wealth of information."

"Like…?"

"Always leave time between contacts---no being rushed into anything. If I'm on the phone and we make a plan to meet, it is always a few days later. If he's in a hurry, red flag. Drop him."

"Okay. Makes sense."

"Always meet for the first time in the daytime. Always in a crowded public place. Coffee only. That way, I can skate in and out in ten minutes if he's awful or dangerous or grabby. No whole-meal dates until later."

"Makes complete sense."

"You'd be surprised how many men don't want to go along with these things. They want instant nighttime sex. A lot of them are married and this weeds them out, too. Red flag. No home phone number means they're married. Red flag, too. And no last name until I know them, no employment information, no telling them exactly where I live. No house calls. No riding in their car. Always meet with my own transportation."

"This guy's smart."

"He knows men. And lastly, no going on any date without first letting someone know where I am going, with whom, and when I expect to be back, calling at that time as well."

"Also good."

"You're it."

"What?"

"You're it," I told him. "You have been elected as the one I am going to call before and after. Malcolm's married so I can't go calling him at home. Shelly's lover Blake would flip out if I called there and described dates with men, especially black men since she's a fucking Mason County knuckle-dragging Neanderthal. And Birgitte is far from ready to hear about happy serial dating, since she's hating men in general and Kyle in particular."

"Well, I'm glad you thought of me *first*, Al," Drake sniffed, his feelings hurt at my practical analysis.

"You big queen, you know I'm crazy about you and there will never be a replacement. Besides, they are all too pedestrian to understand the ins and outs of such things anyway. I'd trust no one else."

"Well, if you put it that way.... maybe I'll watch and learn, maybe take out an ad of my own. I could use a Prince Charming myself. A white one for me but same concept. As long as it doesn't interfere with my trip to Mexico. Only a few more months. Mary Baker *Eddy*, I need to get away. This office job is like wrestling alligators in a K-Y pit."

"Men like the long hair," agreed my hairdresser, eager to get rid of my dated mullet. She'd thrown a plastic apron over me and snapped it behind my neck, twisting the paper into the collar. "We'll give it some layers as it grows out. Men don't understand layers. Anything that's shoulder-length or longer is long to them so we'll keep it manageable as it grows out. How long have you had it...feathered like this?"

"Since God was a baby. Make it different. I'm tired of looking like a dyke."

She'd grinned at me in the mirror, holding my hair tips out to measure by feel.

"My own private research has shown that people wear the hairstyle that reflects their prime. If they were a cheerleader or a football star, they still wear their hair the way they did then, no matter how old they are now. People get stuck."

"You might be on to something there."

When the children were small, I'd read everything I could get my hands on about being a non-custodial mother.

Imprint them with smell and voice repetition, the books said and tell them you love them over and over. Don't make promises, just stay genuine. Use terms like "a different day" rather than being time-specific. Don't criticize the other parent.

I wore White Shoulders perfume, stuck with it for almost 20 years and asked for it every Mother's Day to further bond the fragrance to their mother-memory. Each time we spoke on the phone, I told them: "I have two things to tell you. One, I love you very much and two, you are very important to me."

Soon I could say "One, two" and they'd repeat it back to me in a sing-song voice, "I love you very much and you're very important to me." When we were together I'd show them two fingers, first the index popping up then the middle finger to make two and they'd nod.

I'd started a non-custodial mothering group but the other stories were so horrific, so sad I couldn't bear to hear them. Most of the other women never got to see their kids at all, or were involved in hopeless, exorbitant legal battles that had stretched for years. The meetings became a forum to air pain that had no reconciliation and hearing them made me feel wretched for my low-level good fortune. I stopped answering calls for a while, removed my name from the phone tree and hugged Dew and Peanut even tighter. I was "lucky" their daddy agreed on visitation that seemed to work. Summers and holidays with me, school years with him. I flew in for parent-teacher conference and the kids and I did homework over the phone almost every night.

Joe would measure Peanut before Halloween as she'd agonize over what to be, the measurements sent to me with her request for the year's costume: a cocker spaniel, a harlequin-ed court jester with a three-corner belled hat, or a princess bride. Dew would read me his essays, patiently explain elementary school football plays for the hundredth time and regularly fall asleep with the phone to his ear while I read him Ferdinand the Bull, The Visitors Who Came To Stay, or Uncle What-Is-It-Is-Coming-To-Visit.

We'd cope through the school year in short visits and live for the end of June when SeaTac Airport would deliver them back to my arms. My jubilant Unaccompanied Minors would be towing a stern flight attendant demanding my identification, despite both children already wrapped prehensile around my legs.

We'd weathered their adolescence, Peanut with huge circles of kohl eye makeup, a cigarette dangling from pierced lip between her hennaed ringed fingers, Dew reading Vonnegut, playing football and going to the prom in a Cole Haan suit with a florescent lime green tie. Now they were at college, making adult decisions, finding their balance, thinking about careers.

I finally switched fragrances to one that smelled like Bakir and no longer had to find a partner who could parent. I had the house all to myself now. They had lived to 18 and beyond so I could breathe a little, enjoy myself.

Both kids now were tickled and happy for fresh interesting blood in the family. They'd been amply schooled in diversity when they were coming up, marching as we did with the lesbian mothers in the Pride Parade. Besides learning camping and fishing from Angel, Shelly had taught them a little Spanish and her lover Blake had taken Dew to the macho action flicks I hated. Malcolm had shown Dew how to shoot a rifle and Peanut how to play spoons, and Drake had given them worldly advice on fashion, books and the ugliness of ignorance.

"I was always proud," Peanut told me, "that my mom was different."

"If whoever you pick is anything like Malcolm," Dew said, "he'll be totally cool."

Chapter Three

Since Shelly drove for DHL, I often saw her downtown. We'd squeal, hug and try to fit in a coffee break, though that was rare. Usually we were too deep in the time-terror crunch used universally by freight companies against hourly employees.

Our livelihood depended on pissing clear so it made sense to stay sober and clean. Shelly and I went to AA or NA meetings once in a while to show face, keep an eye on the peers and gossip. We also got the best free group therapy ever invented though we weren't crazy about all the players at the gay AA Alano Club, a huge yellow Victorian house in Capital Hill.

Some of the dykes were cool, like Diane and Babs, but some were loony as bedbugs.

Anna droned on and on about her landlord issues, her victimized rant setting everyone's teeth on edge for months. Diane's ex-lover was a cryer and always seemed to have "a burning desire" to speak at meeting's end, prolonging closure another ten minutes. Reed, who had bad facial tics, had been committed to a mental hospital, locked up for being gay as a teenager by Jehovah's Witness parents. Etta had been in a car accident, her frequent non-sequiturs and rush to anger displaying her real cognitive damage.

Some of the worst cases fit in every meeting the Alano Club hosted---AA, OA, NA, GA, OCDA, Alanon, Adult Children of Alcoholics, Codependent No More, Inner Child Tuesdays, Bradshaw Study Group Meetings, Shop-aholics, Sexual Abuse Recovery, Incest Survivors. At meetings they'd be functioning at a crisis level, in tears despite rugged street personas.

Over lunch one day our commercial vehicles sat at the curb next to each other, me in Shelly's passenger seat. Shelly began talking about people she detested but with whom she had to remain cordial, like the fucked-up Alano Club dykes who dissed her for being bi.

"Or the assholes on route," I said, another favorite subject since we delivered freight to many of the same places. "Do you ever go to that little building just down the street from Regence? Top floor, some architect's office?"

"Yup, I was there last week," Shelly said, taking another forkful of salad. "Man, the bleu cheese really makes this thing. Wanna try it?"

She held a fork toward me.

I nodded and opened my mouth, leaning toward her. As she fed me pine nuts and romaine, her own mouth opened watching me, like mine had done when I'd fed my children.

"Isn't he a dick, that receptionist guy?" she said as I chewed. "He called me stupid last time I was there and I was pissed. I reported him to my boss but that went nowhere since Mr. Personality had already called DHL to complain about *me*. I got a letter in my file over it, too. Bastard."

"It *is* a good salad. He has that little dog, you know? Bit my ankle and then the guy gets pissed at me when I kick the thing away. He called FedEx, too, and complained about me. Closet case." I was finished with my sandwich and flipped through the Time magazine Shelly had on her front seat.

"I need this job and he knows it so I have to hold my tongue and just take it. Closet-case maricon motherfucker," Shelly spat.

"Don't you wish there was some passive-aggressive way to get back at people like that without repercussions? Like the whiners at the meeting? Or that asshole?"

The magazine opened to a Special Edition Barbie Doll, wearing a black skin-tight cocktail dress with the taffeta pouf at the calf. When I was a little girl, Fawn Camp had debated over whether to have Barbie dolls or not, and finally agreed, dressing them in home sewn coveralls. I'd coveted that black dress.

"Look at this," I said, showing Shelly the full-page ad. "We had this doll. Man, I wonder what they're worth now. Mine would be worthless even if I had it since the tits got smashed in. We threw her off the barn roof playing Supergirl."

"Lemme see that," Shelly said, pulling the perforated tear-out order form out of the magazine. "I think I am just about to be *brilliant*."

She studied the little square sheet and grinned menacingly at me, her eyes twinkly with barely contained glee.

"That guy. The one we hate. I've got it."

My dating career began in earnest following all the rules Malcolm had prescribed. After a while, it became second- nature to control the interaction with time, place, limits and first right of refusal. These cautious constraints made a smooth journey from first sip of lunchtime coffee to first time in bed.

And Malcolm had been right. The replies rolled in like clockwork, the pile growing larger every day. I didn't know Seattle *had* that many men of color. There seemed to be hundreds of black men out there hearing my clarion call. I weeded them out online, over the phone and then with coffee.

Though in the back of my mind I would have liked a serious partner, I wanted to have a little fun. I missed sex which with lesbians had been spotty at best. Suddenly there were available men everywhere who were interested in me. It was an emotionally starved woman's dream. Three nights a week, if I wanted, I had a date, dinner out or an evening at home rolling in some daddy's arms. It was incredible how efficient the game of dinner to sex could become, getting to the point faster via the internet. Men had to lay out their pedigree, their portfolio and their ability to charm before they even got an email out of me.

Condoms were employed to keep everything cool.

Every time I'd call Drake before leaving and every time I'd call him that night or next day to report all the juicy details. I spent a whole winter regaling him with my bawdy tales.

The guy on Lake Washington had humiliated Drake at a party in front of other snobby rich men so Drake was focusing on a younger man from Portland.

"He thinks I'm dreamy," Drake reported after they'd talked on the phone all week. "That's the word he used. Am I ready to be adored as The Older Stable Man?"

"You are dreamy, darling. He's right. Stable? Maybe not so much."

"Oh, thanks a lot, Miss Conventional. Speaking of stable, how's the rotating stable of studs going? Found Mr. Right?"

"Nope. Having hella fun, though. I think I might prefer serial dating to marriage. I am certainly eating well."

"There's the thing about being The Older Man," Drake began, dropping 'stable' from the mix. "I am expected to be the paying sugar daddy. That's what *I'm* looking for and here comes this kid looking at me like my receptionist job is gonna pay his college loans? I need a facial and a microderm abrasion, honey. I feel ancient."

"Just be up front about the money. Long distance alone is costing you a fortune. And then you're going to meet, yes?"

"This weekend. He's coming here. I'm terrified. What if I hate him or worse, think he's boring? Or ugly? What if he doesn't like me?"

"That's why I have coffee with these fools first, then dinner....out of state dating is rather...rushed...as far as progression goes, simply by geographic challenge. I don't envy you there. But you boys do it differently, anyway."

"Has he gotten anything yet?"

"I don't think so."

Shelly and I were parked next to each other, our trucks along the back wall of Dick's in the alley. We munched Deluxe burgers, double orders of hand cut greasy fries and chocolate shakes. Dick's Drive-In on Broadway had been the first place Angel had taken me when I'd moved to Seattle and the first place I had taken the children when they'd arrived that summer for our first visit.

A tradition had soon taken effect, with the rear door of my Subaru wagon open and all of us hanging out the back, throwing fries to the pigeons and watching the Broadway freak show pass by. Peanut refused to eat the pre-made burgers unless I scraped all the "icky stuff" off, pulling at the inside of the bun to remove even the ketchup stain before she'd touch it. She liked her food "plain" like I had as a child. Dew always ordered a strawberry shake, his love of strawberry in place since infancy. Every December birthday he'd want fresh strawberries and I'd searched everywhere until I found them, paying any price.

We all loved the Dick's experience. Shelly and I met there for lunch when our routes overlapped.

"I can't wait to see his face when the shit starts rolling in, mamacita. He's such a Type-A personality, he's gonna completely go loco."

Shelly was grinning, congratulating herself on her vindictive idea. I had stood back in wonder at its magnificence, following her instructions at Bulldog News. We'd discreetly pulled out every single tear-away sheet for every subscription and purchase we could find. Marking the "Bill Me Later" box, we'd ordered Mr. Personality with the ankle-biting doggie everything we came across.

Anytime now they'd start to arrive.

Heirloom dolls, Marine Corps electric trains, John Wayne commemorative plates, Ronald Reagan beer steins, Oreck vacuums, plastic hamster Habitrails, a bird-chirping-chime clock, a talking map of the fifty states, a deluxe satin sewing basket, ceramic lifelike newborn babies, zoysia grass, Amaryllis bulbs, Holly Hobby ragdolls, white calfskin leather Bibles with gold page-holders, Precious Moments keepsakes, cubic zirconium bracelets, Princess Diana dolls, Velcro bras, cat calendars, bronzed baby shoes and a Mario Andretti slow cooker were all being sent to his office.

Interest cards were procured for him for the NRA, both WWFs, Shaklee, Amway, The Pride Foundation, NAMBLA, NOW, VFW, American Legion, Masons, Oddfellows and Rebekahs, Jerry Falwell's True Believer's Circle, The Jewish Defense League, The Southern Christian Leadership Conference and the Full Gospel Businessmen's Association.

This jackass who griped about our services and begrudgingly signed our delivery logs would get Esquire, Vogue, Newsweek, Lithuanian Ladies' Monthly, the Catholic Digest, Business Leader, Wall Street Journal, Time, MS., National Geographic, Men's Health, WWD, Reader's Digest, Tiger Beat, Seventeen, Elle, Cosmopolitan, The New York Times, The New Yorker, Mother Earth News, Redbook, Jugs, Bodacious Ta-Tas, Nothing But Skin, Atlantic Monthly, Pussy-licious, Ebony, Blue Boy, Cooking Light, Nickelodeon, Crosswords and Puzzles, Buns of Steel, Playboy, Maxim, Hustler and Playgirl.

The poor man had been secretly signed up to contribute on a regular basis to The Ocean Conservation Fund, both the Republican and Democratic parties, Save the Children, NARAL, the Fireman's Find, The Benevolent Policeman's Association and both The Sons of the Confederacy and The Southern Poverty Law Center.

We couldn't wait to see him go apoplectic over the flood of incoming goods. Fortunately, all the shit due to hit his fan was ordered postal service so Shelly and I were neither suspect nor impacted, unless, of course, we were busted for mail fraud.

"How's the manhunt going?" Shelly smiled, waiting for details.

I told her the latest tale, of the white guy whose email response made me laugh so hard I actually went out for coffee with him. His tag line was: "I'm Jewish and my ex-wife's half black---does that count?" I had to give him props for trying.

"Guess what I saw on LOGO last night," I said, taking a huge gulp of my chocolate shake. "Vonnegut's 'Slaughterhouse Five.' Haven't seen it in years. Man, Valerie Perrine had gorgeous tits. But you know the funny thing?"

"Whazzat, mamacita?"

"Holly Near is in it. She plays Billy Pilgrim's daughter Barbara."

"No shit?"

"No shit. Hair all up in a 'do, wearing tight dresses and horn rim glasses. Her face looked really round."

"Miss 'Gentle, Angry People' in a tight dress? Miss 'Nina' in hornrims?"

Shelly began to sing "Hay Una Mujer Desaparaceda."

"Yup. Man, I loved her stuff. I still have a Fire In the Rain cassette somewhere."

"Did I ever tell you, chica, I went to Carnegie Hall to see Meg Christian and Cris Williamson?"

"Hell, no, you never told me that! What was it like?"

"A sea of tuxedos and lavender cummerbunds."

"How did a downtrodden oppressed lesbian former fruit picker such as yourself ever get to Carnegie Hall?"

"Practice, girl. Practice," Shelly grinned, waggling her fingers as if on a piano keyboard. She burst out laughing as I made a face. "No, for real. My first lover was a white woman from the family who hired my family. She got me special treatment on the job then got me out of the fields altogether. We became lovers, she turned me on to all the lesbian music. Gave me Lesbian/Woman, Rubyfruit and all that. She got the tickets as a surprise. I'd never been on an airplane."

"What a fucking great story!"

"It was heaven. I'd never seen that many lesbians before. I thought Claire and I were the only two in the world. She loaned me the money to get the hell out and on my own. But anyway."

"You told me about her before but you never mentioned going to New York."

"It was a trip, for sure. The concert was awesome and seeing the other lesbians was an eye opener. An endless waterfall of dykes, filling up and spilling over. There were so many fat women there. I'd never seen so many women taking up so much space." Shelly giggled. "Did you ever hear the circus joke about the fat lady marrying the midget? They get married and all the circus people crowd around their tent at night to try and peek in to see them having sex. They can't imagine it, since she's so fat and he's a midget. So they finally get a spot where they can peek in and they see the midget jumping up and down all over the fat lady, hollering 'Acres and acres and it's all mine!'"

"Nice. You are full of surprises, Shell. I think I've heard all your stories and then you pull another one out of your phenomenal brain. No wonder I love you."

"Okay, okay, mamacita. Don't go all mushy-homo on me. Back to work," Shelly said, looking at her watch then wiping her hands on her pants. "My pickups are already heavy."

Birgitte sipped her tea over Sunday brunch, a rare treat we were indulging. She lived north of downtown between Ballard and Fremont, and I was way the hell south so getting together was a luxury.

"I hate it that you're having so much fun while I'm dealing with this lunatic ex-husband. We are never in the same place at the same time."

Birgitte stirred more lemon into her brew and looked out at the incredibly grey drizzle. She continued her melancholy rant.

"I can't believe it's almost Thanksgiving already. I never even got any summer, I was so twisted up with this idiot."

"If we were in the same place at the same time, we wouldn't be able to be there for each other," I insisted, hoping it was the right thing to say. "Divorce is always fucked up even when it's theoretically cordial."

Poor Birgitte had a maniac on her hands, a wild man careening in every direction at once. She'd changed the locks, installed a security system, gotten a restraining order. Her eyes were always looking around and she'd become understandably jumpy.

I tried to speak softly.

"Maybe you could move?"

"I refuse to sell the house and disappear just because *he's* an asshole."

"Good for you, then. Stick to your guns."

"I think I'm gonna go back to school."

"Gitta, that's a wonderful idea. Very strong and focused. Have you thought about Alanon anymore? Shelly says to tell you there's meetings everywhere."

"Hey, I *went.* I found out they were at that church just down from the Troll and I nerved up and went."

"That's great! How was it?"

"Every single woman there…it was all women…they were all singing my song. It was Kyle to the 10th power. He's everywhere."

"Did they say anything helpful?"

"Yup. I'll go again. Let's see…what was it? 'We felt too shameful to let anyone else know, and too fearful of disappointment to take the chance of being let down' or something like that. I also heard that I didn't cause Kyle's drinking and I can't fix it, either. That stuck in my head. I like that idea. I guess I always felt responsible somehow."

"That's how he wanted you to feel. It gives him power."

"Do you know what he told me?" Birgitte said quietly, looking out the window again, her eyes filling with tears.

"Oh, Gitta, don't cry, please."

"He said I would end up a skinny old maid and never find someone to love me."

I started laughing and apologized through my choking.

"I'm sorry, sorry, I'm not laughing at you."

I took her hand across the table. I felt a few eyes on us, or rather, on her.

"Gitta, darling, you are so fucking hot and so smart, you will find *hundreds* of people to love you if you want them. Don't believe a word of that shit, baby doll. That's why I laughed, since it is so ludicrous. He has you wrapped so tight, you can't see what everyone else sees. Kyle sees it, too, and it's very threatening to him."

"Sees what?" she sniffed, blowing her nose. She wasn't ready yet to believe me, still holding back, a little hurt at my laughter.

"He really beat you down, honey. Look up, Birgitte. Look around this room. Slowly. Notice the men cruising you. Hell, even those dykes over there noticed you but they can't figure out if we're together so they don't want to step on my toes by looking too much if I'm your butch. You are a treasure, honey, pure pleasure on the eyes and then you're smart besides. Kyle was terrified that you'd realize how precious you are and that you wouldn't need him. That motherfucker knows what a thing of beauty he threw away over drinking. He's just trying to take you down with him. Keep going to those meetings, babe. They'll help a lot. You're doing great. Now tell me, how're the twins?"

"I put in for a new job," Malcolm told me, sliding into the booth as I tucked into my Chinese chicken salad. "In Anchorage."

"What? How can you leave me?" I asked, setting down my fork.

What would I do without this pretty man to dream about? His restaurant was on my favorites list and his advice had gotten me acclimated toward the other side of my byke world.

Men were now drawn to me like magnets everywhere I went. I swore they could smell other men's scent on me and wanted to mark me with theirs, which Malcolm said was completely true. I felt primal, as if there was a hidden prehistoric sub-script of male and female to which my genetic material urgently had to respond.

"It's a long shot so it prolly won't happen," he assured me. "But the wife wants a change and I could use one myself. Thought I'd apply and see what happens. Roll the dice."

"But who's gonna guide me along?" I teased, trying to cover my devastation with kittenish big eyes.

Friends this true-hearted weren't easy to find in middle age. He was a straight man with whom I could be honest who gave me unvarnished straight-guy advice. How rare was that?

"Go on, girl, you got it now," he smiled. "You are leaving me in the *dust,* man. Been on five dates a week for three months now? Lessee, that's..." he appeared to be adding in his head, his eyes rolled upward and face arranged in a thoughtful pose. "...a lot. It gives my brain lots of pornographic material to replay when...when the time is right. I like living vicariously through you."

"You and everyone else. Get brave and get out there yourself, if you want. I don't understand why you aren't polyamorous."

"I'm married, Al. Bernie can't hack the jealousy. We tried some shit like that. I jerk off a lot. I look at cyber-sex. I read things. But I stay within the legal bounds, know what I'm sayin'? I'm not looking for anyone."

His eyes burned brightly, staring at me.

"But...what if you *weren't* looking and it found you anyway?" I asked point-blank, my face expressionless as my heart pounded.

"Well, then. It would depend on the circumstances."

His thumb started rubbing his fingertips, as if he was thinking of something dastardly. As if he was rubbing a nipple between them. It made me squirm.

"I have a perfect wife. She's a lady on the street and a whore in bed. And I have made her do some nasty shit..." Malcolm looked away, staring at the bar.

"Do you regret doing that?"

"Sometimes. But sex is in the brain, I discovered, not in actual place and time, so she doesn't have to go through that anymore for me to experience it in my head. Understand?"

"Yes, I do indeed."

I was having sex in my brain at that very moment.

"I don't do that shit to Bernie anymore, either, because I don't want her all wrapped around the axle. And because good shit is harder for her to remember than bad shit."

"What do you mean?"

I started eating my chicken salad again, the sex over for me once he started talking about his wife. She was a real person, a woman like me, and I didn't like her on the receiving end of anything humiliating or bad, either. I didn't know her but she deserved dignity, too, just like every woman.

I sighed, going in my brain from fucking her husband on top of the bar like a wild animal to female solidarity in under three minutes. Goddamn Sunshine upbringing.

"Everyone has good shit that happens to them. Birthday presents and kisses and congratulations over good things, right? But there can be that one traumatic event, one horrible, scary thing and it could have happened when they were three fucking years old. But that one bad thing stands out bigger than all the good things all put together and that one bad thing shadows everything they do, everything they choose for the rest of their fucking life. They spend hours in therapy trying to exorcise that one bad thing because bad things imprint more strongly on the brain. Our neurons just burn the shit into the cells."

He made a searing noise with a sharp intake of breath through his teeth, pointing at his eyes. Boys and butch dykes make sound effects, I thought. I'd tried and always sounded stupid. Malcolm continued, audio illustration over.

"Burning the brain, burning it behind the eyeballs so everything the eyes see is now through the filter of that one bad thing. No one says 'Oh, I like cupcakes because I had a good experience with them when I was three.' If you said that people'd think you're fuckin' crazy. But if you say 'Oh, I'm scared of dogs because I had a bad dog experience when I was three,' everyone nods and understands. The bad experience is bigger than the good experience and burns its way into the brain. Cupcakes don't get burned into the brain."

"Agreed. And well put. You speak so *well*," I grinned. Malcolm had turned me on to Chris Rock, who parodied white folks amazed at Colin Powell's grasp of English.

"Fuck you," Malcolm smiled.

"Oh, now, don't go starting something you can't finish."

"Oh, I could *finish* it, AnnaLee, don't you worry. And I've got technique," he said, leaning in close across the table "…since I ain't got no gi-normous dick like the motherfuckers *you've* been finding. Men with the big dicks don't need technique. Now, average guys like me---and I'm not ashamed of it, just honest, 'cause I'm average size, you know, I've looked in the showers and all---average guys like me, we need technique. I've got the *moves,* baby."

"I'm sure you do, Malcolm. Lemme know if you change your mind."

Thanksgiving was around the corner. I wanted to make a little dinner with Drake but Drake wanted to stay home and study, he said, for the first test in the Teaching English Abroad Program. He'd signed up at Seattle Central, sure that his ticket out was a teaching job in the Mediterranean where he could cruise hairy-chested men and get paid for it.

"You can study the other three days, just come over this one day, please? You could invite the new boyfriend."

"Oh, all right. But the boyfriend's history. He's simply too young. He has *roommates,* for god's sake. But you always do make a delicious spread. Can we have apple pie, please, Mother May I?"

I laughed and thought of the childhood game, my favorite being Umbrella Steps. Mother, may I take three Umbrella Steps? Permission granted, I'd pirouette with my hands over my head, fingertips touching.

"I'll bring 'Love! Valour! Compassion!' I got that this week and 'Breakfast on Pluto.'"

"Bring them both."

Shelly called me, her voice crazy with glee saying the first shipments had begun to arrive and Mr. Personality at the architectural firm wondered what the hell was going on. She'd had a delivery at his office the same time as the mailman and Mr. P. had been throwing a shit fit as five magazines and seven boxes arrived with his name on them.

"I didn't order this crap," Mr. P. had yelled at the mailman who'd simply shrugged. It was beautiful, Shelly said, the way the mailman didn't give a shit.

"They have your name on them. I'm just doing my job," the mailman had responded and walked away, while Mr. P. fumed, his desk piled high.

"I wish you'd have had me when you were a hippie," six-year-old Peanut had sighed, winding her long red-gold braids around her head. I loved how my small childrens' minds worked.

I'd been telling her about going to The Farm in the summer as a kid, following Ina Mae Gaskin around and smooching the little newborn babies. We'd gone to Saugatuck, Michigan, too, to loaf around Ox-bow School of Art and followed musicians like Fraser and deBolt and TRex along the west coast. There were Sunshine tie-dyed shirts and flowered skirts and ankle bracelets, I would tell her, brushing her bowl-cut bangs away from her perfect face. Children were considered wizards. Everyone had long hair, knew yoga and ate dense homemade whole wheat bread slathered in oily peanut butter. Our geodesic dome had been ordered from The Whole Earth Catalog. My favorite book had been Alicia Bay Laurel's 'Living On the Earth.'

I'd shown the children both books at Elliot Bay Bookstore.

"Would you still be *you* if I had?" I asked, tugging her brain to work. I loved this beauty in Snow White pajamas and Cinderella sheets. "Your daddy would be someone else and I would have been 16 instead of 30. I was different then."

"I'd have stayed with the Sunshine People. You could *still* be one, Mom. We could still go. C'mon, it'd be fun."

Her front teeth were missing as she grinned at me. I had no desire to gather with the tribe in a redwood forest or scrubby desert for a solstice festival. I liked clean sheets, clean clothes and a paycheck. Besides, they were a thing of the past, the group all but disbanded, scattered to earth's every corner.

"You dream about the Sunshine People, okay? That's the only place they still exist."

I kissed her goodnight and went upstairs to Dew's room in our ramshackle old house.

"Mama, why don't we live with Angel anymore?" Dew asked, his big eyes vulnerable and sad in his baby face. "Now am I from *two* broken homes?"

"They're not broken. There's no such thing. Relationships don't fail, sweetheart, they just get finished. People go as far as they can with each other. I'm so sorry you and your sister get put in the middle of your mother's changes."

I kissed his forehead.

"Angel moved on, baby doll, and found someone else. We've got this nice house of our own now and will make it go from here, just you and your sister and me here. No one can take it away. Every summer you'll come back and it will be the same. There's nothing broken about it. You have two places to live, is all. Your daddy loves you and so do I. Never gonna change no matter where you live."

At the apex of our breakup, Angel had snarled the deal-breaker at me.

"I don't hate kids," she'd said, curling her lip and getting ready to slam out the door. "I just hate *your* kids."

I'd found the little Zenith cottage, called up my FedEx retirement fund and bought the place. It had been abandoned for a few years, the windows broken out but the tucked-away location was ideal for growing children to run around and me to write. Most of all, it was so run down I could afford it by myself.

I mortgaged for twenty thousand more than the asking price since it needed so much repair it scared the children.

When the kids had first walked in, an abandoned piano filled with mice sat cobwebbed in the living room. The windows were so thin they rattled when planes landed at nearby SeaTac Airport. The rickety attached-garage door handle rolled the door sideways like an old-fashioned barn. If I tugged too hard it popped off the track. Knee-high weeds comprised the yard and the "garden" with five untamed fruit trees needed months of work. But it had two bedrooms, a nice loft upstairs, a decent kitchen and it was walking distance to summer day camp and the 7-11.

Yet without the fore-thought and vision of an adult, it looked completely haunted. Holding his sister's hand as they had gingerly stepped inside the first time, Dew looked around and then straight at me.

"Do we *have* to live here?" he'd said.

"Just wait, babies, by summer it'll be looking really nice. You'll like it here, honest. It's still in the same town as all your friends and I'll fix it up, you'll see."

The construction crew had completed a finished garage with a remote opener, insulation, triple-pane windows and paint inside and out. One of the painters bought the piano for a hundred bucks and hauled it away. I'd cleaned the carpets, wallpapered the kitchen, put glow-in-the-dark stars on the ceiling in Peanut's room, a Jeremy McGrath poster in the loft for Dew, and a futon in the livingroom for me.

We got over Angel together in that little house, a house so perfect it was like it had been made for us. I'd roto-tilled the garden, planting corn and tomatoes to, apparently, share with the raccoons. Dew sat in the back of the Subaru wagon in the garage with the new garage door open shooting his BB gun at the big apple tree. Peanut buried her dead goldfish under the monkey-puzzle tree in an elaborate funeral, weeping over her handmade grave marker.

I had gotten each child a kitty cat and they carried their new pets around, inventing kitty games with paper grocery bags, foil and string. We would talk to each other through shadow hand-puppets on the wall at night, Dew choosing Feluga the Beluga as his one alter-ego, while Peanut and I rotated our hand-personalities like new outfits.

That was the summer I'd started writing down the tales I told to the children. Peanut and Dew clamored for bedtime stories and they preferred the ones I'd created. I'd felt awkward and uncreative as I told them, making it up as I went along but their little faces were so rapt I'd press on. I'd try out new material on them and then after they slept pound it out on my Royal Manual typewriter.

Two characters seemed to roll off my tongue and stick: Babushka the Mouse and her friend Aphrodite the Giraffe.

I'd made the characters children in the stories recalling, before he'd gone away, my own father's storytelling with his three stock players: George and Beezy, two hippopotamus brothers, and their monkey friend Cheepee-Weepee who was always swinging down through the trees. They'd go on wild adventures, getting into scrapes and barely escaping with their lives to come home to mothers who washed their mouths out with soap for lying. I'd borrowed heavily from my dad's material, cribbing the pirate ship kidnapping, the underwater submarine trip and the ride along a rainbow's arc.

I eventually bought a Writer's Market and began reading on my lunch hour about how and where to submit material.

"It smells like my patchouli oil in here. Why is your Barbie dressed in tie-dye?" I'd asked Peanut. "And what is that in her hand? Art? Is she an artist?"

Peanut showed me the small square of paper she'd colored black with a big blue and white planet in the middle.

"It's a Whole Earth Catalog. She's Sunshine People Barbie now."

"And the stuffed animals?" I'd asked, pointing to the ring of soft toys piled around Barbie.

"The rest of the tribe. They're at a happening at Mount Reindeer."

Chapter Four

"What's it like to never have to worry about your physical safety?" I asked Malcolm over the chicken crepes. I thought they needed more curry but the sauce was creamy and comforting.

He smiled at me, sliding his arm up onto the back of the booth opposite me, turning sideways.

"I don't know," he answered slowly. "I only know my reality and that's jessa way it is. I don't have your reality of being watchful all the time to compare it to so mine just feels like mine. That's like asking a bird how it feels to fly. He's never *not* flown so how would he know how to describe it? It's just ordinary experience to him."

"You fucker. I so envy you. You never have to watch your back..."

"OOOOO, now wait a *minute*..."

"I don't mean like a black man, I mean like a woman. Black women can understand me here."

"I'm sure they can. Twice over."

"I just can't imagine walking down the street at two a.m. in fucking Chicago, confident, in my own head, not having to think about strangers leaping out from between parked cars to force me into a dark alley and rape me."

"The reality of that? Grim, I imagine."

"I wish I could just set it aside for a while. I want to be the predator. I'm tired of being prey."

"I'll teach you to shoot, if you want."

"No, thanks, babe. I'd just be scared-er...is that a word?"

"You're asking a black man if a word is a word?"

"But you speak so *well.*"

I smiled for the first time that day, it felt like.

Sometimes the pouring rain, the pounding job, the abject loneliness felt too big to carry. I wanted someone else to be on the other end of the folded sheet, my evening couch, the late-night bed. I wanted not to be afraid anymore.

"Yeah, I'm a regular Colin fucking Powell. Only I'm *Oakland* black, baby, black *all* the way down."

"I might have met you in Oakland if I'd stayed, back in the day."

"When were you down there?"

"I met LeRoi and lived with him in the Tenderloin when I was sixteen."

"No shit? The Tenderloin? What the hell was a sixteen-year-old Midwestern white girl doing in San Francisco, for one, and in the Tenderloin for another? Who's LeRoi?"

"I hitched there to try to find Cora, my first lover. She was long gone, though. I met LeRoi in City Lights Bookstore. He kept me, paid me to fuck him and his friends. It wasn't half bad. I made good money then lost it all in Vegas like *that.*"

I snapped my fingers.

"No shit? Yeah, we very well might have met on the street back then. I used to go into town and cruise the prostitutes when I was 16, roll down my window and let 'em lean in and shit. They knew I was underage and they didn't care. They were nice to me."

"I'm sure they were. Studly young man like you. See? You get to be the strong stud even back then. Not fair."

"Life's not fair, Al."

The only time I'd seen writing produce results was in Chicago.

My chef love Cora was about to lose her job and I had to do something to help. I had an ulterior motive, too: Maybe if I was a hero I could tear her away from the butch who kept her down. If I could write well enough to save her, she'd choose me.

The city had torn up Halsted Street in the blistering hot summer, bringing in bulldozers and jackhammers and huge cement pipes, ruining the street and sidewalk in front of the fledgling restaurant where Cora had recently gotten her dream job. Finally the head chef after years of serfdom, she was loving life until suddenly the street sewer project took over.

Piercing high-decibel noise plummeted sales, heavy machinery covered the trendy new café with relentless dust then all the work stopped completely, leaving equipment and trucks full of pipe, huge dunes of sand by the front door and twisted, exposed rebar sticking out of the ground. Two weeks of inactivity went by, then three.

Cora was desperate. Her rent was due and because she hadn't been paid, she had to sell her air conditioner. The owner, Nunzio, was a second-generation Sicilian gay man and his life savings was at stake. When the work simply sat undone, it drove Nunzy nearly mad and almost out of business. Calls to City Hall were getting him nowhere.

I suddenly knew what to do, writing to Mike Royko on behalf of Cora. Taking a bit of liberty, I presented myself *as* Cora.

"Mr. Mike Royko
Chicago Tribune
Chicago, Illinois

August 6, 1984

Dear Mr. Royko;

For the first time, I can honestly say that I love my job. I am very good at the work I do.

Directly outside my workplace sprawls a problem that is threatening not only my job but the entire flow of commerce from Aldine to Waveland along north Broadway. Fired up by a shared-grievance session with the proprietor of the resale shop next door, I called CBS to speak to Walter Jacobson; Mr. Jacobson's assistant referred me tiredly to my alderman, saying he'd already heard from businesses on our street and he couldn't do anything. Jerry Orbach was not in; his assistant said he'd look into it and call me back in an hour, mispronouncing my name. An hour later, he left a message for me----"Thursday."

I, for one, have my doubts that we'll have a new sidewalk by Thursday. I've heard this line before. If you can do anything about this cul-de-sac of non-responsibility, I would greatly appreciate it; let me tell you a sad story.

My occupation is unusual in that I am a woman in food service. The dues I have paid amount to ten years in some of the Chicago-area's finest restaurants. Working my way up from prep, or assistant to the chef or cook, I recently left a secure, well-paid but physically exhausting head cook-kitchen coordinator position after 2 grinding years. To prepare food for a restaurant that seated 98, open from lunch to midnight dinner and weekend brunches 363 days a year---a popular, prosperous Lincoln Park restaurant—left me with biceps that rival a woman wrestler, burn and cut scars, and a permanently damaged wrist, "carpal tunnel syndrome," or chef's wrist. Worn thin, I had thought it was time for a total career change, out of food service altogether. But when I interviewed for this cafe position, the owner gesturing grandly at the future finished product, sawdust and drywall everywhere-- my gut feeling was "Go for it."

Nunzio Cafe e Galleria was inspired by a tour of Toronto the owner Nunzio once took. Pretty little sidewalk cafes beckoned to him everywhere. Borrowing from his parents and a few trusting friends, Nunzio designed a menu with some of his mother's treasured Sicilian recipes, contracted artists to exhibit monthly in the cafe, painted, scraped, wired, plumbed, and constructed to meet Health Department regulations. He bought quality used kitchen and dining room equipment, light fixtures, deco knick-knacks, fifties cabinets, a green and pink neon clock, vases, an espresso machine. The health inspector rated the cafe 99 out of 100---he said he'd give it a hundred, but that'd look suspicious downtown. All the proper licenses went up on the wall.

Nunzio is a small businessperson struggling toward the American Dream. Second-generation Sicilian, he comes from a blue-collar Detroit family. His folks visit every other month, staying four or five days, helping out, his father fixing the freezer compressor while his mother does dishes and runs to the store. They're very proud of their son. I took their picture on opening day as our first customers.

The cafe is four blocks from my apartment, my hours are flexible, I am well-paid for the time I put in, the work crew is capable and interesting, and the creative challenge of menu specials and new desserts keeps me enthused and eager to work—like I say, I love my job. What Mama Fresta didn't teach me from her personal collection of tested recipes, I cull from memory, experimental urges, one of many cookbooks or a magazine for the culinary arts. Since the café only seats twenty-five, my workload is no greater than feeding an enormous extended family.

I am considerably healthier, happier and constantly updated with both praise and constructive criticism from our friendly customers.

By the time the cafe opened in April, there was no money left to advertise. A large, transplanted community from Detroit, Nunzio's friends and fellow business owners along Broadway, my friends and hungry following, and the attractive, bright, wild atmosphere of the cafe itself drew a good deal of business. An underground grapevine sent us a late-night crowd of punkers, gay men and women, and young people who found ours to be a new hot spot. A more conservatively attired crowd enjoyed early evening dinner. Things looked great for the future of the cafe; we were gaining neighborhood celebrity status and so my job was secure.

On July 1st, a street crew materialized and tore up the sidewalk in front of us with a jackhammer and a bulldozer. No Parking signs went up on every meter for blocks, concrete tubes and metal rods appeared in piles, dump trucks and enormous, noisy equipment multiplying daily.

"Better get used to it," Nunzio groaned. "It'll be like this for at least two weeks, they said."

The Broadway business hotline from Buckingham to Addison buzzed the information down our way. It was our only source of real information and commiseration.

We battened down the hatches and held on, kept the door shut to keep out dust storms that rivaled a big Okie blow, turned on the air conditioner for ventilation and blared the radio to block out the unbearable noise level. Tremors from the heavy machinery shook down two of the plastic letters over the door, shattering then on a table before they hit the floor. Nunzio patiently re-glued the hand-designed and-cut logo pieces and remounted them. They fell again, three days later, under the heavy artillery attacks.

Then suddenly one day the trucks were gone. Our sandpit for a sidewalk remained untouched. Bumpy cement pieces jutted out of the dirt, rusted wires an inch around snaked dangerously out of the ground. Two weeks had gone by and nothing was anywhere near completion. Mounds of leftovers blocked traffic, just sitting there. All the activity had shifted to the south; Nunzio asked around and found there were hurrying it up down further south for the upcoming Broadway Street Fair. And it would be at least another week before we got our sidewalk or street back.

Needless to say business dwindled then plummeted to nearly nothing. There would be one, maybe two hours of work for me to do. I began worrying about my rent, my American Express bill.

The cafe's skeleton crew began taking all their meals at the restaurant, there being no cash available.

Nunzio began talking about getting a waiter job. He started sweating the rent, the gas bill, my salary. Our hardcore customers still wandered in for a meal now and then but it couldn't cover the overhead. Even Nunzio's catchy idea of spreading Oriental rugs across our sand-bar, placing two plants on either side of the door "for the total Sahara effect" did not help.

"Tuesday," Nunzio reported last Saturday as the word spread. Tuesday came and went. No Parking. No road crew. No sidewalk.

I paid my rent this month by selling my air conditioner. And I got an additional jab to supplement my meager income from the cafe, my first priority. But that job doesn't start until September.

The alderman's assistant told me that Miller Asphalt Co., hired to re-do the street, is not responsible for the sidewalk. The sidewalk contractor ("Some Italian company") went bankrupt, and their crew walked off the job for non-payment of wages due. I don't blame them for walking, that's a helluva good reason. But for some reason, a Lakeview organization hired the private contractors and this makes the city also not responsible since they didn't directly order the work done. Or that's what the aldermanic aide said. He promised a sidewalk by Thursday. I think he was trying to pacify me. "Try Streets and San," he told me.

Yesterday, outside the cafe, two elderly ladies struggled across the sandpit one with an armload of groceries.

"Do you think they'll ever finish this?" I heard one remark.

"Not in our lifetime," came the reply. I'm starting to feel the same.

Isn't there something I can do?"

   I signed Cora's name, sent it off and hoped for the best.
   The fact-checker at the Chicago Tribune called Nunzio three days later to confirm that yes, he *had* actually spread an Oriental runner across the sand dune outside the restaurant door and added a palm tree "for the full Sahara effect," and yes, his chef *had* sold her air conditioner to pay the rent. He assured her that yes, his parents spoke little English and the restaurant had been their life's dream. Bewildered, Nunzio wondered why Mike Royko's office had taken an interest in him but he shrugged it off, too panicked about going under.

   Next day, just in time for the week's restaurant reviews, Mike Royko wrote a nice piece about Nunzio's café, taking the city to task for dashing the poor immigrant's dream and demanding immediate action.

"Chicago Tribune
Friday, August 17, 1984

Pasta *a la* dusta just doesn't sell

THE QUESTION keeps coming up: Is Chicago
the city that works?
It depends on whom you ask. If you are from
City Hall, don't even bother to ask Nunzio Fresta.
Nunzio is a small businessman. A few months
ago, he opened an Italian-style cafe on Broadway
near Addison. It's a pleasant little place. A dozen round
tables. Original art on the walls. A limited but
interesting menu. Not meant to be a full-service
dining room, it's patterned after European
sidewalk cafes. Business was pretty good in the beginning.
Then came progress. And disaster.
The city recently began tearing up that stretch
of Broadway. It's part of a program to rebuild
some streets and sidewalks that are in bad shape.

ON JULY 1, A crew showed up in front of the
restaurant and tore up the sidewalk.
"We better get used to it," Nunzio told his chef
and waitress. "They say it might be as much as
two weeks before the new sidewalk is in."
Naturally, business dropped off. With the sidewalk
and part of the street torn up, the
slightest breeze created a dust storm. There were
mounds of rubble and no place to park.
The two weeks passed. No new sidewalk appeared.
And the sidewalk work crew had disappeared.
Nunzio tried to find out what was going on with
his sidewalk. But nobody could tell him.
He called City Hall and got the runaround. He asked

the remaining workmen, but they were vague.

And every day, business got worse and worse.

"We lost our lunch business. And some nights we
only had two people for dinner. I couldn't pay the
help. My cook had to sell her air conditioner to
pay her rent."

WORSE. NUNZIO couldn't get any answers. He
had no idea when—if ever—the sidewalk would be
replaced so customers could come in without tripping
over rubble or gasping on dust. Nunzio asked if we could get
some answers for him, and here they are. The contractor for
the Broadway project said the problem was caused by the
subcontractor who was responsible for sidewalk work.
"The city now requires that all general contractors,
such as myself, must give about 25 percent of the subcontracts to
minority businessmen," the contractor said.
[This is a policy put in by Mayor Washington's
administration.]
"Well, there aren't that many minority firms
capable of doing the work. The first one I contacted is reliable,
but he has more work than he can handle. So they recommended
somebody and we took them.

BUT THEY TURNED out to be under funded.
They didn't have enough money to pay their workers.
So when they couldn't meet their payroll, the workers walked off the job.
"We funded him for a couple of weeks. We
advanced him $2,500 a week. But they still couldn't meet their payroll.
And that's why the sidewalk wasn't finished."
The subcontractor said: "I took this job on the
spur of the moment. I told them up front I didn't have the money
to meet my payroll. They told me they'd handle it. Then the city advanced
them money so they
could advance me money. But then he told me he
couldn't advance me anymore. So I didn't have
any capital and I couldn't get a loan from the
bank. So I couldn't pay my men and I couldn't do
the sidewalk. I thought I could call downtown [City Hall]
and get money. But it doesn't work that way."

NO, THAT NORMALLY isn't the way it works.
Usually, you have to do the work to get paid. But the city
finally advanced enough money so that the subcontractor
could pay his workers. And on Aug. 10, more than five weeks
after the sidewalk was torn up, it was finally replaced.

"It took them only one day to get the concrete
poured," Nunzio said. "One day is all it took. And
we had to spend five weeks waiting."
Now they are beginning work on the other side of Broadway.
And the same subcontractor will be doing the sidewalks.
When told that, Ald. Jerry Orbach—who has
been deluged with complaints from Broadway businessmen—gasped.
 "I was told by public works that the guy was bankrupt or something
and they're getting another subcontractor."

NO, HE'LL BE doing the rest of the work.
"Well, if that guy's going to do the work, it's
scary."
Meanwhile, Nunzio doesn't know if his business
 will recover from the five-week slump. It's like
starting over again, except he's spent all of his
capital just trying to survive. And *he* can't call anybody
in City Hall for an advance."

People had streamed to the restaurant in droves despite the hardship in
negotiating the streets, eating everything Nunzy and Cora could turn out.
Cora had fifty people ask her if she had really sold her air conditioner to pay her
rent as they stuffed money in the front counter tip jar. Nunzy took Royko's column
to Sir Speedy and had it blown up onto foam board, leaving it easel-ed in the
window.
    By Friday evening all the heavy equipment had smoothed a path to the
restaurant's door. By Tuesday the project was mysteriously, amazingly done, but
alas, though she was grateful to me, Cora had stayed with the bully.

        "It makes me want to move to Canada!" Drake moaned, his anger and anxiety
heightened with every administration blunder. "My stomach is grinding glass.
Bush is such an idiot. I can't believe I once thought he was handsome."
    "You *did*?" I couldn't believe what I was hearing.
    "Have you ever seen his college pictures, Al? He was a cheerleader in a white
cable-knit sweater and those yummy pleat-front white pants. Took a wrong turn,
that's for sure. Now he's all down-home yuck-yuck with that priss of a wife and
leading us straight into hell with this war."
    I knew what he meant and agreed but I took a longer view.
    "We all lived through the sixties and seventies with Viet Nam and Nixon when it
also felt like the end of civilization. Things are cyclical and each generation thinks
theirs is the crisis of all crises, *much* worse than any previous. It seems to me like
we just kept repeating the same story."

"He's going to blow us all to hell. I just know it. But enough about him. Back to me. Here's my new idea. Why not heat whole buildings with computer equipment, Al? If they could harness this room alone we'd be able to light up Vashon Island. Honest to Val Kilmer's 'Gotham,' how is a girl supposed to stay fresh as 'National Velvet' when these machines crank out so much hot *air?* "

Drake was surrounded by a fax machine, a laptop, a desktop, a flat screen monitor, a copy machine, a printer and the entire security system's five screens with my FedEx truck at the loading dock visible from his desk. He waved a hand-painted Japanese bamboo folding fan and intermittently patted his forehead with his light blue hanky, slipping it back in his jacket pocket at a perfect rakish angle.

"It's pouring outside," I informed him then looked out the 40th floor window behind his desk. We were completely enclosed in a surreal grey cloud. "About fifty degrees. Wanna switch jobs?"

"No, thank you, darling. Despite how hard it is on my complexion, I still prefer indoor civilization to your blue-collar underworld. And you get so *dirty* on your job. I might break a nail."

"How's the kid from Portland?"

"He's sweet as a little puppy and thinks I'm to die for. I feel terrible."

"Why?"

"He's just so…young. He wears Converse All-Stars, AnnaLee, and has a MySpace page with pictures of his old dorm room on it. He teaches inner city youth and eats ramen noodles because it's all he can afford and he's happy. It's not my scene. Good in bed but still. I can't deal with it. Anyway," Drake sniffed, waving his hands to push it all away. "I'm focused on my Teaching English classes and getting certified to get the hell out of this country. Not so much as a dust bunny ties me here and I could just as easily be teaching swarthy Aegean goat boys on some blue-water island. I'll stick to having fun. I've got to leave before I go mad."

He patted his forehead dry once more and stood to stare out at the eerie cloud surrounding us.

"'But it's so lush here in the summer! It's liquid sunshine!'" Drake quavered, imitating the cheerful Seattle weather optimists we both hated. The dreary, near constant rainfall spawned the city's most popular tourist t-shirt: Seattle Rain Festival, Jan.1st-Dec.31st.

"I know you want sunshine. Why not Florida or California?"

"Because this country…I can't bear to watch the Republicans destroy it. We are doomed, we are all doomed."

"I go to Swedish Hospital parking lot when I feel like I'm gonna cry on the job," Shelly said, sniffling. "No one bothers you if you're crying in a hospital parking lot. They assume personal tragedy and steer clear."

"I know just the thing to cheer you up," I told Shelly over the phone, after she and Blake broke up.

I didn't want her getting nostalgic, returning to the hurtful familiar just because it was a known. In their break-up, Blake had deserted her in the Tahuya State Forest on a camping trip, throwing a shoe at her head and pushing her out of their motorhome on a moonlit night, committing crimes I called "aggravated stupidity."

But Shelly still remained sure a little domestic violence couldn't be overcome. Their dysfunction seamlessly meshed. I wanted to help her break the cycle.

Garland Academy Homecoming was a fall phenomenon in Seattle, the Adventurer's Club on Elliot rented out for a huge Saturday night. The gay event, referred to as Homo Homecoming, was always a smash, the huge ballroom and multi-storied hall agleam with crepe paper streamers, glittering disco balls, color gel lights, class election posters, wooden desks with attached chairs, orange plastic scoop chairs with swing-away writing arms, grey graffiti-ed walls of lockers, a glittering trophy case, and piped in announcements from the principal's office. Every room was themed for a different school function---Cafeteria, AV Room, Nurse's Office, Teacher's Lounge---with the apex the decorated school gymnasium and dance floor in full tissue-paper-chrysanthemum-ed glory.

Hundreds of people would turn out, dressed as every imaginable character from high school. There were two rival football teams and cheerleading squads, wearing Marlene Dietrich High's lavender and Judy Garland Academy's green. The rest of the student body was rounded out by smokers, stoners, jocks, nerds, hoods, popular kids and beauty queens.

An entire faculty was also present, featuring lots of teacher beehive hairdos, enormous pastel cat-eye glasses on chains with delicate clasps, huge fake boobs, cardigans with clasps and stern brown-suited ultra-butch authority figures walking salaciously around with paddles.

A Homecoming King and Queen were chosen at the festivity's apex, after secret ballots and much jostling for position. As the sobbing (male) Homecoming Queen was presented with a dozen roses during her victory walk with the (female) Homecoming King, the sarcastic fake claws-out congratulations from the losers would have the entire place in stitches.

There would be too many tuxedoed dykes there already and I didn't want to be another penguin. For my costume I went to Value Village and bought a suit, going for a button-down bookish nerdy kind of look. Under my Oxford shirt I wore a dickie and added a bit of duct tape to my glasses, topping the ensemble off with a nice porkpie hat.

Sticking a piece of Scotch tape onto the ends of my hair, I cut a quarter inch off in a short row then carefully smooshed it into a sticky moustache held by spirit gum. With my hair pulled up into the hat, looking back at me in the mirror was my male twin.

Shelly met me wearing a bright red taffeta number, pinched at the waist and brimming with her beautiful brown décolletage, cut down to *there.*

"Too bad we're friends," I sighed, looking at all that wasted opportunity right in front of me.

"You make one handsome hombre, chica. Look at that moustache! It looks *real*!"

"It is real. It's my own hair. I figure I'm on the school paper. I'll carry a little notebook."

"Kiss me."

"What? C'mon, Shell."

"No, kiss me, for real. I want to see how your moustache feels."

I kissed her, gingerly.

"It is real! Hey, can you run into the 7-11 for me? I need cigarettes and these heels are killer."

"Sure, babe."

I pulled up to the convenience store as she checked her makeup for the thousandth time. She looked stunning. I sighed again. Too bad.

"Newport 100's," I growled at the counter, lowering my voice and putting a macho-stern look on my face to cover my timidity.

"Box or softpack, sir?" the clerk asked me without batting an eye.

"I passed!" I crowed, as I got back in the car.

"Far out, chica. I'm proud of you, my handsome little stud-muffin."

The inside of our wrists stamped with the school's day-glo dolphin mascot, we chose the country-themed dance room first, sitting on hay bales to watch the line-dancing lesbians and gay men. There were lots of queens with tiaras, a sea of lesbian tuxedos and even one incongruous Minnie Mouse in huge shoes, all doing the Tush-Push.

I got us two tonic waters since we were out in public. The AA grapevine was very swift with eyes everywhere and I didn't want to answer to anyone.

Blake appeared in the City Scapes room, her mullet freshly dyed blonde at the tips. I'd smelled the strong whiskey smell on her breath as she'd leaned proprietarily toward Shelly so I grabbed Shelly's arm and moved her along with purpose, as if we had other places to be

Once lovers, always a chance, I supposed but not if I could help it.

"She looks good," Shelly yelled in my ear as we entered Disco Inferno, complete with a lip-synching Donna Summer drag queen and glittering mirror ball. Shelly looked a little guilty.

"Fuck her," I yelled back. "Other fish in the sea. Look around you."

"I see a hot butch across the way, the one with the shop teacher coveralls on. Look at those biceps."

"You just like her because she has a wrench in her hand."

"I think it's the streak of grease on her cheek. I love a woman who works with her hands."

"Go dance with her."

"Ya think?"

"Holy shit, Shell. Yes."

Shelly sashayed across the floor to the grease monkey and soon they were frugging to the repetitive techno beat heard in every gay bar since 1980, a mix of old disco songs pumped up with a hard edge. The butch steered Shelly back to me and wrote down her phone number, slipping it into Shelly's cleavage with a sly smile before she walked away.

"See. Other fish."

"I think I see your point," Shelly flushed, throwing back her hair. "Let's go rest a bit."

We moved on to see the rest of the school setting. The decorations were incredibly well done, as always, streamers over our heads and school election posters on the wall in the hallways.

The Cafeteria was quieter.

"Peak season starts tomorrow," Shelly said, her rustling dress crinkling as she sat down at a long table. 'Cafeteria ladies' in heavy pancake-makeup, beaded hairnets, white dresses and nurse's shoes had lattes and pastries for sale, the proceeds benefiting the AIDS hospice.

"Geez, I hate the thought of it. How many more of these can I do? My knees hurt and the early morning wake-up…I have to get another job. Or find a rich husband."

"You'll do that, chica," Shelly said. "You'll see. Maybe this will be your last peak. That's how I get through. I convince myself that *this* year is the last time I have to hump Harry & David boxes. I escaped the fruit picking fields to end up delivering the goddamn stuff by DHL. I am wearing myself out with sixty-hour weeks."

"Don't forget the genuine Maine wreaths from L.L. Bean. Sending a fucking wreath from the east coast to the west. It's the height of American depravity."

"I daydream I no longer have to do this for a living, like this is temporary," Shelly sighed, explaining her coping mechanism. Her eyes looked far away, scaring me a little. "I convince myself that this peak is *it*, I'm done, and I never have to do this again. The job sure pays the bills but it about kills me in the process. C'mon, I've had enough high school. Let's go home."

Daydreaming of never having to work again got me through as well but I knew it wasn't temporary unless I made things different. As AA had taught me, if nothing changes, nothing changes.

But how could I change things while at the same time working physically, brutally hard, pushing, running, sweating through my clothes, loading a ton of freight in my truck at o-dark-thirty from a moving conveyor belt that sped faster, it seemed, every morning, then delivering the same freight, unloading it piece by piece, computer after computer. I would work until the truck was empty, meeting stricter, more demanding time commitments then spend my lunch hour napping in the back of the Grumman, my stashed sleeping bag rolled out onto the floor. Waking to my digital watch alarm, I'd leap up and repeat the process in reverse until 1730 hours, rushing to pick up packages and refill the truck to bursting, taking it back to the reversed conveyor belt. Repeat five to six days a week, 12 hours a day.

After more than a decade at FedEx, I knew the stress of peak season was so high that three things nearly always happened along the conveyor belt by the time Christmas Day itself rolled around: there would be a physical fight, someone would cry and someone would quit.

That Christmas was also a difficult emotional time since the kids were at college and no one was decorating a Chanukah-bush at my house. The holiday itself was simply a day to sleep through after the yearly work marathon.

There wasn't time to date, either.

Desperate for pleasure and comfort, I realized I was not "dating" anyone anymore, simply fucking them, usually at my house. I had my coterie of fun fellows who knew how to throw a woman around a bedroom and there was no small pleasure in that. But no one was taking me out, there were no restaurants, no conversation, just booty calls.

It left my outer shell intact but there was no substance, like a hollow chocolate Santa.

"How the fuck can I get off this hamster wheel?" I griped to Malcolm.

The beef stew was excellent, the perfect warmth against my soaking wet uniform. December in Seattle simply meant colder rain.

"First of all, eat that hot meal and shut the fuck up. You look a little peaked," Malcolm said and smiled his million-dollar smile. The toothpick slid to a corner of his mouth. His hair was freshly cut, neat and perfect and his nails looked suspiciously buffed. "Can't say that to a black person," he grinned. "How you gonna tell?"

"I'm sure black people *feel* peaked, though. You just have to speak up."

"Like being ashy. If a white person look all ashy, how would you *know*?"

"Hey, I get ashy and I can tell."

"Listen and keep eating. I worry about you, that this internet thing has taken a turn I never meant it to. I had something else in mind, a steady one-on-one relationship rather than this bed-hopping. We talked about that. Captain of industry, remember? Sure, you're getting laid, and that's good, nothing wrong with that. And I have to say, I sure enjoy hearing about all your escapades. I can get hard just imagining them."

His fingers rubbed his thumb in his little gesture of excitement.

"I'm sure you do. I'd like to see that sometime."

Malcolm just stared at me.

"We've talked about that, and I'm unavailable. That's what makes me so exciting to you, my being unavailable."

I set down my fork and wiped my lips on the aqua cloth napkin, stiff with commercial laundry starch. The new hostess was folding them at the bar into half-fans.

"I'll tell you what makes you so exciting, Malcolm. You are fucking gorgeous, for one, you're smart as hell, for another, and you have a sensuality about you that drives any woman from 10 to 80 wild. I'd still want you even if you were available."

"My *point* is…" he sighed, leaning into the table and speaking softer. "…you are going in the wrong direction here. I see potential for ugly things. You aren't valuing yourself highly enough. And I feel responsible, I suppose, for wanting my own gratification in your erotic tales. For that I apologize."

I was too tired to argue with him. My legs felt like lead, and my feet were throbbing. I needed new work shoes but who the fuck had time to even take a decent shit, much less go shoe shopping. And finding women's all-black running shoes with good support was a real chore. Men's shoes were mostly black and women's were almost always white. And did other peoples' feet hurt as badly as mine? Were they as tired as I was? Maybe I should see a doctor.

"Now let's head into the right path, shall we? Take a step back, as it were."

He sat back in the booth and watched me eat, sip coffee, and try to rest.

"What you need isn't to have a date every night, or get laid all the time by a different man. You need a husband."

I opened my mouth but he protested.

"We *talked* about this. I don't mean that in some sexist, fifties perversion of your lesbianism or because you were raised by wolves. I am not saying you are 'unfulfilled' or some Feminine Mystique Madison Avenue bullshit where you wear a frilly apron and wait for Ward to come home. I mean, you need someone who loves you, truly loves you, and happens to be a solid breadwinner, some go-getter type with a good job who wants to be a patron of the arts and support your writing career. Lets you blossom as a writer without you having to sweat the bills. Take you out of this goddamn job that runs you ragged in the best years of your life and terrorizes you with numbers, numbers, faster, run, and then tells you afterward you didn't meet goal. I wanna find that Fred Smith and wring his fat Skull and Bones neck."

Sometimes I did, too. It felt like Uncle Fred had unrealistic goals, his multiple ex-wives' alimony taken out of the workers' hides. I put my fork down and listened. Patron of the arts sounded not half bad. Neither did the word "husband," for that matter. I needed a butch around the house.

"He has to be able to build things, fix things," I blurted out.

"Who? Fred Smith?"

"My husband."

Malcolm smiled.

"It would get you off this treadmill that keeps going faster and faster to nowhere. You are running too hard. Time to stop."

"My job pays my bills. I don't know any other way to survive. I'm listening but I have ten minutes before I have to start pickups, so hurry up with your plan. Then I'll think about it."

"Girl, we're gonna get you out of FedEx and writing that Great American Novel."

After the third email from Movement Guy, I was deeply intrigued. He had been a member of SNCC, knew great stories and he lived a few suburbs over. His deep gravelly voice made him Barry-White sexy over the phone, and his credentials seemed completely solid. The invitation to his home caught me on the Saturday before my lonely Christmas holiday, dateless and hungry after working a sixth day in a row.

Everything went well until he shut the deadbolt with a key lock then pocketed the key.

"I know it's late, Malcolm, and I'm sorry to bother you," I sobbed, pounding on the restaurant door just after closing.

"No, no," he insisted, unlocking the door. "What the hell are you doing out at two a.m.? You look…not right somehow."

"I'm sorry, I didn't know where else to go. I nearly got raped," I choked out as he steered me to a booth and took my coat.

"I didn't follow the safeguards and I had to climb out a window with a madman screaming at me in the street. He was strong and he…he held me down. I got away after a while. The door was locked so I had to break a window and climb out. I think I cut my leg."

"Lemme see it. Come on. Don't cry, babe. Jesus, I'm sorry. You gonna call the cops?"

"And get my name in the papers as the idiot who got attacked on a booty call? No way."

Malcolm knelt down and motioned me toward him. He'd looked worried, which scared me even more.

I was too old for drama like this. I'd been really stupid and desperate and now I was ashamed to show that, to be that vulnerable in front of Malcolm. He'd told me I was heading for a danger zone. I hadn't listened.

I slid to the edge of the booth and pulled my dress up to my thigh. The dress was torn and there was blood on my leg.

"Oooo, ouch. Yeah, Al, right there on your…inner thigh, you have a good gash."

His fingers brushed my skin and I stopped crying. My leg opened slightly as I looked down at the cut.

Malcolm pressed into my thigh.

"Does that hurt? It's bruised right there and the cut goes up to….I'll get the first aid kit," he said, standing abruptly.

His shoes clicked across the polished oak floor. For the first time I registered that we were alone in the dimly-lit restaurant after hours.

He returned with the white metal box and opened it with studied concentration.

"You want something to drink? Lemme make you a Lemon Drop. That'll help. I'ma have a Jack."

He left the first aid kit and went to the bar and came back moments later with our drinks.

"Here's to…us. And your health. Don't let this night throw you, AnnaLee. He was just a little turn-out in the road, is all. Don't get all wrapped around the axle over this. Remember how we imprint the bad shit stronger than the good? Let this one go, babe. Consider it a lesson learned. A turning point. Cheers."

We both downed our drinks and he went back to the Band-Aids.

"Let's see. Okay, now, I never thought I'd get to say this to you but," he knelt down again in front of me and looked up smiling. "Spread your legs."

Slowly I opened my knees, the quiet of the place suddenly very loud.

"I'ma lift your dress up just a little more," he said, eyes never leaving mine while his hand slowly slid the silky fabric higher. "I think there might be some damage on…the other thigh, too."

Finally he looked down, his thumbs firmly holding my legs apart. I couldn't feel the cuts and the fear of the bad experience was dissolving under his touch. I tried to remember what color underwear I had on. Black, I thought to myself, it was black so he still hasn't seen anything, really, just a shadow. I relaxed my legs a little more.

"This is gonna sting 'cause it's alcohol," he said, letting go and soaking a cotton ball with disinfectant. "You just relax and I'll get you all cleaned up."

"Ow, Jesus, ow!" I yelled, clamping my legs together.

"Al, you've got to relax. I know it hurts but that's killing the germs. God knows what-all you picked up on window glass. Open your legs. Please."

I took a breath, swallowed the rest of my drink and gingerly I let him swab my cuts. There were three of them, toward the back of my leg where I'd straddled the windowsill after throwing a vase through it.

"I'ma rub some Neosporin on 'em now. It has anesthetic in it so they should stop hurting in a bit."

His voice sounded detached, too clinical.

When his eyes had met mine, I felt the electricity. It took everything in me not to look down at his crotch.

"I can feel the soothing part already," I said as he circled the cuts with his fingers, spreading the crème.

"Jesus, this is killing me," he groaned. "Al, here you are all hurt after some guy tried to force himself on you and I want you so badly I almost want to do the same thing…"

I grabbed his Italian silk tie at the neck to pull Malcolm toward me. He smelled like whiskey, another comforting smell of Cora's that had always turned me on.

"No, Malcolm, it's not like that at all. You aren't forcing yourself on me. Jesus, it's the *opposite*," I'd said. "You're taking *care* of me. C'mere."

His hands then left my legs and held my face. Rising from a crouch, he pulled me up with him and kissed me deeply, pushing and insistent.

"But I want to fuck you hard, I want to force you open and fill you with my dick, Al," he'd whispered directly into my ear as he'd trembled in front of me. "I've wanted you from the moment I saw you but….."

"Fuck me, please, Malcolm, Jesus, I need this, please, baby…" I begged against his perfect chest.

Malcolm ran to the bar, dimmed the house lights all the way, pulled the blinds and tore open a condom from the bar's fishbowl. Sweeping his arm across the top of the bar, he cleared everything in seconds, the fruit-garnish tray and the few remaining cocktail glasses hitting the terrazzo tiled floor in a shower of broken glass. Tearing the condom wrapper open with his teeth, he spit out the corner as his fingers tore the package open.

"C'mere," was all he said.

"How about if you and I go out for Christmas?"

Birgitte called a few days before the holiday. She pressed on with her logic before I could answer.

"Look, neither of us wants to cook or do anything, and neither one of us has any family around. The twins are with Kyle over in Eastern Washington. I swear, they bonded with all his bad habits and I lost them in the divorce to their damn step-father. Anyway," she sniffed. "I don't care if its Denny's at this point, I'm so damn broke from owning this house by myself. I'm gonna have to get a roommate, I think."

"Sure," I told her, "Let's have Christmas dinner together. Out. Let's find a Denny's between us and meet half way. I'm so tired of driving."

"Mexico City. Mere months away!"

I hadn't told Drake about the near-rape or the torrid incident with Malcolm. I hadn't told anyone, wanting to savor the details myself, balancing the horror-show of the night's beginning with its raw wild end. I was imprinting the wicked fun, the date's scary part growing miniscule in comparison.

Drake crowed his excitement into the phone.

"All I have to do is live through Christmas and soon I'll be in gay old Mexico! And my English Teaching class is almost over. I'll have a certificate so I can get the hell out of this dog-town. I know everyone and it rains all the time and I need excitement, Al. I can't wait. I'm thinking Italy."

"What are you doing on Christmas?" I asked, wondering if Spokane pressed on him this time of year. His family had to do everything right, lots of protocol followed and tradition reinforced. He tried to stay just out of range, sending deep regrets and FedEx-ed gifts.

"I've got nothing, darling. There's an old Francois Truffaut film at the Uptown. Maybe Dick's will be open."

"Birgitte and I are going to Denny's. Wanna go? Christmas Day. Whaddya say?"
. "Sure. Sounds funny and sweet. Christmas at Denny's with the homeless people. Maybe we could just go to McDonald's instead," he sneered but I knew he was glad to have the offer of companionship on an emotionally loaded day. He hadn't found an ideal boyfriend yet, either, preferring his Netflix account and a pull-apart cinnamon roll.

On Christmas morning, both of us having lived through another peak, I called Shelly. Alone and afraid of old Christmas blackout drinking, Shell had just finished agreeing to meet Birgitta, Drake and me at Denny's when my other line rang.

"Al, it's Malcolm," he said huskily, as if he was out of breath. "I'm at Swedish Hospital. It's Bernie."

The pouring rain disappeared behind us as we shook out our wet clothes inside the silent Blue Canoe. Closed for Christmas, everything looked still and spare in the grey light of day. Malcolm switched on a back kitchen light while we waited in the dark foyer.

"Come in, come in," he urged, beckoning us all toward the kitchen. "Let's make Christmas dinner, shall we?"

Malcolm's wife Bernadette had fallen off a ladder while adjusting the angel on top their Christmas tree, breaking her hip and arm. After hours of surgery to pin her back together she was going to be okay but Malcolm was shaken up. With Bernie sedated, Malcolm didn't want to be left alone for Christmas. Delighted to hear other orphans were in the same boat, Malcolm warmly offered to open his restaurant for our private party with himself as host.

None of my friends knew each other. Their only connection was that they all knew me.

The first thing Malcolm did was to go in the office off the kitchen and roll a joint from the stash he kept in the safe.

Shelly and I, drug-tested at random, looked at each other and shrugged.

"What the fuck, it's Christmas, right?" I said, letting job security disappear for a moment.

"Roger that, chiquita!" Shelly glowed, relieved to be able to share the moment with me.

Drake took off his topcoat, neatly folded it and set it on a pile of clean green linens wrapped in brown paper and twine. Pulling out a festive pine-green apron, he turned to the rest of us.

"I'll be the barmaid if that's alright with you, Malcolm." he asked, grabbing an order pad and doing a brief curtsy. "Where's the Tanqueray?"

"You are *so* hired," Malcolm smiled, handing Drake the joint. "Bar's out there on the floor, on the left wall. Just flip on the little switch down by the bar sink. That'll light the area without looking like we're open. I'll have a shot of Jack."

"Cosmopolitan for me!" Birgitte smiled, hopping up on the cutting board countertop and passing the jay to Shelly.

"Let's see. Are we doing this up right, chica?" Shelly looked at me for company. I nodded, approving. "Then I'll have a 7-7."

Drake wrote on the pad and waited for me.

"Lemon drop," I said, looking at Malcolm. "They remind me of happiness."

Malcolm cut his eyes sideways then back at me shaking his head.

"Al, come with me to the walk-in and we'll see what we can rustle up."

Once inside the cool refrigerator, Malcolm took hold of my shoulders.

"Look, Al, I....I had a great time, don't get me wrong, and I loved every moment of that night, but my wife....it scared me, this fall. She doesn't deserve this, I mean, she's never done anything wrong, always done what I asked her to and some of it was nasty shit. This hospital gig, it made me realize how short life is and how comfortable I am and I don't want to fuck it up. And I want *you* to have this domestic scene of connectedness, too, that's the thing, but we can't have it together. I already *have* a wife," he said, looking me in the eye. "So are we clear? Friends?"

He looked panicked, with no Plan B if I didn't agree.

"Friends." I kissed him lightly. "It was fucking awesome, literally. I'll never forget it. You erased the whole bad experience for me so don't go thinking you wished it never happened. It was necessary for me."

"I don't wish it never happened, no way. I just can't do it anymore."

"Deal."

Malcolm handed me half-pans of food covered with clear plastic lids. I shoved the silver vacuum-seal door open with my hip and we carried our loot out to the huge cutting board table. Malcolm began turning on the equipment, firing up the convection oven, lighting the griddle, flipping on lights, getting out chef's knives. Drake, looking for all the world like a professional, carried in the perfectly poured drinks on a shoulder-high tray and set them down next to Birgitte

"What?" he said at my open mouth. "I did this in college to pay the bills,"

"Thanks, Drake," Malcolm said, pausing a moment to recognize the warm bliss of an event none of us had planned. "To friends, old and new. Don't matter whether we ever met before, our bond today is a gift from the gods. Bottoms up," he said, looking straight at me.

The rain slogged down all through January, doing exactly what Seattle does all winter. With Christmas over the tinseled festivities died away and I faced a long string of months with monotonous sameness.

The next big FedEx push wasn't until Valentine's Day so business was slow. My seniority made me able to take a lot of days off. I was exhausted from somewhere deep down. My feet never really stopped hurting except after a long night's sleep and my knees made crunching noises when I walked up stairs. FedEx was on a productivity witch hunt and I was falling behind in numbers, my stops per hour down. I already had one letter in my file. The writing was on the wall. I needed to get out of there.

The holiday had left me tired and seven pounds heavier, despite running like a madwoman. I wanted nothing but comfort food, thwarting my efforts to diet. My house grew steamy with meatloaf and mashed potatoes, macaroni and cheese, chocolate cake, oatmeal raisin cookies. I had trouble fitting into my uniform and all I wanted to do was sleep.

This lethargy also left me dateless since I felt fat and unattractive so I slept, taking a morning nap on Saturdays after breakfast and an afternoon nap before dinner, then television until two a.m. and sleeping again until midday next. My name remained at the top of the boss's call roster for overstaffing, always ready to volunteer to stay home.

I cooked instead of writing.

There was now plenty of time to write, the rain pounding outside my bay window, making a comforting noise on the roof, my fireplace insert toasty-warm. But I had nothing. I was dry. No words appeared or even could be recalled. There was nothing interesting about which to write. My life felt blank, no material to mine in my completely mundane world, everything a flat, dull grey.

With gritted teeth and determination to change I headed out in the bone-chilling rain for the new Writer's Market. I would produce something, dammit, I would sell. I would figure out my own Rubik's cube of literary success. Others seemed to break in naturally, or had the right New York connections, or their style was perfect for that moment. Many others were so awful in their popular prose that I was sure they had slept with the right person at Random House or Esquire Magazine. It simply did not seem that merit equaled success. Who did I have to blow to get something published, to get paid?

Rejection letters trickled in as I re-sent re-worked older pieces to different venues. Unable to squeeze any more juice out of what I had already done, I needed some new material.

Chapter Five

"It's official," Drake crowed, "I'm registered at Saks if you want to get me a graduation gift."

"You're certified! Hey, that's wonderful."

I was holding the phone to my ear as I stirred some chicken and dumplings. The recipe was Drake's, its origin traceable back to his Mayflower ancestors.

"Thank you. Finally, I'm going to do something with my life. No more sobbing to Elliott Smith while it pours. Rain be damned, I'm putting on my Mackintosh and heading for the bookstore, darling, to research living abroad, visas and all that. I hate this moss-covered cow town and the badly-dressed yuppies drinking five-dollar coffee. I can't wait to get out of here. I'm so psyched! It feels like everything's wide open, my whole future awaits. I haven't felt like this since I graduated from U Dub. Back then I moved to San Francisco but…ah, well, that's when I was young and carefree. Castro Street was something else, I tell you."

"Yup. I remember Chicago pre-AIDS, too. It was a different world."

We both got very quiet, thinking of that wild, innocent time. Sylvester blaring at the discos, coke in the bathroom, lots of Tenax and musk oil and feathered hair spilling over upturned collars. We were all so thin and beautiful. And there were so many of us then who now were no longer on the planet. Every one of my queer boy friends in Chicago was long dead. It had made my urge to reproduce that much stronger.

"Well. Anyway." Drake cleared his throat. "I'm off to let a guidebook decide my middle-aged future. The men are hairier in Greece than Italy or is it the other way around?"

"I'm just so *tired* of doing this," Shelly moaned over the phone. "I hurt all over and I've been fighting with my supervisor. I just don't want to *work* anymore."

Her funky mood was leaking out everywhere, with a few extra pounds on, loneliness that made her cry at night and a leftover exhaustion from peak that wasn't going away. I knew how she felt but to her it made her past life on the streets suddenly look a little better, a little more fun.

"Mishellina mine, stick with it. I feel crappy all the time, too. It's nothing that a sandwich and a nap won't cure. Sure, today looks a little hard but tomorrow will be better. Then it's Saturday and you can sleep in."

I stuck with laying out short-term goals. She had given me this same pep talk in the past, and later we'd analyze it, mining it for improved data for next time.

"I just wanna get really drunk."

"That might help in the short-run but it'd fuck up everything in the long run. Think the drink through, Shelly. I don't have the money to come get you in Texas. Let's go to a meeting. Or out for a milkshake."

"No. No meetings. Fuck them. Fuck AA and NA and all the goddamn A's." She started to cry. "I'm so tired, Al, and everything hurts all over."

"You thought about seeing a doctor?" I suggested.

"No. They scare me," she sniffed.

"You have *insurance*, Shell. That's one of the benefits of these hard delivery jobs. Go see a doctor. If you don't have one, go down to the Country Doctor. They're really nice and they'll take you."

"You'd go with me?"

"Make it on a lunch hour, sure."

"She's much better, thanks," Malcolm beamed at me across the booth. "A bunch of comfort people come by and fluff the pillows while I'm at work, a visiting nurse or something. I got her one of those smooshy beds with the foam and she's got the t.v. and good drugs so she's fine. How's Drake doing with his foreign move plans? Man, I envy him. And Shelly? You said she was ill or something?"

"They did a bunch of bloodwork and tests. She'll know in a few weeks if it's anything. I think it's just wintertime blues. She'll get another lover and things will feel better. Drake's thinking of Mexico first, his big vacation, so the Greek boys who need English lessons are having to wait."

"Man, that was the funnest Christmas I've ever had."

Malcolm watched my face, knowing I couldn't bear it.

"Funnest is not a word," I had to say at last, and he smiled.

He looked off into the distance and reassessed our happy holiday, obviously pleased with my friends.

"Shelly gets wild after a few drinks, don't she? And she does have nice titties, even if she doesn't think so. And that Birgitte? There's a woman who needs a black man to show her a good time. That overgrown frat boy she married, man, he's a piece of work from what she says. I'm glad she liked my coq au vin. I'd cook for her anytime. She was so appreciative. Oh, and speaking of that, Drake sent me a lovely thank-you note on hand-made paper. I think it was even scented. I had to wash my hands afterward so I wouldn't smell all flowery."

Our holiday had ended up raucous, despite timid beginnings. Over appetizers in the Blue Canoe kitchen, we'd swapped small biographies, the details getting more vivid with each round of drinks. First nostalgically painted in colored ribbons and longing, our compared childhood Christmas details seemed sweet, but then the reality surfaced for each of us, laughing as we described drunk hands-y uncles, family secrets erupting, competition and fistfights over decades-old slights. With reefer and holiday liquor, we got to know one another as we all chopped vegetables, sliced fruit, split chestnuts and prepared coq au vin. Our awkward Christmas dinner turned warm as we bonded, sealing the surprise love-fest.

By evening's end, Shelly had danced topless on the kitchen's long prep table, Drake had recited "The Cremation of Sam Magee," Birgitte had done dead-on celebrity impressions, I'd described an entire Sunshine Festival from beginning to end, and Malcolm told stories of dealing coke out the drive-thru window of an Oakland Burger King, joining the Navy soon afterward to avoid arrest.

"Drake is nothing if not polite. Old-money upbringing will do that to you."

"Why doesn't he have any of it?"

"What?"

"Their money."

"Because he is the black sheep, the queer they don't talk about. He refused to stay in the family closet and bear heirs. He is the first-born and only son and a screaming queen. After college he couldn't go back to that life and after San Francisco, well, no turning back then. He'd rather struggle along and be true to himself. Maybe when they die he'll get some."

"Poetic as hell, but damn, I'd take the money."

"Suppose you had to act gay all the time and fuck men to get that money, and sneak off once in a while to secretly fuck a woman?"

"Okay, you're right. I'd leave, too. You ready to start my plan, speaking of fucking men?"

"I thought about it and…yes. Do I need to write shit down or what? Is it a 12-step program?"

I grinned at Malcolm.

"Maybe more steps. Lots of steps. I'm making it up as I go along so I'm not sure how many."

"Okay, lay it on me, brother."

"First, stop fucking everyone. Men, women, everyone. No more booty calls, no late-nights, no old friends."

"How the hell…"

"Hear me out."

"Listening."

I ate my Cobb salad as Malcolm leaned forward.

"Stop fucking. Period. No one, nothing."

"Why?"

"It will clear your vision and send a signal out to the universe that you are beginning the process.."

"What process?"

"Getting serious."

"Fine."

"Then, write down everything you want in a mate. Everything. Even the little shit you never consciously think of, like he's got to be taller than you or have a deep voice or hates televised sports."

I made a mental note of that one. I *did* hate televised sports and people who slavishly devoted their lives to it.

"Write it all down. Make a list. Build your dream man. It's all in your own head, and you never have to show the list to anyone so write everything down. Let yourself add more things as you think of them, and you *will* think of them, because we are turning your brain a certain way. We are sending out the vibe that you are serious, girl. And when you cast your bread upon the waters, it will come back to you in good measure, pressed down, shaken together, running over, as they taught me in Vacation Bible School. But it's true, even if you throw an Eastern flavor on it, go all woo-woo-twinkle-ding-dong about it. What you send out, what you *expect*, is what you get back. Expect garbage and that's what you get."

I grinned at him.

"My therapist told me 'Honey, you've been eating shit for so long it tastes like chocolate.' That was one of the most helpful things she pointed out. That and that I don't owe anyone anything, even to the point of answering when someone speaks to me. I have no obligation to answer them at all. I had never known that, being the victim I was."

"You were the bunny."

"The what?"

"The bunny. You were prey that predators would jump on. They could smell it on you. You were the bunny, never the wolf."

"I want to be a six foot built black man in my next life."

Malcolm smiled his newly intimate smile at me, our one-time experience so satisfying we still savored it.

"You're right about that. I was never the bunny. Now listen. Make a list. Stop fucking anyone. No booty calls, no midnight runs. Pay attention to yourself. Read. Eat well, lots of fruit. Get a lot of sleep. Go to the gym. Capiche?"

"A'ight already. I'll do it. Hey, one question. What do I do with this longer hair? It keeps falling in my face and it makes me crazy."

Malcolm stared at me like I was insane.

It dawned on him at last that I was serious.

"You've been a dyke a long time, haven't you?" he asked, still staring.

"Yes."

"Well," he gently told me, "There's a whole women's culture out there for straight women, magazines at every check-out stand that will tell you what to do with your hair. Girly stuff. Barrettes and shit. I don't know, Annalee. I'm a man. All I know is men like the long hair. Do some research. Go to the beauty shop or whatever it is *other* women do."

"Alanon keeps telling me I didn't create it and I can't cure it. I don't care if Kyle chooses to keep drinking, but when he shows up at 2 a.m. and I have to call the cops, I have a hard time separating myself from it."

Birgitte had been holding up well but she started to cry. It was late at night and she was frightened to be alone.

"Last night he got hauled away for violating the restraining order and all the neighbors were watching. I have to go to court next month. And the boys are siding with him now, that I'm a hard-hearted bitch. My own kids. He took my *kids…*"

Her mournful sobs were unbearable.

"They'll come back, Gitta. You'll see. It takes a while for everyone to figure shit out but they'll see soon enough that he's a fucking loser. You're doing a great job handling all this. Keep up with the meetings. I think there's a lot of strength there."

"Those boys are my whole world, Al. What do I do now?"

"You chop wood, carry water, Gitta. One foot in front of the other. You get through the day fifteen minutes at a time if that's what it takes. I recommend a therapist just as a matter of course but let yourself be angry. You're entitled, I'd say. Did he hurt you?"

"He never got to me, he just pounded on the door and I called 911. The neighbors must have called, too, because the cops were here in like, seconds. I was sound asleep and he just made me about have a heart attack. I looked it up online today, though, and he has had his sixth DUI, Al. Sixth. And the man is on the street, still has his license. He always slips loose somehow, some fucking technicality or something."

Birgitte blew her nose.

"But doesn't violating the restraining order send him to jail?"

"Yup. He's in King County right now for the weekend."

"So this means," I said soothingly, hoping it was the right thing, "tonight at least you can sleep well, knowing he won't be back. You know where he is."

"Good thinking," she yawned. It was almost midnight.

"Take a hot bath," I suggested. "With bubbles and candles and let yourself cry. This shit is temporary, Gitta, until he finally goes to prison or gives the fuck up. One or the other will happen soon. He will hang himself. You don't have to do a thing.,"

"Thanks. I don't believe it myself so I'll just believe you, because you always steer me right. I'm gonna go get in the bathtub."

"It's not good, chica."

We stood outside the Captial Hill AA Big Yellow House, waiting for the Saturday night meeting to let out. Shelly's eyes welled up as she blew into her coffee. The misty February rain looked soft on her bronze skin but her face was full of tightly controlled fear.

"You got the test results back?"

"It's Hep-C."

"How serious is that?"

"I can have six weeks of god-awful treatment where I want to die, my hair falls out, I lose thirty pounds and I puke the entire time. It sounds like withdrawal, sort of."

"Then what happens?"

"Either nothing or I'm completely cured."

I brightened and grabbed her arm.

"But Mishellita, that's *wonderful!* You're saying there's a fifty percent chance of being well? Go for it. What's six weeks?"

Her face remained dark, and she wouldn't look at me.

"I don't want to go through that," she said flatly, her chin pointing out with determination.

"Go through what? Dying? You might not have to."

"The treatment. It sounds worse than the disease."

It was beginning to dawn on me she was serious.

"Are you crazy, Shelly? You have to give it a try."

"Crazy?" she snorted, turning fiercely on me, her eyes hot with tears and rage. "Loco, I am now? I come to you for support and this is what I get?"

Shelly tossed her coffee into the flowers and spit on the ground, walking away from me. I was too stunned to move.

"Shell! Come on, woman, talk to me. I didn't mean it like that."

I took off running after her.

"Get your fucking hands off me, traitor," she yelled when I caught her arm. "Touch me like that one more time and I will slit your fucking throat. Are we clear? You think we are some buddy-buddy friends all cuddly and shit but when the shit goes down for *real* you tell me it's wonderful I have a goddamn 50-50 chance of *survival*?"

She was standing in the middle of 15th Avenue, fists at her sides. I put my hands in the air, walking backwards toward the curb, trying to coax her out of the way of oncoming traffic.

"Problem here?" came a voice over a loudspeaker, a patrol car pulling up to Shelly with the cherry suddenly turned on.

"Goddammit," I whispered to myself as the cops shone a light in Shelly's eyes. This would *so* not be cool, to haul her away as she's digesting this shattering diagnosis. She desperately needed a break, not harassment. But her anger issues and her police record seemed about to collide.

"I got no problem," Shelly said, shielding her eyes as the cop walked slowly up to her.

"Hey! Four-Way!" the cop said, and began to laugh.

"Officer Smartley?" Shelly asked and they pumped hands, Shelly's crisis suddenly turning into old home week.

"Everything okay, Shell? You look a little pissed off and standing in the middle of the street isn't the way to get home alive."

I watched Shelly's face melt into her calmer persona, the transformation genuine.

"Just having a bad day, is all. Hey Al, c'mere. This is Officer Smartley who scooped my ass off the street and sent me to rehab four times over."

"Nice to meet you," the barrel-chested black cop said. "Looks like it took. Fourth time seems to be the charm. I'm no MixALot but I still count. You ladies need a ride home? I've got an extra ten minutes and you can tell me your troubles as we go, Four-Way."

"You turn the siren on?"

"Only for a sec. But I'll leave the lights flashing for you."

Drake drew in a deep breath and sighed into the phone.

"Darling, tell me again why I live here? This place is as grey as my grandfather's flannel suit and I'm about ready to go all Dorothy Parker."

"Now, now, Precious, you might as well live. Even Dorothy said so. What has you so wrapped around the axle?"

"I feel like an animal caught in a trap and I want to gnaw off my own leg to get out. I hate my job, except for when we go out to lunch at The Metropolitan, I'm fat and ugly so no one will ever love me and the weather makes me want to open a vertical vein. I have lived here how long and the weather still gets to me."

"When's your vacation?"

"It can't come soon enough. How's your world, darling?"

"Let's see….I heard Diane has decided to…are you ready…get a sex change. She, excuse me, he will now be referred to as Andrew. The pill stages have already begun and he is sprouting a fine moustache."

"Get out of town on a *stagecoach,* sister! You are *kidding!* The woman you were just out with a few months ago, the motorcycle babe who owns Lesbian-in-a-box bookstore?"

"Yup."

"Where did you get this dish?"

"From Shelly, who heard it in the Madison Beach meeting gossip mill."

"Well, I just have one question."

I burst out laughing.

"Of course, as does everyone. The whole lesbian community, whatever that means, is fighting over this and there's a write-up in the SGN about it. The headline was, 'Local Lesbian Lineage Threatened.'"

"Omigod, this is wild. What will become of the lesbian store if it's owned by a *man?*"

"How's the man-free space feel?"

Malcolm sipped Jack and coffee, keeping me company over my lunch.

"Kind of odd, really. It's weird to turn down sex and company. Like throwing away good food. I have a hard time with that. However, I'm keeping the big picture in mind. Speaking of which, I'm thinking about writing a piece called 'The Five Rules of Safe Driving As Applied To Life.'"

"Five rules?"

"Patented. Swear to God. They're called 'The Smith System,' after Uncle Fred himself."

"Lemme hear 'em."

He relaxed back into the polished blond-oak booth and smiled at me.

"Well, they make it easy to remember with All Good Kids Love Milk, using the first letter of each rule as a prompt: AGKLM. They couldn't make it a snappy acronym which FedEx loves to do so they gave it that memory phrase."

"Making it easier by complicating it further, elongating the things to remember, in my book. Not only do you have to memorize the rules themselves, you have to remember All Good Kids Love Milk? Man, that Smith guy is wack."

"Aim High In Steering."

"That's a good life motto. Go on."

"Get the Big Picture."

"Always necessary."

"Keep Your Eyes Moving."

"Ain't *that* the truth."

Malcolm started to grin.

"Leave Yourself An Out."

He whooped and I smiled back at him.

"I knew you'd like that one," I said.

"Make Sure They See You."

"Damn. You *could* write a self-help book using those rules. White women'd buy it like crazy."

"How's your wife?"

"Speaking of white women? Much better, thanks. PT and some pushing from me and she'll lose the cane pretty soon. How's Shelly?"

I stopped eating and looked out the window.

"I can't reach her, Malcolm. It almost feels like she doesn't want to live through this. Go out all James Dean, quick and young. She seems almost comfortable, like the other shoe finally dropped."

"Is she gonna go through treatment?"

"That's what I mean. No, she's not. She's not fighting for her own life."

"What's that about, you suppose?"

"I dunno. Maybe…maybe she doesn't feel she deserves to live?"

"Maybe. Who can know what's really in another person's head?"

Malcolm's fingers rubbed together and he raised one seductive eyebrow at me.

"Stop that. If it was a one-time deal, no fair teasing."

"I'll always tease, baby, sorry, jessa way I am."

"Okay. I'll just…soak it up."

"Seriously, how is it without a man every night? The voices getting quieter, you can listen to your inner self better?"

"Matter of fact, yes. It does seem to center me somehow, to focus more on me. But how will this perfect man I'm conjuring find me if I am just going about my own little life? Will he knock on my door?"

"It will just happen, Annalee. Trust me here. And I have to say, you look radiant lately."

"It's the exercise."

"It's good. Keep it."

"I need a bar crawl," Drake informed me. "I'm totally restless waiting for everything to happen, waiting for vacation, waiting to begin my future, waiting for Prince Charming to awaken me with a candy kiss. Let's just go out and get loaded and hit all the gay bars."

"I can't, I'm in a new program to get centered."

"How is a pub jump through gay bars going to jeopardize your latest Man Trap? We'd be going to boy bars so a.) you're not gonna see any of your sober lesbo friends and b.) the boys there don't even know you exist. I can't see what harm it would do. The worlds do not meet."

"Agreed. I can be ready at eight."

"Call the gang. Make it nine and meet me at The Cuff."

By the time I met up with Drake, Birgitte was already waiting, leaning on her car.

"Shelly's already inside," she said, pointing at the bar. "She seemed kinda drunk already when she got here. Is Malcolm coming?"

"He's working tonight."

"Too bad. I'd like to see the men go wild for him."

"Poor Drake's gonna have three women hanging off his arm. I'm sure it will make him totally popular."

"Do you think he uses women as a shield? 'Stay away from me' kind of thing to other gay men?"

I was stunned. I'd never thought of such a thing. Suddenly it occurred to me that nearly all of Drake's friends were middle-aged white women.

"Well," I answered, leaning on her car with her, "it makes sense. He leaves town to be gay, do gay things. This trip around the gay bars is a departure for him but I agree, if he wanted to see some action, he would not have invited us along."

"There he is," Birgitte said, brushing off the ass of her perfect jeans.

"Drake, darling, you look mah-velous," I said, hugging him close. "Just the thing, a night on the town. What a great idea."

"Well, I figured we all could use it. The rain is never going to stop, is it? Everyone had their disco nap? I heard there's exotic dancers at Ram and tonight's wet t-shirt night at Steel. I'm leading the way, girls," he tootled, throwing an imaginary boa around his neck and pulling us into the pounding music of the dark, black-lit cave.

"Shelly ever come home that night?" Birgitte asked two days later, when we'd all recovered from massive gin hangovers.

"No. Not til this morning. Shelly went home with some meth head gay boy and swears she was trying to get him sober. I kinda wonder, ya know, Whiskey Tango Foxtrot, what the fuck. She's really got me all wrapped around the axle, Gitta. She's not the person I knew and she's getting sicker, I can see it in her eyes. She's lost some weight and she's on leave of absence from work. And I couldn't tear her away from the bar at any of the places we went to."

"She missed the dancers entirely. That was so cool, those men in body suits with the air machine blowing those long scarves around. Like Isadora or something. And the dry ice was a nice touch. Very modern. I had a great time. I just wish Shelly hadn't disappeared."

"Drake sure had fun, though, didn't he? That stripper boy with the spangly g-string was nice to him."

"It was the money Drake was waving in the air, Al. But who knew Drake was brave enough to put it in the guy's banana sling with his teeth?"

"Give him one too many Tanquerays and he's a wild man of sorts. I had fun, too. I especially liked the ball bearing wrestling pit at Mandrake. "

Like an adult fun-ball pit at Chuck E. Cheese, the greased wrestlers had rolled around in slippery little silver balls. In the blue light you could almost tell they were stripping each other.

"I swear I saw some dick flash around."

I got serious again and sighed, my mind fretting over my friend.

"She'll be okay, Al. Shelly's a smart cookie, she'll turn it around."

"I'll have to believe you, Gitta, because I don't believe it myself. I have a bad feeling about this."

"Stripper-boy's number turned out to be *bogus*," Drake informed me. "Why do people *do* that? Just say no, if you aren't interested. Leading an old man like me on like that. I was once a pretty boy just like him but I never did that. It's simply bad form."

"Well, then, he isn't as refined as you are and he's not worthy of you. Thank goodness he showed his true colors before things got serious."

I wondered if Drake had gotten a number at all. Was this all for my benefit?

I decided to change the subject with the best distraction known to gay men.

"Hot gossip alert."

"*Tell* me!" he squealed.

"I ran into Andrew."

Drake's gay-excitement voice dropped a few levels.

"Who is Andrew?"

"Diane!"

"Holy shit, you saw her?"

Drake's curiosity meter ran back up to full.

"Him."

"Him. Tell me."

"Well, actually I ran into him at McClellan's hardware store in Kent, literally ran into him. I turned a corner and smacked full-body into this really handsome white guy with a moustache and muscles and when I took a step back, apologizing profusely, it was him."

"How did he *look?*"

"Like a guy. It was unbelievable. It was still Diane underneath it all, I mean, the person was the same and now there was facial hair and a slightly deeper voice and something about him was more…square."

"And…?"

"What?"

"C'mon."

"*What?*"

"Annalee, you're a self-proclaimed byke. You went on a date with this hot woman and her motorcycle not even a year ago and you drooled over her then. Okay, so now you run into her as him. My *question,* Miss Density Award, which should be obvious and go without saying, is: were you attracted to him as a *man?*"

"I'm not sure. But we're getting together for coffee on Thursday."

Drake shrieked, holding the phone away and laughing hard.

"Oh, honey, that's hysterical! I want to know everything."

"It's just coffee."

"What about Malcolm X's Rules For Dating?"

"Andrew and I are friends. It's just coffee."

"Tomorrow's your birthday, right? Come to my office in the evening. I've got something to show you. Can you come after work?"

I sighed. It was the last thing I wanted to do.

After work I couldn't get home fast enough to peel off my uniform and take a shower. Dinner was something heated up, eaten in flannel jammies watching yesterday's re-run of Jon Stewart. My friends knew I didn't answer the phone during The Daily Show. It was my special down time.

Besides, it was my *birthday* and it was on a school night. I sighed again.

"Drake, why on earth would you be in the office at seven at night? I don't get off until then and I just want to go home after work. What do you have to show me?"

"Can you come? It's a one-night one-time offer, for this birthday only. Something you can tell your grandchildren later."

"Okay, okay."

On my birthday evening, Drake was waiting outside the Ban Roll-On Building as the sky started to get dark. I was rarely downtown at sunset in my personal vehicle, as FedEx people called their cars.

"Peaches, I'm so glad to see you. We have to hurry!"

"What? What's the hurry? What's the thing you're showing me?"

"It's...how do you say at FedEx? Time-sensitive?"

"That one's old. The latest is time-definite."

"Oh, it's definitely definite. C'mon."

Taking my arm, Drake let me in the secured building after hours, signed in with the lobby guard and held my elbow as we got in the freight elevator.

"This is the last place I want to be after work," I insisted. "What the fuck *is* this? Some birthday. I hope next year I have a freakin' husband instead of a gay companion."

Drake pulled from his pocket the building engineer's key and stuck it in the elevator firefighter lock, turning it one click to the right. The secured top floor button lit up and we began our ascent.

I instantly knew what this meant. My mouth fell open in amazement.

"How did you...? Are you kidding? At sunset? Holy shit, Drake. That's phenomenal. Omigod. How did you pull this off?"

"The janitor wanted a blowjob the other day." Drake smiled. "We negotiated."

"For me?"

"For you, Your Highness. Happy birthday. I'm glad you can appreciate what I had to *endure.*"

The elevator door opened to a green glow. I inhaled sharply, amazed at the aquarium feel under the rounded tinted glass on top the Ban Roll-On building. Industrial compressors, machines and blowers made a steady hum as we walked to the edge of Seattle's famous skyline dome and looked out over a little rail.

The sun was turning Elliot Bay a brilliant orange on top the shimmering blue water. The mountains were out over by Bainbridge Island, snow-peaked and postcard perfect. Seagulls circled the ferry coming in while a ferry heading out blew its deep horn. A Foss tug pushed a freighter loaded with orange and blue Hanjin rail cars. A rainbow-colored parasail drifted by above the piers. To the south Mount Rainier was beginning to turn pink.

It was the most beautiful, panoramic Seattle sunset I'd ever seen.

"Drake, it's sensational. The view is amazing." I turned back toward the curved green glass dome feet from me, huge, radiant. "The tour boats say there's a law library up here inside the dome."

"I've heard rumors it's a swimming pool in an exclusive health club."

"It's just compressors. What a disappointment."

"The white rim on the edge?" He touched it and it shifted in his hand. "Its just plastic covers for the huge fluorescents. At Christmas they put red covers on to make the red-and-green Santa hat."

"It seems so…pedestrian somehow. I expected more glamour."

"Well, now you can say you've been inside the Ban Roll-On Building dome. Only you have to swear never to tell what's here. It's a tradition."

"I swear. It's the best present ever, Drake."

"Do you still have your motorcycle?"

It sounded totally lame as soon as I said it. Why would a gender switch change that? I felt stupid.

"Of course I do. Why not? Just because I grew some facial hair doesn't mean I don't like to go fast."

Andrew took a swig of his coffee but there was no Adams's apple bobbing up and down. I wondered if he'd had the big surgery yet. His tits seemed to be either bound or gone altogether. He'd grown a moustache and sideburns while some chest hairs sprouted at out his open shirt collar. There was even hair on his knuckles.

"Everything else okay? Your work going alright?"

"I'm getting a lawyer. I'm suing my silent partner. I'm being forced out of the business now that I'm not a woman."

"Good for you. Go get 'em. Find a girlfriend yet?"

The hotness was gone for me with Andrew as a man. Somehow, I'd liked butch Diane better. Maybe it was all the facial hair.

"Not really. Not looking."

"Oh."

"What, you thought maybe you and I…?"

"Oh, no, not at all…" I blushed deep red and took a big drink of coffee. It burned the roof of my mouth and I started coughing.

"No offense, Al," Andrew said, pounding me on the back, "but I just can't think of you that way anymore. You seem kinda confused to me, dating men and women."

I was astounded that someone who had physically morphed their birth gender was judging my sexual ease between worlds.

"You're kidding, right?" I laughed, blinking hard as I tried to swallow the rest of my coffee without killing myself.

"No. I mean, I've always known who I was, even in my female body I knew I was a man who loved soft, feminine women. I had to be with dykes to have women at all but now I can get a straight woman. I'm a *real* man now."

"Good luck with that, Andrew," I smiled, hugging him and leaving a five-spot on the table as I got up to go. I was glad we hadn't fucked back then and I could walk away from this transaction with my side of the street clean.

All the same, I wondered what would become of Lavender Labrys.

"Mom, I need to call AAA because my car got broken into and I need the keys but they're locked in my apartment and everyone's stealing my stuff and no one understands, no one gets it, but I cut my hand when I broke into the car and Spot needs water but no one will give it to me, no one understands, I've talked to seventeen people and no one understands, I'm a poet, an artist and a writer and no one understands...."

Dew started crying.

Cars were honking and I heard his dog bark.

I held the phone tightly to my ear, heart pounding in insane wild terror as the scariest red flag of all waved madly before my eyes.

He was the perfect demographic, white male, 18-25 and I hadn't heard schizophrenia talk since the Sunshine People, when Ziller took too many peyote buttons and never came back.

Setting my enormous fear aside, I aimed right for the practical. Find out where he is and get his ass off the street.

"Where are you, Dew?"

Completely exasperated with me, as if I should already *know* where he was in Chicago, he said he was at Taylor and Racine, where else? He had his dog, and no one would listen, he couldn't get into his car so he'd smashed the window himself, and seventeen people didn't understand...

"Stay there, sweetheart, and I'll get on a plane."

"Because you understand, no one understands but you," he began crying again, then straightened back instantly as someone approached. "Hey buddy, hey buddy," he called, setting the phone down, and I listened in horror as he handed over his PlayStation II and his TV to a complete stranger.

"It's so great, Mom, I'm free, I'm free, they need this stuff but I don't need this stuff, I went to Trader Joe's and got organic sandwiches and passed them out to the homeless people and I got all my money out of the bank and gave it away, just gave it away, isn't it great? What am I gonna do, Mom, Spot's so thirsty and I can't get in my apartment. Here's my new phone number because I don't have my old phone anymore, I need to go under the radar because too many people are looking for me. And I never need to eat again, do you realize we spend all our energy eating and I don't have to do that anymore. I'm gonna live on protein powder and water, that's all I need. And we spend a third of our life sleeping so if I just stop sleeping I can get it all done because I'm a poet, an artist, a writer and no one understands..."

"I'm getting on a plane. Stay there, stay in touch with me."

With utter calm that covered my sheer terror, I hung up the phone and called Amanda.

"Amanda, I know I haven't talked to you in years but I need you, Sunshine style. My family doesn't live there anymore and I can't get to Chicago until tomorrow morning."

"What's the matter, Al?"

Amanda was all ears.

"My son Dupree's gone Ziller."

"Where is he?" Amanda asked, her vibe tensing into action instantly, the time between us unimportant.

"Taylor and Racine, by some apartment I thought he'd just moved out of. There is a girlfriend somewhere, from what I can gather, and a few friends who don't understand. I think its mushrooms."

"I'm on my way. I'll take Colin, they're about the same age. Is he still a redhead?"

"Yup. Six foot. Skinny. He's got a Golden Retriever with him."

"Gimme an hour."

I called Dew back and kept him on the phone, my heart breaking over and over as he raved, taunted passers-by, described the violent vengeance he wanted to wreak on everyone in his reality, sobbed into his dog's shoulder, and paced around his car with the shattered glass. He still hadn't found the keys, for which I was grateful, since he wanted to go to Wisconsin to see his sister, Seattle to visit me, California for his dad, even France, because he hated America and wanted out, no one understood. Finally, my other line rang.

"Annalee? It's Amanda. We're with him. I'll call you later."

Nail-biting eternities later, after five hours of listening to his spin, Amanda, her husband Josh and son Colin had delicately coaxed Dew into their car, set the child locks so he couldn't jump out and drove him to the hospital ER, where he was admitted into the psych ward.

My early morning flight and rental car got me to the hospital almost 24 hours after Amanda had "run into" him on the street.

It was Memorial Day weekend and the hospital was short-staffed. His assigned doctor wouldn't even be in for two more days. My six-foot-four baby was in a single locked room in two hospital gowns, one backward, and a pair of hospital pants and hospital non-skid socks that barely covered his size 13 wide feet.

I finally placed my hands on my firstborn child.

"I told you not to come," Dew snorted, appearing after the psych staff retrieved him from his room.

He stood stretching in a doorway as I rushed to hug him tight. He didn't reciprocate, just waited for the touching to be over.

Dew didn't stop talking for a single instant, saying the same loop over and over, begging every fourth sentence to get out, how can he get out, what do I need to sign, why aren't you on my side?

Now a complete babbling stranger, Dew grew enraged and almost violent within ten minutes of my arrival. I heard doors locking tight and a Code Something, some color, was quietly announced over the PA. The floor went into lockdown.

Two beefy security guards in rubber gloves appeared and manhandled Dew down the hallway where I could not follow. They pushed him into his barricaded room and sealed the door.

I was asked to leave. Dew was screaming, his voice muffled as he threw himself against the metal door time after time.

"Come back tomorrow. He'll have calmed down by then," the nurse said, buzzing me off the locked ward.

I waited in the silent hallway for an elevator, weeping in huge gulping sobs, astounded that two days previous my deepest concern had been losing ten pounds.

Amanda handed me a cup of hot tea.

"How about Chinese?"

"I can't eat. I can't. Jesus, Amanda it was like listening to Ziller all over again. I was young then but it stuck with me. Three days he raved and then he got quiet and we were all so grateful he'd shut up, remember?"

"I remember. It was frightening listening to the elders discuss if we needed to get the authorities involved."

"And then he got quiet and he never spoke another word. Just glazed over."

"Fernfeather is still taking care of him, I heard. The Canopy had a little blurb about her dedicated service on the website. Ziller's almost 70 now. I hear he's fat, too, since he sits in a chair all day."

"What if Dew never comes back?" I whispered then started to cry.

"He'll come back. He has to. It's gonna take a few days for the 'shrooms to get out of his system. How long can you stay?"

"Thanks for the housing on short notice, A. I'm staying until he's done. Work can suck my dick."

"He'll be okay, Annalee. He's young, healthy, bright. He just got overwhelmed, maybe?"

"Maybe. But he's so far gone. He smiled at me with this maniacal smile, like an evil clown. It gave me the chills. He kept telling me he was lying to me, that he lies all the time, that he's an actor, a poet, a writer, and no one cares. If I use logic, like saying I care, he gets angry. I have forgotten how to think Sunshine."

"Ah, thinking Sunshine. The path of least resistance. Go along with whatever he says. Agree with him, don't contradict. See if that calms him down."

"The drugs they're giving him are calming him down to sleep. I just called there and they said he was sleeping. Or maybe they say that to the parents so *they* sleep. Jesus, it's creepy there. And my kid, my kid is one of them. Omigod, what can I do?"

Amanda set my tea down and pulled me closer, letting me weep on her shoulder.

"I have to do it," I said. "I waited all this time, waited to see how he was with my own eyes, waiting to be there before any of his family found out."

"Call him."

I wiped my eyes and found my phone, calling Dew's father to break the news.

Next morning I went to visit Dew, hopeful something had changed overnight, ready to face the challenge of having a grown child go completely insane. We'd make it work. I'd take him home with me to Seattle, it was his second home. I'd find him a good doctor. Or maybe he'd suddenly snap out of it, start back to school, apologize to the frightened girlfriend, buy a new t.v. and we'd all skate away clean. Everything would be alright.

We were allowed to meet in the dayroom, where Judge Judy was blaring on a ceiling-mount t.v. Another gowned patient sat in a wheelchair, watching the show. I asked if we might go in the lunchroom instead to be able to talk and that was allowed. I still couldn't go to his room.

Dew was as crazy as he'd been the day before.

Everyone hated him, when could he get out of here, what were they giving him, why couldn't he have a t-shirt, what did he need to do to sign himself out, the food was awful, he couldn't sleep, no one understands, no one was listening, it was all him, he was the only one who knew anything, he was a dealer, the doctors and patients were all his clients, it was all written down in a New Yorker, where was his magazine, where was his dog? He sobbed, he begged me to get him out, he tore his clothes, he swore he'd escape. He'd written a poem and drawn a picture in art therapy, did I want to see?

Peanut arrived down from Madison with her boyfriend Chad, both of them deeply concerned. They'd socialized as a couple with Dew many times, and said they'd seen no evidence of any trouble. Chad didn't feel comfortable going into to see him, so he slouched his six foot frame into a waiting room chair, hunkered down for whatever came next. He wanted to be there for Peanut, supporting Dew's support system, and said firmly many times through the course of the troubles, "Whatever Penelope wants."

Dew was happy to see Peanut. He seemed almost himself for a few minutes before going into an angry tirade about his dog.

"Amanda had your dog and now he'll go with me. I'll take good care of Spot. He has water and food and toys."

"He needs *me*," Dew wept, banging his fists into the wall.

"You all need to leave now," said the nurse who magically appeared when Dew began making noise. "Dupree, let's go back to your room."

"Goodbye, brother-man," Peanut sadly said, leaping up to hold him around the waist, her head barely reaching his shoulders. He stood motionless, allowing Peanut to touch him but not touching back. Their red hair was exactly the same color. The nurse pried her arms away and led Dew down the hall. He never said a word or even looked back.

Peanut rubbed my back while I wept outside the secured door, Chad unwinding himself from the orange plastic chair to stand uncomfortably near by, helpless to do anything.

"You need to let this out, too," I admonished Peanut through my sniffles, pulling myself together enough to go on.

"Not in front of other people," she growled, turning her fear and grief to anger.

"Then get alone soon."

"I will, Mom. Let's go to Amanda's and you can rest up."

"Can you stay overnight? I know you drove down from Wisconsin in a hurry but do you want to come see him in the morning?"

Peanut looked at Chad, her eyes imploring him.

"Whatever Penelope wants," Chad said to me.

"Amanda's got room. She's Sunshine, it won't be any problem."

There was Dew's car to deal with, the sunroof bent, the window smashed, shattered glass all over the seats and everything of value stripped away.

A friend who'd turned on him, from what we could piece together, had his computer and his guitar and refused to give them back. Dew's passport, license, and sentimental items were also being held by this new enemy, one of the seventeen people who hadn't listened

The girlfriend tearfully called, now safely in the suburbs with her parents after Dew had held her down and screamed in her face, she said. She was traumatized, taking a semester off, and told me we had until Friday to withdraw him from next semester's classes without penalty. If there was anything she could do....

His apartment involved some mysterious 11th-hour deal he'd made with his old landlord and needed undoing. The landlord was amazed, saying he'd been a great tenant all last year, impeccably clean, responsible, reliable, but if Dupree was unable to sign a new lease, well, this was the busy rental time for him, so would we please make a decision? The next four hours were spent trashing half the apartment's contents and boxing up what was salvageable with a promise to the landlord to pay for the splintered front door. I told him we'd be out of there if he'd release Dew from any commitment, verbal or written. We shook hands. Two trips to box up and move Dew's belongings to Amanda's basement were required, Chad pitching in without a word of protest. Peanut and I worked at a huge wine stain in the carpet, swept and gathered, then carried piles of trash to the alley, stunned into silence over the filthy condition of the apartment.

Peanut and I went back to the hospital Sunday evening.

Dew was doped, barely able to hold his head above the table in the lunchroom. Another patient in the room was fiddling with the radio and landed finally on WFMT, Chicago's Fine Arts Station, which had played in the Fawn Camp when I was growing up. Rossini wafted into the room.

The gowned white woman yelled out "He's a good boy, your Dupree. He helped an old man get up today and he gave me his Jello."

"Thanks Marcel," Dew grinned, raising his head. "Hear that, Mom? I'm a good boy. I'm a poet," he said, the loop going slower now as he put his head back down. "I'm an actor and a writer. No one understands. Marcel understands."

"We understand," Peanut assured him, rubbing his back through the gown. I noticed he needed a man-wax, his back hairy and overgrown, stretching up to his hair line. My metro-sexual child had let himself go.

"Did you see my bruises? I tried to escape four times," Dew grinned, the maniacal leer trying now, it seemed, to *intentionally* frighten me. I stayed unswayed, though that face would haunt my night-sweats for months to come.

"Yes, you did," I replied but he showed me again, the purple spots big as my fist all up and down his shoulder, arm and side.

He showed Peanut again.

"How's Spot?" he asked her suddenly, and I was very pleased that he remembered Peanut had his dog.

"He has plenty of water," Peanut replied, tapping immediately into Dew's primal fear. The bony shoulder blades relaxed as his head went down again.

"I have to go to sleep now," he announced and stood up, wobbling to his room, now fully acclimated to the zoo.

"I don't think he's going to come back," I told Amanda into my glass of wine.

I still couldn't eat food. Peanut tried to get me to eat anyway and I pushed her away.

"I thought by today he'd have settled down, 48 hours off the mushrooms and with anti-psychotics in him but he seems exactly the same only slower."

"Yes, he will, Mom," Peanut demanded. "He'll be fine. He has to be."

"He has to be," Amanda seconded.

"Ziller wasn't," I moaned, laying out my darkest vulnerability. Not my golden boy. Not my Dew. The genius goes mad and never returns.

"When are you guys going to tell us about Ziller?" Peanut asked, taking more salad with her chopsticks, the black lacquered ones with the mother-of-pearl inlaid roses she always kept in her purse. "Chad doesn't know what you guys are talking about. You always refer to him but you've never explained who is."

"A, you tell" I said, passing off to her, my head in my hands. Amanda rubbed my back and said she'd tell the story.

"Ziller was The Sunshine Tribe's John Kennedy, man, a tall looker the color of caramel. He had round John Lennon glasses, a little afro and always wore a little cap, like a...what do they call them, Al?"

"Greek Fisherman's cap," I prompted her "And he had an Indian motorcycle."

"This guy was the coolest thing on two wheels and we were all crazy about him. Sorry, poor word choice under these circumstances."

"Oh, wait!" I shot up my head. "I have to tell you something before I forget. Can we set your story on the shelf just for a moment?"

"Sure, Al."

"I went to Target today to return all that crap Dew bought in his buying frenzy...well, first I went to Walgreens but they said they can't take the phone cards back once they've been activated at the register. Nine hundred dollars in phone cards, he bought. Jesus. Anyway, I went to Target and I didn't have the receipt but I had his temporary credit card Peanut found in his trashed apartment. Sure, she could take it back, she told me and then she said, 'Wow, he really went crazy, huh?' I couldn't believe it. I wanted to say 'yeah, actually, he did.' I started laughing or else I'd have cried."

"That's awful and hilarious, both," Peanut said, hiding her chewing mouth with her outstretched delicate, be-ringed fingers. One of those gold bands was the wedding ring her dad had gotten me an eternity ago, another was the diamond from Angel. It all looked better on Peanut, who had her nails decorated every two weeks. Today they were turquoise with silver stars.

"Yup. Go ahead, Amanda, I'm sorry to interrupt. Tell about George Wilson Ziller."

"We worshiped him. He was the son of a Black Panther and a Jewish women's rights activist and he was raised in France. Just the ultimate cool, you know? Like Hendrix and John Lennon put together but the accent was slightly Parisian. His eyes were hazel. Anyway, he came back to the Sunshine Tribe Council one year and sat with the elders in the ring of fire, you know, presenting himself as a rightful heir and they lapped it up. The power everyone gave him was unbelievable, like a new messiah had arrived. And bear in mind historical perspective," Amanda added, looking over her square granny glasses at my beautiful daughter and her beau. A's braids were naturally streaked with gray and she looked fabulous at nearly fifty.

"What do you mean?" Chad asked, his eyes intent, interest peaked by the story. He was so tall he folded nearly double in the chair to be appropriate table-height for eating, like a cartoon character. His body was rock solid from working out. No wonder Peanut liked this handsome, nice guy.

"It was the mid-sixties and the swell of cultural shift was enormous. Everywhere was upheaval and change, unforeseen even five years previous."

Amanda sounded like her well-worn I Ching.

"Civil rights protests, civil disobedience, heightened awareness of Viet Nam through first-time-ever grisly, realistic television coverage. Women were beginning to wake up and want more. Young people of color were banding together for all kinds of purposes, which scared the hell out of the old white guard. Others were dropping out of society altogether, going back to the land, like we did. We kept our finger on the pulse of what was happening out there but we preferred organic vegetables and world peace over dinner, on a more local level. The things others protested out there, we quietly re-worked and adapted---integration, mixed marriages, gay freedom, women's liberation, free health clinics, daycare, pre-school, agriculture and bread-baking seminars. It was an agrarian, equalitarian hideaway, under the radar. Each according to their need."

Amanda sighed and took a sip of wine. The younger ones were rapt, waiting for the climax. I knew this story like I knew my own name.

"Then along came Ziller," I whispered.

"Yup. Then along came Ziller. We all adored him, hung on his every word. He spouted European ideas, modernization, global marketing. He had a plan that could move us quietly into the black, buying land in Costa Rica and South America, saving the rainforests and having a good investment at the same time, stuff like that. Way the hell ahead of his time. No one else knew anything about stocks or gold bullion so he was instantly crowned king of the People. The hero worship got really large, and a lot of infighting began, petty jealousies that began to eat away at the foundation. The crowd of worshippers was huge, though, and then there were a few distracters making mayhem, and alliances started forming, for and against. It split the Tribe, and hurt feelings webbed out, poisoning the whole circle. Even the little kids were irritable that winter, remember?"

"I remember. It was so white, the snow was so deep. Five feet that winter."

"We had a tent meeting, with a fire and Smoking of the Drum Pipe, and everyone said Ziller took peyote buttons that night but we never got the story straight. Anyway, Ziller came to the Drum Pipe ceremony and he was kinda off. He was sweating a lot and he kept taking off his clothes and pacing and everyone was on edge anyway. We all thought he was birthing some new concept he was going to lay on us, getting ready, and then he started screaming. He took the firesticks from their poles and started doing this kind of hula dance with them and it was dangerous in the tent. We all started backing away from him with the men eyeballing the exits and the height of the tent, calculating danger if flames took over while the women were herding the children away as fast as they could. Ziller screamed and waved the firesticks around for an hour, yelling incomprehensible stuff, violent, radical damnation stuff, and then all of a sudden he took off into the snow. The quiet was as loud as the screaming had been and even though I was little, I can still hear the dead silence after that wild night. I stood outside hoping he'd come back, be himself, feeling like the Ziller we knew was already dead."

"It would have been better if he was," I sighed and stood to stretch. Was my Dew in for years of similar mania?

"He sat in the snow all night and he threatened everyone who tried to talk to him with a sword he'd gotten at some surplus store and hidden outside the tent. When he came straggling back next morning, he raved non-stop for three days then was silent and he never spoke another word. Still hasn't. Magic gone backwards, is what it was. And there went our one leader, down the tubes, eating pudding from a paper cup with a plastic spoon. Even the hospital didn't know what to do with him, once the Council got him into a car next day. Take care of him, was all the doctors said. Maybe he'll come out of it, maybe not. He never has."

Peanut shifted in her chair, her delicate hands in her lap.

"But Dew will," she said. "It wasn't like that. It was just drugs, not a messianic calling that got him. He'll be okay."

The next day he was *more* okay, anyway. About an eighth of the time, he seemed to comprehend things, know who I was and why I was worried, know that he was in a "loony bin," as he called it, and had realized he had fucked something up. The enormity of it still wasn't anywhere near the surface and Dew's crazy talk continued, but at a slightly slower pace. He knew he'd spent a lot of money that last day. He knew the girlfriend had thrown him out. That his friend Trent had become his enemy and was holding his important things.

But the crazy talk still took over.

"Take my poem home," Dew whispered, pushing it into my hand, afraid a doctor or nurse might try to stop him.

My skin is yellow, nobody is listening.
The blood screams dry! Nobody hears.
The cup I once drank from has gone from full to null.
Nobody is there to buy the null.
Preoccupation, defecation all locked away in solitude,
When I finally die, they'll hear my shouting and stammers.
At rest at last, finally I sleep.
And everybody feels my disease.

"Do you want to come back to Seattle with me?" I asked.

"I signed a lease," he moaned, coming clearer the last few days. He vaguely recalled negotiating with his old landlord. "Didn't I?"

"Taken care of. No, you didn't. Nothing's holding you here. You want to take a break from school and come west?"

"Yes."

"Then we'll make it happen."

"I need to go to sleep now. This drug they give me is awful."

"What is the drug he's on?" I asked the psychiatric nurse assigned to Dew's corridor.

"What is your relationship to him?" the prissy woman asked.

"I'm his mother," I hissed. "Look at his file. I am his emergency contact and I hold his insurance information. Now. Tell me what drug he is on."

"Seraquel. It's an anti-psychotic."

Drake was not answering his phone and I wondered if this was the week he was in Mexico. How long had I been in Chicago? It felt like I never had left this enormous slum, as if my Left Coast life was a blur, a dream. I had lost all sense of time, the days now one long stretch of harrowing anxiety and incredibly difficult mundane tasks.

I withdrew Dew from college, got the landlord's forwarding address to make Dew send a check later for the bashed in door, visited the hospital at least twice a day, let FedEx know I was going to be delayed, sent emails with updates on his condition.

My phone remained blessedly silent, all the Sunshine People and my friends acknowledging my firm directive for phone silence. The call of distress went out but everyone respected my grief. Any questions or commentary were to go to Amanda, who'd agreed to field any concern.

My brain was barely functioning.

I'd lost my taste for drama completely.

Relating the horrific details to Dew's father was enough. My sense of humor was gone, my face set at flat affect, tears sprouting at inopportune times.

I wished I had Gitta, Malcolm, Drake or Shelly to tell it to.

Shelly's phone was now out of service, scaring me, but I had enough on my own plate. I didn't need to add more worry beads to my invisible rosary of hope that pleaded in a non-stop loop: Please, Universe, I am casting honest bread upon the water, asking for a miracle for my boy, please bring him back, please hear my plea. I didn't need to add Mishellita on top of that, not now. I'd check on her when I got home.

Gitta's voice mail was full, kind of odd for her, but I didn't have the energy to wonder about that, either.

Malcolm was always working and couldn't talk there, and I didn't want to bother him at home.

Still, I wished for a touchstone, something to remind me of my real life in Seattle going on without me. Chicago was filthy, a weighty chain around my neck, trying to suck me back into its misery. Everywhere was poverty, burglar bars, aggressive signage full of NO's, concrete, pavement, miles of brick buildings, no trees, huge potholes, shitty roads, angry people, fear and danger. The small beauty one might eek out of the city was limited and unavailable to most city inhabitants, being tucked close to the lakefront. Seattle's geographic beauty and welcoming spirit were nowhere to be found in the flatlands.

Except with Amanda. By contrast, Amanda's quiet background hospitality was a godsend. Dinner appeared, the fridge was stocked with farmer's market bounty, wine was placed in my hand. The bathroom was bursting with organic products, the towels were huge and fluffy. Colin found me some pot to quiet my nerves and the slow burn down my throat gave me no regrets. Interesting books were everywhere, quiet places were offered, exercise possibilities laid out.

All publicity about Dew's event was fronted by Amanda. She never let it touch me.

I slept the sleep of the dead, waking instantly at sunrise, dressed and ready for another exhausting round of hoping for tiny changes in my firstborn, my golden boy, my life's blood.

He had calmed down considerably and even used some old family in-jokes, smiling slightly, a little bit shy, as if it was awkward coming back to himself. Peanut and I were deeply relieved to see each moment.

His slight stutter returned.

We'd told the doctor this phenom, that his lifelong minor speech impediment completely disappeared during this psychosis. His psychiatrist had clearly taken a mental note of that, an interesting tidbit to recount to his colleagues later.

Yet there were still moments of spontaneous tears and frustrated rage, such as this one.

"You'll never trust me again," Dew wailed, near tears as we sat in the dayroom

"That's not true!" I immediately rushed to assure him, though I knew instantly, feeling it physically in my gut that yes, it was exactly true.

I *would* always wonder if he was going to lose it this way again. That child could still read me like a fucking book.

Chapter Six

Measure upon measure, here a little, there a little, Dew came back enough after five agonizingly long days to be released from the hospital into my care. There was the family counseling session, the meeting with the social worker, our plan for after-care, the shrink appointment back home. We shook hands with the doctor, thanked the staff, and Dew got his clothes back.

"How's the outside world look?" I asked as we drove up Lake Shore Drive. A roadside electric construction sign flashed "Workers on LSD Next 2 Miles."

"Too bright," he said, squinting his forehead. "But good. Good to be out. Can we stop for some cigarettes, please? And can you loan me ten dollars until I get the bank thing straightened out?"

He'd maxed out his credit card and taken too much money out of his debit account in too short a time, buying wildly the two days before he was hospitalized. His money was frozen, his bank cards useless, despite five grand sitting in his savings. We hadn't had the long moment yet to go to the bank and deal with it. I was also worried because Dew's patience was about minus fifty and the least little glitch enraged him. Facing a bank's bureaucracy might land him in jail if it didn't go well.

I couldn't take that chance, alone with him in such a gloomy, miserable town. I didn't want to have to chase after him or have him go off again.

I handed him cash.

Amanda's home expanded to include one more and we began relocating Dew to Seattle.

The basement boxes had to be sorted through. A pile was made, bagged and driven to a thrift store. Dew's whole life, as he put it, sat in another pile of keep-able, ship-worthy goods. Angry, near tears, and resigned in short bursting cycles, his arms flailed about as he vented.

A car caravan lugged the seven boxes and one bicycle crate to FedEx. Even with my discount, it cost Dew a significant amount, his first indicator that this manic episode was going to be expensive as he cleaned up his trail of despair. This helped feed the victimized angry cycle he seemed to be looping.

Though flattered he felt comfortable enough around me to be himself, the energy he gave off was exhausting.

I cried when I had moments alone, still trying to reach my friends.

At night I made him take the terrible drug that paralyzed his body but left his mind active, forcing him to lie down and endure the terrors with no way to fight back.

Seven days, I made him promise me, seven days of taking the drug at night, remember how the doctor said the psychotic break affected your brain chemistry and the Seraquel was needed to balance it out?

Seven days, he agreed.

Grateful, I couldn't believe this towering giant still listened to his mother.

Peanut and Chad returned to Madison when I promised that Dew and I would come see their new place once we got his shit together in the city. I loved her more after this family event than I ever had.

The first night I sat in Amanda's darkened front room, the leather couch pulled out to make Dew's bed. I "lit" the electric fireplace, watching the fake flames glow in the dark. From an easy chair, I watched my firstborn draw one breath after another, not moving except for his chest, recovering in horrible, tiny increments from the fried circuits he'd put himself through, his brain firing off like Pop-Rocks, his body paralyzed with Seraquel.

I wondered in the dark if our family would ever be the same, if he would have permanent damage from this one episode, if these things were one to a customer.

Hours I sat there, staring at his skinny form, the streetlights bleeding in through the window's closed wood slats, the tinny fireplace making a humming sound. I turned it off after Dew made moaning noises. I needed to hear his every utterance. My child needed to live. No Hendrix scene here, no vomit-choking on my watch, and hopefully, Universe willing, no Ziller redux, either.

I left a voice mail for Cora, this being an occasion when my need to hear her voice was greater than my respect for her coupled relationship. Her Sherry had always gone green-eyed whenever Cora and I were in touch, but forty years of friendship was greater than Sherry's paranoia.

"It's bad, Cora. It's Dew. Call me."

The trash cans were oozing slimy food garbage and underneath were ruined mementoes of Dew's childhood, high school and college years. Torn and smeared were photos of prom, the second girlfriend, the current one. His writing, art and sentimental doodads were ruined, unsalvageable. A favorite pair of Dew's raggedy-ass jeans sat on top of one trash barrel in the alley behind his former friend's apartment, the pouring rain making our already dreadful task even more miserable.

A painfully skinny black homeless man came walking down the alley, a belt wrapped almost double around him.

"That's my coat he's wearing. And my belt, too. How much cash do you have, Mom?"

That question still hurt him after being responsible for his own finances and life for the past six years, now dependent on his mother. But he didn't have time for pride.

I handed him everything in my purse and he walked quickly toward the guy.

"Hey, mister. Buddy. I'll give you forty bucks for that coat."

I waited for him in the car, wanting to stay out of the transaction. My own child, buying his clothes back from a street person. What horrific chain of events had led up to this point? How ephemeral everything was that we think solid---jobs, money, relationships, even geographic locations. A couple brain chemicals later and ka-blooie. Two weeks previous his life had been perfectly set in Chicago, and now, nothing held him here, not one shred or person.

I looked in the rearview. The skinny man was holding Dew's hand and praying for him.

Dew hopped into the car.

"It's a two hundred dollar Cole Haan jacket, Mom. Thanks for the money. I'll get it dry-cleaned. I got a blessing, too."

"Maybe it's the start of something good. We could use it. Okay, so you own one extra pair of jeans and now a jacket. What does Trent still have?"

"My laptop, my guitar and case, and my passport."

"His girlfriend won't let you in?"

Dew had hopped the secured fence and pounded on their back door while I'd waited. They had no front door accessible without a key, either, no bell to ring. It was a fortress, and his valuables were walled inside.

"Nope. She said if I come back, Trent's gonna call the cops and arrest me for trespassing."

"What a great idea. *We're* going to the police."

It was the antithesis of the event's beginnings, the yang to the yin in my own head. Chicago police could be brutal, but we had been spared that outcome by Amanda's rescuing Dew off the street. It could just as easily have ended a different way, with him in Cook County Jail and then Cook County Psych Ward.

But now, the cops were on *our* side.

Twenty minutes later, we met two Chicago police officers out front of the barred apartment. Dew sounded a little crazy, giving far too much detail and dangerously too much personal information.

"Cut to the chase, Dew," I interrupted him after lengthy minutes, the cops getting impatient. In a motherly gesture, I removed his sunglasses, making sure he made eye contact with the two officers. "This kid who lives here, Trent, has his laptop, guitar and passport. He won't give them back."

"Is this true?" the cops asked Dew. He nodded, quieting down.

The cops jumped the stair railing and pounded on the apartment door.

Star, the girlfriend, fronted as best she could but when she eventually caved and produced Dew's guitar, the cops began to understand Dew was telling the truth.

"Star, I'm Annalee, I'm Dew's mother. Now you *know* there's a case that goes with that guitar. Just turn around and go back inside and get it, please."

I knew young women were frightened by grey-haired mothers like me so I puffed up as big as I could, giving her the steely eye. Saying she'd take another look, Star disappeared into the apartment while the cops lectured Dew on letting his shit out of his sight and taking drugs to get into this mess. Head hung, Dew concurred, apologizing, swearing never to do this again.

A moment later Star suddenly found the guitar's case but swore the laptop was nowhere inside. Trent would be back at seven, she said, and she'd tell him to find the laptop.

"There're drugs inside," Dew said flatly after we'd left, all of us agreeing we'd try back at seven. If we needed to call the cops again, they said to do so. "That's why she was scared."

"Why didn't you want the place busted? I would think you'd be pissed and feel righteously vindicated since they are trying to rip off your stuff."

"Star's cool. I had a huge crush on her freshman year. I still like her. It's not her fault Trent's an asshole."

"Well, I wanted to throttle her. She knows the stuff's inside."

It made me furious, some twenty-year-old white girl punk trying to stand up to the cops, playing against a boy who still has the hots for her, manipulating the situation.

"Don't take it out on Star, Mom," Dew angrily snapped at me. "And talk about humiliating, Mom, taking my sunglasses off in front of the cops and Star? Like I'm fucking six years old."

Dew spat out the window, suddenly seething next to me.

I was stunned but he had a point.

"You're right about that. Sorry. I hadn't even thought of it. I apologize."

He wasn't ready to let go of the anger yet, his dignity still bruised, his world throbbing over his complete reversal of fortune.

To fill time before our seven-p.m. climactic meeting, we went to Manny's on Roosevelt Road. Dew wolfed down the vegetarian special and I refrained from ordering tongue for the sake of my sensitive vegan boy. It felt wonderful to be in that homey Jewish deli again.

Chewing my corned beef, I wished I'd gotten the pastrami. My throat was so tense and dry the extra grease would have helped me swallow. I wickedly thought about mayonnaise and smiled to myself. I'd be thrown out for such a sin.

"We can go to Target," Dew said, his head hanging low over his plate. "It's right by here. I have to return more stuff. And GNC is around the corner. Do you think Walgreens will take the phone cards back?"

"No. I asked them three days ago."

I'd pulled the assistant manager aside and asked for a quieter place to talk before I had burst into tears. No, ma'am, I'm sorry, she'd whispered, we can't take them back after they've been activated at the register but good luck with your son.

"GNC needs a manager's approval. I went in there, too."

We sipped tea and waited, trying to stretch out four hours of waiting until the big confrontation at Trent's over Dew's remaining possessions.

I parked the rental car on Taylor Street, then Dew and I walked to the alley behind the apartment complex. It was starting to rain.

Trent was on the back stairway, just going into the apartment door.

"Hey, Trent," Dew yelled. "Gimme my stuff."

Trent held up his hand and disappeared inside, closing the door.

"Was that 'gimme a sec' or fuck you'?" I asked, sure we would have to call the goddamn cops again.

"I think it was gimme a sec," Dew said, surprisingly optimistic.

It seemed highly unlikely to me that we'd get what we came for, but the scene had to be played out or, I knew from adult hindsight, Dew would always regret it. It was like the assortment of his things we'd boxed to ship back to Seattle: dishes, banged up thrift store kitchenware, a few books, minimal clothing, posters, a toolbox, the sewing machine I'd gotten him. In the end half of this stuff wouldn't mean a thing to him but since his life was reduced to ashes and rubble, it all became important.

Suddenly the door opened and Trent came toward us like an automaton, carrying the laptop's box and a basket with Dew's passport, license, and some receipts. I was completely baffled as he brought it right out to us and handed it to Dew. We must have frightened the bubblehead girlfriend enough earlier to scare him vicariously. I felt triumphant.

"Trent, I'm Dew's mother. Sorry to meet under these awkward circumstances. Thanks for bringing us our stuff. Open the box, Dew and check it. Trent, you stay right there until he does."

Mothers of friends are formidable. I stared at Trent without blinking, holding him there with my eyes.

"It's all here. Call me sometime," Dew non-sequitered-ed as Trent turned and walked away.

Dew didn't mean that but he was feeling magnanimous. After the loss of so much, we'd finally won one. The passport was a relief, and the Mac seemed to be all there, every accessory still nestled in the foamboard cut-outs.

"Totally cool," I smiled as we walked out of the alley, the rain pouring down in sheets.
"That was *awesome.* He just handed the shit back, like it was the right thing to do. I never thought we'd see your stuff again, frankly."

"Me, neither. I wonder what got into him?" Dew puzzled until we reached the street.

Sitting in front of Trent's apartment was a Chicago police car on completely un-related business, the cherry-top flashing right into Trent's living room window. Made more distinct by the grey rainy dark contrast, we realized Trent must have been scared out of his mind that they were coming for him. What a stroke of sheer coincidence.

"Thank the Universe for that one," I said, laughing for the first time in days. "I never thought I'd be so happy to see a Chicago police car. Maybe," I giggled, trying to imagine the hyper-paranoia with which Trent must have been seized, "Maybe he flushed all his drugs."

I told Dew's dad to deal with Dew's car. It was in his name, anyway. One call to his clan and they dispatched a member to drive it away.

There were advantages, I supposed grudgingly, to that family.

Dew and I headed up to Madison to see Peanut and Chad's new place, maybe have a little vacation before we flew home and give Dew a chance to say goodbye to his graying dog. I spent two days helping Peanut clean the funky Victorian's first floor, taking her to Target for household goods, showing Chad what he needed to handyman-up to reach satisfactory levels. Talking non-stop, Dew followed his sister around, still uncomfortable in his own skin, still resisting the anti-psychotic he needed to take at night.

When we all went out for breakfast Dew went to the restroom and there was a moment alone. I implored Peanut to take him off my hands for three hours, my eyes filling with tears, saying I had to rest, I needed silence back at the hotel, alone time. Her pretty white fingers covered with rings grasped both of mine as I cried for a minute, her bracelets jangling across the table.

"Of course I can, Mom. I'll find him something to do. You go rest."

It was the first alone, silent peace I'd had in over eight days.

Getting naked was a priority. My skin had been bundled into clothes 24/7 because of proximity to everyone.

The bubblebath was soothing, while an episode of "Law&Order" let me further drift away into zombie-state. None of my friends answered their phone, except Malcolm, who wished me well, said he was in the middle of lunch rush, and had news for when I got home.

A two-hour nap put me right and I woke to the telephone and the sweetest voice that ever whispered erotica in my ear.

"Annalee, it's Cora. Is he alive?"

"Yes, he's alive. And that's the bottomline. Drug overdose, psychosis, five days of commitment. I'm a wreck. Where are you?"

"On my way to the airport. Effete cooking contest I'm judging in New York. Are you sleeping? Eating? Mon Dieu."

"Sort of."

Cora had played on the singing sandy-white beach with me as a Northern Indiana child and we had done guerilla theatre on Chicago's L, pulling strangers into our private play. Since Cora was exceptionally beautiful, her hair like spun silk, she could captivate any audience. In her Help Me Mister gig, she'd exclaim with joy at seeing an old friend again, the stranger taken aback, insisting she was mistaken, then she'd stage whisper that she was being followed, point to someone shady-looking and beg the innocent pawn to play along. Her puppy-dog eyes were irresistible and the poor schmoo would talk loudly and effusively, riffing on people they theoretically knew, both of them making things up for the entire ride.

In jail for five hours for hitch-hiking on Interstate 94 outside Chicago, the Sunshine lawyer bailed Cora and me out as soon as they'd heard. With our parents' phone permission to thumb a ride, the cops had to let us go, free to stand back on the Interstate just in front of the "no hitch-hiking" sign. Double-daring fate, we'd stick our toes over the imaginary line, then yank them back in glee, hoping we drove any passing cops crazy. A suburban matron with two dogs in the back of her station wagon stopped for us, driving us all the way home to the Indiana Sunshine Enclave. Cora and I told her every good story as pay-back for the courtesy ride.

One private lightning-storm afternoon on Cora's waterbed remains burned into my sexual mainframe, words unable to capture the fire.

Bonded for life, she lived inside of me everywhere I went. Never really apart, our lives had simply taken different paths. We were instantly re-attached at every contact, though her jealous lover made things more difficult. Mostly I left her alone but when shit hit the fan, she was my ultimate support. A few words from her could last me for years.

"Try. He will be fine after a while but it will take some energy. You must have been terrified."

I started to cry, blew my nose.

"I'll call when I get back," she promised. "I love you, Annalee."

I headed back to Peanut's to help her make dinner before Dew and I had to leave for O'Hare.

"Nothing," Dew said quietly three weeks into his Seattle stay.

His voice was full of anger. All the signs of feelings-denial were in play--- heightened color to his face, eyes wetter than usual, jaw locked and flexing, puffs of cartoon steam virtually coming from his ears.

When they were children, I'd gently tell Dew and Peanut "Your words don't match what your body is saying," and then they'd spill.

"Dew," I asked again, waiting a full ten minutes, after he'd sighed numerous times and paced about, then threw himself into the big chair. "Sure there isn't something on your mind you'd like to talk about?"

"Everything's so *hard* now," he wailed, cheeks coloring and tears filling his young-man brown eyes. Tucking his knees in close to his chest, he looked away. "That fucker reconfigured everything on my Mac and my whole life is gone. Everything's gone. Not a single picture or document. A job isn't materializing. I have no clothes. I lost everything."

"The magic's gone? Doors aren't opening?"

"Exactly. I can't find a good job, every resume I sent out up til now has the wrong phone number on it so it's all meaningless. I desperately need a car. I dreamed about my car last night. I was driving up the hill by the Alien Park and going really fast."

We'd hiked when he was a child to the bottom of "Earthworks," the concentric circles like an upside-down wedding cake carved into the ground off Military Road. It was completely silent, soundproof, at the base. Both kids were sure it had been made by an alien spaceship landing.

He shook his head. It was all too big.

I moved to sit beside him, un-pretzeling his long legs across my lap. He wanted touch but not full body from me, his mother. If it was Peanut, I'd hold her. His man-signals still crackled with bruised ego, ready to flare to anger again at any moment. Avoiding the emotional landmines, I hugged his legs and rubbed his cold feet.

"Well, I have tools and resources from living here a while. I've been walking the fine line between being helpful and staying the fuck out of your way. If you want more help from me, I'll be happy to help."

Dew nodded, defeated. Any assistance would feel better. PTSD, heartbreak, grief and misery were blocking his exits from this nightmare. Given a fresh start after years of Midwestern domicile, his second hometown now seemed impossible to navigate. He'd gone on a disappointing interview downtown, then come home without going to the next because, he'd said, Seattle was too overwhelming.

"We'll find you a vehicle. You can use mine for now. We'll find you a decent job to start, Dew, and then later a good job. It's in little steps. Can I explain what I mean here?"

Dew nodded.

"It's like…remember the collage you made in the psych ward? The big picture of what you want is like that collage, all the pieces torn out and pasted together."

They hadn't let him use scissors at the hospital. The collage looked like one from 'Thief,' James Caan's patchwork of Willie Nelson shown to Tuesday Weld, the hostess at Chicago's Belden Corned Beef Center.

"The job, a car, your girlfriend---how is she? You two talking?"

"Things are back the same as they were."

"When you were good?"

"Yeah. And better because we talk all the time. But there's nothing there for me now, just her, and I can't move back there just for her."

"She has no interest in coming out here?"

He shook his head and his cheeks got pinker.

"It'll still work out," I said. "Just not today. Like the collage. Back to that. She's in your collage of what you want, a piece, and it all looks huge."

I waved my arms out in a big sun.

"Now, there's today, which is tiny."

I brought my fingers together in a gesture of smallness.

"What you do today, in tiny, tiny increments, will get you closer to that big picture of your collage. It doesn't *feel* like it at the time, but when you look back, you will be able to see the chain of events that led to that point. You will get your big picture, your collage, but not today. It'll all work out, Dew, but it's going to take longer than you are used to. You were golden, honey, and that has disappeared. Now it takes work, like everyone else. I know that must be hard for you. So. Today. What can you do today to help get closer to that big picture? Email me your resume and I will help you job hunt. Job equals money which equals personal power."

Cora called from LaGuardia to ask after Dew, so I told her what Ziller had said. Cora laughed her tinkling, perfect laugh as she rushed to get on a plane.

We would never be lovers again, I knew, her life tied so tightly to Sherry she couldn't get free. A renowned, world-class food authority, it burned me that Cora was pussy-whipped at home, cowed by Sherry, who pushed too hard.

Grateful for small conversations that slipped past the censor, I closed my eyes and swore I could smell her oaky perfume through the phone.

Fiercely wanting her, I knew it would never go away.

I still hopelessly yearned once in a while, waiting for the past to be different.

I stayed up all night repairing the torn up jeans we'd rescued from the garbage, washing them, pressing iron-on interfacing into each threadbare thigh, covering the knees with dark stiff adhesive patches, replacing the missing seat with huge squares of jean material carefully sewn on the inside.

Grouchy with general discouragement in the morning, Dew's face lit up when he saw his jeans, as if magic fairies had come in the night. He looked at me grinning and said a sincere "Thanks, Mom."

"Drake, you're home!"

Finally, he answered his phone, even if he sounded a little tentative.

"Darling," he croaked. "It is you. Sorry. I've been avoiding contact with anyone."

"When did you get home? Did you go to Mexico? I've been….out of town myself. I'll explain everything but tell me all about your trip. I'm so tired of me and my shit I could use a good vacation story, all sunshine, museums and parties."

There was a long silence on the line.

"Drake?"

Something was very wrong. My throat began to close.

"It was bad, Al. I got jumped."

"Omigod, honey, are you hurt? What did they do to you? Do I need to come over there?"

"No, no, no I don't want anyone to see me this way. I am a hideous nightmare, truly Elephant Man. My face is unrecognizable."

He started to cry.

"Don't make me cry!" Drake told me, trying to regain control. "Just let me talk and maybe I can get through this. I haven't told anyone. I've been back for almost a week. It happened the second day I was there."

"Go on, if you want to, I mean, Jesus, Drake, are your teeth alright?"

He loved his pearly smile, obsessing over his ivories, always whitening, bleaching and brushing after every meal.

"I lost two of them," he said, sniffling. "But my dentist says he can reconstruct them. I have twenty stitches in my face, in various parts. I look like Mother of Frankenstein. My right arm's fractured, I'm in a Velcro back brace, and my left leg is broken from when I fell."

"You fell?"

"They tripped me. That's how this all got started. I was walking across this beautiful plaza and there was a long park at the end. The bar I wanted to go to was on the other side of the park and I thought, stupid me, I'll just cut through the park. These three guys appeared out of nowhere and started walking behind me, and you know how athletic I am, darling, I run like the little white girl I am, but I ran. The park started looking like the evil forest in the Wizard of Oz---'I'd turn back if I were you!' Then they caught up to me and tripped me. When I was on the ground they kicked my face and broke my arm, calling me an American over and over. I didn't understand that part. Do they really hate Americans that much? I thought those Mexican people love our country, since they climb every mountain and ford every stream to get here."

Shelly's Spanish suddenly surfaced.

"Maricon," I said quietly.

"Yes! Just like that!"

"It means 'faggot.'"

"Oh." Drake got very quiet. "You mean to tell me I got gay-bashed on my vacation and I didn't even *know* it?"

"Yup."

"Well, Pamela Anderson's tiny tits! I can't believe this! Now I feel even more stupid. I'm never showing my face in public again. I'm a laughingstock in the entire Queer Nation."

Drake started to cry.

"No, no, darling, don't feel stupid. This way you can feel *twice* as victimized. Call the Gay News and get a write-up from that butch reporter. You can demand an apology from the Mexican Consulate and create an international incident."

"I *could*, couldn't I?" he sniffed, pulling himself together.

Even through the phone, I heard Drake smiling, the wheels in his brain as visible as Mr. Machine's cogs.

"So where have you been, darling? Tell me of your world for the past two weeks."

"Gitta, where the hell have you been? I was starting to get worried. I know you're popular but your voicemail being full for *weeks?"*

"I was back east of the mountains," she huskily answered, her voice thick with tears. "Sam knocked up some dirt-riding hill-ape over there so they got married without telling anyone."

"Wow. Big news."

I wasn't sure why that would make her as miserable as she sounded so I aimed for a neutral comment.

"It gets bigger. Kyle started haranguing Sam. How was Sam gonna party now with a brat on the way, that he'd ruined his life, that he was following his dick, that now he better step up and be a man. Sam has no job skills, really, since he and Adam both got derailed into drinking their lives away with their step-dad, and so Kyle gives him the brilliant idea to join the Marines. The *Marines.* Not the Air Force or the Coast Guard, something cleaner and out of harm's way, no, the damn *Marines!"*

"Jesus. Don't tell me..."

"Yeah," Gitta sobbed. "And not only did Sam sign up, Adam signed up with him. Both my boys, they'll be cannon fodder in two weeks. I was over there trying to make sense of it all, Al. They weren't raised this way. Is it my fault they got so screwed up?"

"Stop that shit, Gitta. They're grown-ass men making their own choices. You don't like their choices but you aren't responsible for them anymore. When they were seven and put that dead fish in their cousin's bed, remember that? Okay, *that* you were responsible for, since you'd used the phrase 'swimming with the fishes' at dinnertime. This you have no control over. But you can grieve. It's a hard blow."

"I went over there to essentially say goodbye, since I knew they wouldn't come back here to tell me in Seattle. If I hadn't gone over there I might never see them again. The one motel there, funky little place with rabbit-ear t.v.s and mildew smell and it was awful. The girl's relatives are nearly toothless, and there was a washer and I think a refrigerator thrown down the ravine on their property, all rusted, like they've been there for years like fucking Mason County. Seven cars on blocks in the yard. You know the drill. So this chubby chick named Rhonda is my new daughter-in-law, carrying my grandchild. She's 17, Annalee. 17. Pregnant and shining, since she's reached her goal in life---married to a Marine and having his baby. If it is his."

Gitta cried harder.

"What do you mean?"

"She kind of...got around. Adam told me he flirted with her but never, you know...did anything, and he said she was popular. He smiled at me funny when he said that. But Sam thinks she's the greatest thing since the cotton gin. He asked me for the name of that catalog where I got their cool baby clothes."

"Hanna Anderson. You *did* have the cutest baby clothes of anyone."

"It makes me want to puke to think of Swedish onesies on a Wenatchee brat."

"I assume she's white, Gitta."

"Yup, and complete and total Neanderthal. Everyone there is. Still covered with fur, far as I'm concerned. Barely have a grasp of language. Her parents' house had a huge Confederate flag flying on a homemade pole and there were chickens and mean dogs. It almost made me want to laugh, it was so stereotypical. They hate niggers and the beaners that pick the fruit."

"Shelly told me about people like that, harassing her through her whole childhood."

"How is Shelly?"

"Unknown as of yet. Drake got hurt in Mexico, though."

"What? Is he alright?"

"He'll be alright but at the moment, no. He's apartment bound because of facial injuries and he's in a cast or two. It was a gay-bashing. They took his money, his id's, credit cards, and left him bleeding on the sidewalk in a Mexican park. He's lucky to be alive."

"I can help out, take him some sandwiches, clean his bathroom, that sort of thing."

"He needs help. I'm taking him some soup and library books tomorrow."

"Well, anyway," Birgitta blew her nose. "That's my story. What were you doing the whole time I was in Wenatchee?"

"Shit stacks up," Malcolm smiled, as I wept in the wooden booth. He kept an eye on the bar, the front door and the serving floor but his interest in my exhaustion was genuine. "Nothing happens easily, Al, problems don't come one at a time. It's not like television where you have one premise, one dilemma, and then you clean that up, ready to go on with your smooth playing field. No, life is hard, babe, and it's hard for ever'one. Let me stress here, no disrespect, you ain't unique. *Ever*'body got shit raining down on 'em but *you* don't see it, is all. Listen, now and hush the crying. I hate that shit."

Malcolm took my hand across the table.

"I don't mean to add to your pile but this is good news for me and I hope you see it that way so Ima tell you anyway. I got the promotion. We're moving to Alaska."

I wanted to sob.

"That's good for you, Malcolm. I'll try to be happy about it. Sucks for me but we're not talking about me for this one little instant."

"Thank you. Okay, back to you. Things stack up. That's what drives people over the edge, makes people lose it. Dew didn't have one thing hit him and his brain kicked over, no, there were lots of factors that all lead up to the event, right? So just know that. The other thing is, you might not be done yet. There might be more added to the pile. Life's like that, Annalee, my precious. When things get too big, too heavy, the smart thing to do is take a step back."

Malcolm let go of my hand and held both his rippling arms out in front of him, fingers pointing up in a Yosemite Sam back-off gesture.

"Take a step back," I repeated, my mind dulled from overload, the pressure too great.

I was back to work, doing everything by rote, a complete automaton. Fortunately, a good deal of my job lent itself to that: route repetition, stacking freight, driving. Dew was struggling to find employment while living with me in Seattle, his world completely disconnected and gone, his future tethered by a very thin string. I had not a moment to myself. Now Malcolm was moving away, Drake was broken into bits, Gitta's children were facing daily death and Shelly was still AWOL.

"That's right. Breathe. Set it all down, and don't make any decisions when you're in that fight-or-flight mode. Low-level panic and decision making do not mix. Adrenalin is not your friend when things get all heavy, man. And there's very little that a sandwich and a nap won't cure, right? You told me you heard that in a meeting. You eating? Sleeping? Letting yourself grieve at the appropriate alone time? Well, good, then that's all you have to do right now. Chop wood, carry water. It will all calm down and your brain will return to you. Now, how about some hot cider before you shove off?"

The words wouldn't come. There seemed to be no time to write, everything compressed and hurried, not a single quiet moment to create. Yet given the gift of time on a Sunday morning, I sat mute in front of the machine, eyes staring out the picture window at nothing I could name. My legs fell asleep sitting at my desk with nothing produced, the pages all blank.

I kept seeing Dew's face grinning at me, frenzy and disturbance radiating off him in waves, his hospital gown knotted at the side, his enormous feet stuffed into non-stick socks. When I closed my eyes, I felt like I was smothering, pressed into a little coffin, my air supply suddenly threatened.

I went to work but had no idea how I made it through the day. Laundry got done, clothes washed and folded, carried upstairs, but the basket sat on a chair for days. Hot and fresh from the dryer, the clothes grew cold, the wrinkles set-in. Food was made but without any interest. My brain couldn't seem to focus, everything felt disconnected. Tears sat behind my eyes everyday, overwhelmed at the bigness of life and death, how precious everything is and how little we realize it. Joni was right that we don't know what we've got til it's gone.

Sleep was the one thing I could do well. I slept at every opportunity, completely exhausted.

When I got quiet, Sunshine messages from my childhood came back to me in flashes, warm inspirational phrases suddenly forefront. Things I hadn't thought of in years floated 8-Ball to the surface. Time takes time. Willow trees bend in the breeze. The circle remains unbroken. We are all looking at the same stars. Chop wood, carry water. Be kind. Take care of yourself and the rest will be taken care of.

When shit stacks up, take a step back.

I smiled when that last one came to mind, since it wasn't Sunshine.

It was from the book of Malcolm.

"Have you seen the Gay News?" Drake warbled over the phone. "Page three, upper right hand corner. 'Local man gay-bashed south of the border.' The picture isn't very flattering with the grainy black and white newsprint and the glare off my casts, but I am the belle of the sympathy ball, darling. Thank you so much for suggesting such a thing. I went public with my story and the phone hasn't stopped ringing. The local news stations have scheduled a time, isn't that something? College friends have called. As soon as I have my facelift after the stitches come out, I'll make a debutante debut at Mandrake and be interviewed by the society hounds just like Don Lockwood in "Singin' In The Rain." You know our motto, darling: "Dignity. Always dignity." I'll be thirty pounds lighter and look ten years younger. This year I'll be sitting in a huge open clamshell at the Pride Parade, a human rights banner strung across my six-pack abs. I'm a star, darling! It's my little fifteen minutes."

"You sound wonderful. Turned things around quite a bit. Did you call that reporter gal to get your personal story splashed all over the press?"

"Yes, I did. She's the one covering Lesbo-Land now owned by Andrew the FTM and you can tell which side *she* falls on in the debate. Butch Wax on *all* her wheels. Easy two hundred pounds, five one. Wears those plaid Pendleton jackets with the square pockets, looks like she could pull a locomotive with her teeth. But she says she might be able to fan the flames of my personal injustice and get me an apology from the Mexican Consulate, like you said, and make it a huge international incident."

"That would be a hoot!"

"Honey, I just want a crack at Anderson Cooper. Mother of Adonis, that man is a living Dreamsicle. He's as handsome as Cal Anderson, bless his soul."

"Maybe you'll hear from some relatives over this. Will that bother you?"

"No. Fuck 'em, Princess. I can't carry the weight anymore. This is my big coming out story, forty years later. Cinderella has arrived at the dance, darling, thanks in part to you."

"Al, its Blake."

I was upright in my sleep. The phone was in my hand, mind awake in an instant, a Pavlovian response one never loses after raising children.

We had never been friends, Blake and I. She treated Shelly like shit when they were lovers, drunk and belligerent with her crazy Mason County family. There could only be one reason Blake would call at two in the morning and it wasn't good.

The Broadway Funeral Home was packed with Shelly's Spanish-speaking Wenatchee family, a hundred clean and sober friends, a few skinny die-hard using buddies in sunglasses, twenty or so DHL drivers and customers from her old route, even, I noted with some shame, Mr. Personality, the guy we'd screwed with subscriptions. That explained the little dog tied to a railing outside.

Smartley the Seattle police officer was one of the pallbearers along with Shell's brothers and three drag queens Shell had partied with at Gay Bingo, now in the somber reverse drag of suits and ties. Anthony Ray was in sunglasses with a well-dressed posse in the back and had sent a prominent heart-shaped wreath be-ribboned: "My Great Loss. Sir Mix-A-Lot."

A white woman I assumed was Shell's first lover Claire sat in the back.

A photo of Shelly laughing in front of Dick's Drive-In had been blown up and easel-ed near the white pearlescent closed casket, a wreath of yellow and red roses framing her moment of joy in garish DHL colors. "Want fries with that?" had been her response to their new uniform's color palette. I'd told her she looked like a Hot Dog On A Stick vendor.

I pushed Drake's wheelchair to the far aisle and we went up to the fourth row, right behind Shelly's sniffling family. This was Drake's first public outing since his "international incident" and he'd worked hard to be presentable. Dark glasses covered much of his bruising and stitches. We'd eased the clothing around his splints, casts, braces and sore areas as best we could.

My black button-down dress was starched in Shelly's honor, lips red to compensate for my lack of eye-makeup, which had gone smearing down my teary cheeks in moments. I couldn't stop crying, angry as hell at my best friend for choosing junk instead of years more life, angry I didn't get to say goodbye, sobbing into a monogrammed hanky Drake had given me for the occasion. Malcolm sat on my other side in a dark navy suit, holding my hand and Birgitta was next to him, red-eyed but perfectly splendid, her blond hair spilling onto a somber clinging dress.

Children in the rows ahead of us cried for their Tia Mishellita, hanging on solid brown women who moaned under black mantillas. Grown men with brown calloused hands wept as Spanish-language hymns were sung, bearing their beloved baby girl to heaven. A harpsichord played mournful church tunes and held incomprehensible sorrow for us all.

A table full of photos and candles was laid out near the casket, ready for reflection after the genuflecting pause at Shelly's bier.

I could not believe Shelly was dead.

I almost couldn't bear it.

How much harder must it be for her tiny mother and grandmother, sobbing in the first row, nearly falling prostrate in grief as they reached for the casket. Shelly had gone to the city to make good, to better herself and the whole family but instead they would bury her, the train to Mexico scheduled for this evening.

"We're going to the Blue Canoe after," Malcolm leaned over and whispered to me, pointing to Gitta, who nodded at the arrangement. "Tell Drake. Place is closed. I'll make sandwiches. And double Mojitos. This is so sad."

"Roger that. What's with the photographers?" Drake whispered, gesturing toward the back. Two cameramen were slowly making their way forward, trying not to seem disrespectful. They had press credentials slung around their necks and seemed to be from competing papers, jockeying for position.

Suddenly the photographers moved to the far aisle where we were, Drake's wheelchair blocking most of the way.

"Excuse me. Con permisso," one of them said, right behind us. Drake leaned away as if to let them pass and a flashbulb went off in Drake's face. Four more lights flashed, the two men elbowing each other to get a shot of Drake.

"This is outrageous!" Drake hissed. "Stop this at once. This is a funeral, gentlemen, and your cameras are not welcome."

A microphone, then four, were stuck in Drake's astonished face, local television station logos visible.

"Is it true, Mr. Astor, you are from the wealthy Spokane Astor family? And is it true that they have not accepted that you are gay? And if your incident in Mexico is to be believed, what are you doing here at a Mexican funeral?"

Malcolm forcefully stood up and moved me behind him, placing himself next to Drake.

"Move along, ladies and gentlemen. Nothing to see here." Malcolm said gently but with frightening authority. "You are interrupting a family's private grief, the height of rudeness in any culture." He bowed his head in the direction of Shelly's family, staring at the scene. "Mr. Astor is tired and recovering from his injuries, and he is here mourning a dear friend. If you have any other questions, you can contact my office."

"And you are?"

"I'm Mr. Astor's agent. All calls through my office. Let's be going, Drake. Heads up. Ladies?"

Malcolm motioned for Gitta and me to follow him. Then head held high, he pushed Drake's wheelchair straight through the newscaster throng and out of the funeral parlor as we trailed behind in a blur of flashbulbs.

"Brilliant strategy," I complimented Malcolm as the Mojito started to sink in. The Blue Canoe had a sign on the locked front door: "Closed: Death in the Family"

"We walked right past all those news people like we do that everyday!"

"Yes, Malcolm, thank you for extricating me from that delicate situation." Drake wiped his mouth with the pale blue linen napkin.

"Will we be on t.v.?" asked Gitta, her eyes sparkly with anticipation.

"Always take the high road," Malcolm said, smiling at us over the turkey clubs on grilled garlic focaccia he'd whipped up in the darkened Blue Canoe. "You know, Malcolm X wrote about stealing carloads of stuff in the white neighborhoods when he was coming up and if they saw a cop, they'd flag the cop car down and ask directions, saying they were completely lost and in the wrong neighborhood. The cops even escorted them a time or two. Gotta take the obvious way---no one ever suspects a thing if you can play it off."

"Well, you can be my agent any day," Drake sighed. "This fame business is exhilarating but I can see how it would get tiring. I have a *whole* new sympathy now for Elizabeth Taylor. How she must have suffered."

"What's the sauce?" Gitta asked Malcolm, lifting her bread to study the ingredients.

"It's special sauce," Malcolm smiled. "Thousand Island with a splash of balsamic vinegar, so it doesn't taste like Mickey D's special sauce. Seriously. We buy Sysco Thousand Island by the five-gallon bucketful, then Alphonzo, the prep guy, has to beat five cups of balsamic into it, then we call it our own."

"Why do funerals make people hungry?" Gitta wondered, putting her sandwich back together.

"It's the circle of life," Drake sang out, one arm outstretched, doing his best Elton John. "We see death, we are reminded of our own lives and the need to sustain them."

"Why didn't she want to live?" I asked everyone in general, my sandwich untouched.

"She hit the wall, Al. Nothing you could have done." Malcolm said matter-of-factly.

"The treatment looked bigger than death itself. Dying's easy. But who really knows another's insides? We all have terrors we don't tell others, or maybe we aren't even aware of them until something threatens us. What's that AA definition of fear you told me?"

"That we won't get something we want or something we already have will be taken away from us."

"Right. We can't know on what level staying alive felt more threatening to her than passively dying. None of us have been in her shoes. But I gotta say, if I'm gonna die, a heroin overdose is the way to go, especially if I'm looking at a prolonged wasting disease eating me alive from the inside."

"Go out James Dean, young and beautiful," Drake nodded.

"But why not want to get the treatment, no matter how temporarily painful, so you can live to see what happens next?"

"Some people get tired, Al," Malcolm said quietly, taking my hand across the table. "She's gone. There's no more *why*. She's gone, is all. Start there and move on."

"It's for you," I told Dew, my face a stunned blank.

Amazed at the miracle about to unfold, I couldn't believe the span of years between the two incidents, yet they would now be forever connected. I handed my cell phone to Dew.

"Who is it?" he asked, holding the mute button, bewildered someone would call for him on my phone, his eyes taking my emotional temperature as he scanned my body language.

"It's Fernfeather. She says George Wilson Ziller wants to talk to you."

A King County executive saw the blurb from the funeral on the news and asked around to see if he could meet Birgitta.

A friend of Malcolm's saw us on TV and asked if he could meet *me.*

We decided to make it a double blind date and all go for drinks at The Edgewater.

"I'm Simon," smiled a tall black man in glasses, holding out his hand. His teeth were perfect. "You must be Annalee. Malcolm told me you were stunning in person and he was right. Curves in all the right places."

"Hello, Simon." I kissed his cheek, feeling optimistic for the first time in what felt like years. Something rolled over in my belly, flipping the happy switch. All my sensors lit up full-on.

"This is Jerry," Simon said, gesturing toward him then Gitta, "whom I just met here five minutes ago. We are double-dating, I understand?"

I nodded, grinning like an idiot, clutching my little bamboo woven bag. I was glad I had spruced up, silk blouse slippery on my skin. Suddenly I felt confident, a surprise path opening in front of me as far as my eye could see. We would have a child together, our joy encased in a white picket fence, Graham Nash warbling in my ear about two cats in the yard.

Gitta seemed to be as star-struck over her guy as I was about mine.

"I'm Birgitta," she said, smiling brightly at the handsome white guy. He looked straight off sixties Madison Avenue, a muscular Elvis Costello with perfect retro tie and horn rims, a pipe in his mouth.

Both men might have stepped off the pages of GQ as they busied themselves with taking our coats and getting them hung. Gitta looked wide-eyed at me, enormously pleased. I could tell she could hardly wait to excuse us for the powder room

"Well, ladies, what'll it be?" Simon asked as he hailed the bartender with one hand and pulled out my chair with another.

"How's my brother?" Peanut asked first off.

She was on break from her new gardening job at the nursery, smoking a cigarette out back.

"He's coming back, honey. He's almost rational now and he's calmed down quite a bit. The non-stop talking has ended, too, thank the Universe. I think he is going to want to come back to the greater Chicago-land area."

"Good. I miss him."

"You guys!" I laughed. "You grew up with him in the same house and you barely spoke through your whole adolescence and now that he leaves, you miss him. I mean, I'm glad you two are so chummy now but I'm still stuck in the old days. I'd be talking to you on the phone and you'd ask 'how's my brother?' and I'd tell you to go in the next room and ask him."

Peanut giggled.

"I know. And then I'd ask you what he was reading and how's his girlfriend...."

"It drove me insane, you two. But I'm glad you're friends now. How's your dog? Dew talks about him a lot."

"He's good. How're my cats?"

"Old. Fat. Lazy. They're having a happy old age."

"I really like my job. I get to wear this cool sun hat, it's, like, woven or something, with a chin strap that's two leather thingees and a bead. The plants are so *lush.* I could just stand there and smell them all day long. I love getting my hands dirty."

"*Your* hands? Dirty?"

I couldn't imagine those delicate white hands with the weekly nail job enjoying ground-in topsoil.

"What do you do with your rings?"

"Oh, I wear gloves. Cotton ones, then rubber over that. I mean I love getting my *gloves* dirty."

"How's Chad?"

I had stepped on a nerve. Her cards retracted, pulled in closer to the vest.

"Fine. Not sure how this will all shake down but for now it's cool."

Peanut didn't want to sound committed to this relationship. She was always the free spirit, one foot holding the door open. Leave Yourself An Out. I thought of that minor-key country song "Melancholy Child" when Peanut went dark and moody, holding back, wary of others, protecting her little crab-shell. Fast change of subject. She was done.

"How're you doing, Mommy?"

We had lived through hell together and she was checking.

"I'm…okay. Kinda spaced out, bumping into things. Very tired. But this will all pass and things will balance out again. But for now, I'm tired."

"I think soon you will have things to look forward to."

Her crayon drawings always had sunny skies and hopeful smiling animals, like dolphins and happy puppies.

"That's a nice idea. I'll hold onto that. And something good *has* happened. His name is Simon."

"Oooooo, tell me everything. But later, when I get off work. Gotta go." I could hear her grinding out her cigarette. "Love you, Mommy."

"How was it?" Drake begged to know, his wheelchair parked at a Blue Canoe booth. Malcolm set down the drinks and joined Birgitta, Drake and me.

"Straight out of the Barbie Prom Game. We both got Ken the Dreamdate," I said, sipping my Lemon Drop.

Gitta nodded rapidly, her eyes big as she smiled into her drink.

Malcolm hopped up to help a busboy with a heavy tray then came back.

"What did I miss?" he asked, grinning. "How was your date with Simon, Al?"

"Where were you hiding him all this time?"

"He called me out the *blue*, man, I swear, haven't heard from the guy in five years."

"Well, he seems to have our Miss Thing here in a state," Drake cooed. "And what about Jerry? Lord, does anyone name their child *Jerry* anymore?"

"He's wonderful," crowed Gitta, dabbing her lips with the linen napkin. "Everything Kyle wasn't. He can dance, too!"

I started laughing.

"Simon can't," I said. "He told me he doesn't play basketball, either. I questioned his identity as a black man and he laughed. I told him about being a byke and how they've revoked my membership card, that I don't get the Gay Agenda emails anymore. He was lovely."

"And he's single because…?"

Drake was suspicious about a man in his forties still unmarried.

"He's divorced, like me. Ex-wife was a byke, like me. Has grown kids, like me. Retired from the Marine Corps, *way* unlike me but he's actually a pacifist. Works logistics for the city of Enumclaw. Malcolm, Simon is the nicest thing to happen to me in a long time. It's been a hard couple of months."

"You're welcome. Your turn, Gitta," Malcolm said, reaching his arm across the back of the booth to rest on Drake's wheelchair.

"Jerry is so nice! He works for King County in the Assessor's Office, something totally boring that pays really well. He's divorced, his wife was a crazy pill freak who killed herself ten years ago. He's finally ready to date again and said he hadn't found anyone worth dating until he saw me on t.v. and he felt something."

"I'll bet he did," Malcolm laughed, his fingers rubbing together as he smirked at Birgitta. She really was stunning to look at. *Any* man would feel something, and a lot of women, too.

"Well, *I* have news, if anyone wants to hear it," Drake sniffed, pulling himself up in his chair. "Let's focus on *me,* shall we?"

We all looked at Drake, fully attentive. He swirled the remains of his Tanqueray and tonic, clinking the ice around.

"I got a teaching job in Greece. Sunny white-washed buildings and uncut hairy Greek men everywhere."

"What? Drake, that's wonderful!" I squealed, happy for his turn of fortune. Without Simon as a bright spot, I knew I might have seen this as a blow. I felt blessed to have a balancing counterweight in my favor. First Malcolm, now Drake, but still I saw that sun-sparkling path ahead.

"Wow! Greece. Good for you. Looks pretty in pictures. Now I'll have a reason to go," Gitta said.

"When does this happen?" Malcolm asked, skipping anything emotional and heading straight for man-practical, his hand absently grasping the wheelchair handle in unconscious male connection.

"In September. I'll be healed by then, I think. Oh, I can't wait!"

He'd been to a shrink and hated it, had no use for 12-step meetings and the complete physical showed no abnormalities. Dew seemed calmer. Six weeks of loafing around without drink or drug while haphazardly looking for a job and watching a lot of movies had given him some free brain space.

The call from Ziller had come at exactly the right moment.

"Mom, I'm moving back to Chicago. I mean, thanks for the care and all but I need to go back to school. I'm still a resident there. I'm still registered. I need to start my life again."

"All this from one phone call? What did the Mystic Man say?"

Dew smiled at me.

"All he said was 'Get right back on the golden horse.'"

"That was it?"

"That was it. Smart guy."

"He hasn't spoken to anyone in *decades.* You know that."

"Yup. Guess he was waiting for the next incarnation. Ta-dah!"

"Well, Mr. Enlightenment, let's leave 'shrooms out of the picture from now on. You got George Wilson Ziller to speak once but don't push it."

"My family came to town, Al."

There was weight in Drake's voice.

"I've been disowned, written out of the will, or so I was informed. My distasteful political activities have disgraced the family, etc. As if I asked to be mugged. Honest to Xena, I felt like I was in a Tennessee Williams play. And some of my idiots cousins came along, eight people in all, like an intervention. These people are tilted from inbreeding or something but I swear on Nancy Sinatra's white plastic go-go boots they have the social skills of mashed potato sandwiches on Wonder bread. If Ghandi had had to hang out with them, he'd have boxed their ears. It was that bad. These people are crazier than a carton of worms! My own flesh and blood. So anyway. I am disowned."

"Omigod, Drake, that's awful. Was your father here in town?"

"No, just the bulldyke sister who refuses to come out, the 'bohemian,' everyone calls her, and my married sister with her husband and children and cousins. They delivered the news by proclamation. I had to sign the Magna Carta with a quill dipped in my own blood, then they were gone."

"How do you feel? Are you alright?"

"Honestly? I feel better than I ever have in my life. So I won't inherit millions. I feel a great weight has been lifted off my back. I'm fully out now and it is just a *relief.*"

"How's Cutter's sound?" Simon asked, the phone wires between us only five miles. The man seemed perfect in every way, including proximity.

"Ideal."

"Pick you up at six?"

"Perfect."

Over the course of a few weeks, I found Simon to be generous, cheerful to a goofy fault, peaceful, easy-going and interesting. Working in his favor was also the six-foot-some frame, easy good looks, white teeth and elegant clothes. He said he had given himself one more month to find a partner before giving up, and then he'd seen me on television and *knew*. Just knew, instantly, I was The One.

At four I'd learned to read by staring at the Fritz Perls poster, one of many on the wall of Fawn Camp, the comfy Sunshine children enclave.

We were Ponies, as we called each other, finding a new word to describe our thread of connection the law didn't recognize. "He's my Pony-brother," we'd say. Yin-brothers shared some genetic material from one parent or another and then there were full Blood-siblings, all of us roaming the enormous nursery. We were corralled in the Fawn Camp's huge, multi-colored soft fabric womb, free to create, interact and nap.

An Elder would read patiently while we climbed their legs, rode them piggyback, or attacked squirt gun-style in a surprise ambush. The Elders were interchangeable, working on loose schedules that fit their bio-rhythm, some Roosters by nature and others Owls. There was never a time we were bereft of adult supervision, even if the adult was sometimes barely into puberty themselves. Someone slept in the Counselor's Bed every night, dimming the lamps and telling us a story to quiet everyone down.

We would join the others for meals in the Friendship Lodge then be Pied-piper-ed back to our comfortable warm world, our bellies full of warm veggies, beans and rice or honey-grilled peanut-butter whole wheat sandwiches.

I read all the posters that lined the tubular hallway to the Friendship Lodge…flapping your arms can be flying…if we happen to meet, it's beautiful…if you love something, set it free…it'll be a great day when schools get all the money they need…war is not healthy for children and other living things. Under the poems were photos of naked children, arms spread wide in the sun by the seaside, or flowers or butterflies in a Peter Max style, colors swirled in vivid Day-Glo on black backgrounds. The words just spelled themselves out for me long before school began.

I don't recall ever *not* reading.

All us children cuddled naked at night under the communal covers, the weight of the huge Hudson Bay blankets holding us firmly in. Our irregular heat source was a small Franklin stove in the corner of the room, so in the cold Midwestern winters we depended on each other for warmth.

I don't recall ever *not* touching others.

Our tight little bodies intertwined, flat chests and pink pudenda meeting pokes and tiny testicles. It was simply how we discovered each other. All of us were taught to be kind.

After the assassination of Martin Luther King we had a television in the nursery. The Elders met long into that terrible night, deciding we needed outside exposure to meet the world halfway. As balance for the Huntley-Brinkley Report we got to see cartoons and Ed Sullivan.

The Sunshine Tribe caught societal run-off from every caste. Those who came from wealth had purchased our hundred acres in Indiana, ten miles from the nearest small town. They gathered gardening implements and a few goats and got back to the land. The grown-ups busied themselves with making the world a laid-back paradise.

The black dirt produced Rodale organic vegetables for the Farmer's Market and local grocery. Goat milk, cheese, and brown fertilized eggs followed, then came the sprouted whole-grain baked goods and organic preserves. What could be bartered, was.

Cash was exchanged with Townies only when necessary so as not to upset cosmic balance and because Townies were a concern. The Sunshine mailbox was regularly loaded with buckshot or bullets clear through. The Elders would send a group of us children out to repaint it, making the new holes into flowers-middles or an open eye in a happy face, meeting hate with sunny vibes.

Townies called us names when we went to barter goods, whispering and pointing or outright calling us out: "Hey, hippie, do you ever wash them clothes?" Any Elder I was ever in town with would stop, smile, walk directly toward the name-caller and shake their hand in introduction, unnerving them completely. The interaction would usually end with begrudging good will but it took a toll.

Us kids alone were a target for Townie kids so we always traveled in groups to soften the blow, learning guerilla theatre tactics from the Elders to ward off the bad ju-ju and include the haters, deflating the situation. We young ones made forays into Chicago to toughen ourselves up, see the rest of the world and then take the South Shore train or hitch-hike home to Sunshine safety, processing what we'd seen.

The Townies never refused our money, though, and had to admit that our products were absolute top notch. Our enterprises grew based on good business and high quality organic commodities. The waterfall and sunshine logo on t-shirts, glass-jar labels, bread bags and vehicles became ubiquitous.

And there were town services we needed, so keeping the peace only made sense. The Sears Catalog outlet, the thrifts stores, the feed and tackle shop, the Co-Op where we bought grain by the truckload, the dentist, the pharmacy all were worldly services we needed. Sunshine dollars became a town staple as well.

The UPS lady was our friend, plied with cookies and free samples to make her regular drive out to our place worthwhile in all kinds of weather. We loved to see her truck come down the winding, long lane under the hundred-year-old oaks and maples, the diesel engine noisily, distinctively UPS. She was our updated Wells Fargo wagon, bearing winter blankets, cloth diapers, bathing suits, parts for the tractor, a horse trough heater, galoshes, chick incubators, a nursing bucket for weaning animals or tools we'd ordered in town at the Sears Catalog Storefront, waiting six to twelve weeks for delivery. Sometimes we'd be surprised by the content, nearly forgotten so long ago had it been ordered.

At each season solstice was a Be-In, or if it was summer, The Big Sun-In, our back acreage sprouting booths, tables, stages and microphones. Sunshine people streamed to our commune from all over the country to celebrate the seasonal shift and trade their necklaces, incense or t-shirts and listen to music in the fields, camping under the Indiana stars. The nursery would swell with children named Guevara, Sparrow, Kennedy, Owsley, Rainbow, Jimi, Karma and Karl. Our toys and bed in Fawn Camp would be shared with new friends.

The Story-tellers, Poets, Historians, Seekers, Diviners and Animal Guides held court in iridescent, starry, American flag or harlequin costumes, imparting Sunshine wisdom to uplift or challenge, waving colored streamers or perpetual water-wheels. Cold metal folding chairs gathered in circles were filled with blue-jeaned and peasant-dressed musicians. Blended into a hypnotic siren call were fat-bottomed striped mandolins, Martin and Guild guitars, hammered and mountain dulcimers, mournful lutes, autoharps, homemade clay ocarinas and bluegrass fiddles with darkened chin-rests. One year The Incredible String Band came to play and I sat at their feet for hours.

I liked the food the best, booths trading or selling honeycomb, fried apples, peppermint tea, hot buttered tortillas, peanut butter cookies, bright red cherry jam on cinnamon flaxseed toast and other seasonal delectables. But mostly I liked it because Cora was there to taste the banana bread or lick the cream-cheese frosting from our shared carrot cake. Children were indulged at festival time so Cora and I ran from booth to booth, eating ourselves sick, holding sticky hands and twirling our embroidered Mexican skirts together.

A lump of lovesickness took over my chest every time my eyes fell on her, my heart not understanding how something so precious to me could hurt so hard inside my ribcage. I wanted to keep her holding my hand, eating sweetmeats at the festival forever, locking our love in time, though I couldn't tell anyone. It wasn't Sunshine to want to possess someone tight so I stared at her, my chest aching, bursting with swollen want that engulfed me, hoping with desperation that she would choose me, too. Her knee touching mine under the Be-In picnic table made me unbearably warm.

Cora came from somewhere near Boston, her mom hitch-hiking through with Cora in tow. My heart-wishes came true for the next decade, since Cora's mother Raven fell in love with Grey Wolf and stayed on. I got Cora as my next-to-me bed partner in our own waterbed, my aching chest giving way to whole body urgency flamed by our nightly kisses.

She became my reason for everything I did. Our budding adolescence was a warm awakening of sensual beauty. Every moment I experienced was drenched in her woody Bakir perfume her mother'd brought from the East Coast.

Our Sapphic devotion was regarded as sweet by the Elders, their philosophy naturally embracing gender-blending. After all, they themselves were falling into bed with anything that moved, their minds and legs open.

Babies came, midwifed underwater to humpback whale sounds in the Mother Hut and little ones were loved by all. Sex with or without reproduction was honored as the Natural Way. Consensual acts of any kind were gently encouraged and forcible violations simply never occurred. Any communicable diseases were taken care of at the Fountain of Wellness Clinic, the supplies donated by our wealthier supporters who couldn't live the life but wanted to share the peaceful vibe.

The Morning School was bright green inside with a yellow sun mural covering one upper corner, the smiling orb looking benevolently down on us. Chairs, cushions, bay windows and tables were available and we sat anywhere we liked. Classical music on WFMT played quietly behind us every day. Old and young teachers, balanced carefully for optimal understanding, led us toward math, science, writing, reading and other worldly necessities while trying not to squash our independent spirits.

I loved school, especially with Cora next to me, making cat's cradle yarn patterns between our outstretched thumbs and forefingers.

Sometimes during lessons she'd let me sit behind her and braid her silky long blond hair, the feel of it charging my erotic batteries from head to toe. I would lean forward and smell that wonderful shampoo advertised on Ed Sullivan, the one with Donovan singing "Wear Your Love Like Heaven." Or it might be the new one called Lemon-Up that came in a yellow bottle with a big plastic lemon for a cap, the citrus goodness shining Cora's blondness to a painfully beautiful luster. I don't recall ever *not* loving her.

George Wilson Ziller's arrival and sad crescendo reverberated throughout the commune, power grabs suddenly primary as the Elders turned on one another. Ziller's influence up the chain within national Sunshine itself vibrated everyone at different levels, jarring fissures into the foundation. Voices once calm and easy-going now clashed in angry bursts. Goods became possessions. The urgent need for declarations of ownership followed in everything from kitchen equipment to love relationships.

Things fell apart. The land was put up for sale. Everyone disbanded, hard feelings left simmering. No forwarding directory was kept.

Cora and her Yin-sister left with Raven and Grey Wolf's older brother Hardy, bound for California. I sobbed brokenhearted as my family pulled us to Chicago, heading for Uptown to work with the poor, my mother's nursing skills needed at the indigent clinic while her new boyfriend Faustino would translate for patients.

Good-paying social work was hard to find, my mother told us as our world was left behind, so we had to be grateful the Universe had provided "clean" work that still felt connected to the *spirit* of Sunshine by helping the less fortunate. And there were, after all, five children to feed: my elder Yin-brother RayRay, me, my twin little Blood-sisters Summer and Rain, and our deaf Pony brother Joey, whom no one had claimed in the disbursement.

Wrenched apart from the love of my so-far life, I felt nothing but despair as the Sunshine homestead splintered into dust, shadows and memory.

I took Illinois state tests and placed off the charts. Awarded a high school diploma in the mail, I soon learned to carry it in my pocket to ward off truant officers. At fourteen I spent my days wandering the streets of Uptown, watching Superfly daddies work the women in full-length pimp coats and platform shoes, long-haired Jesus freaks peddling their full-color rag "The Cornerstone," panhandling junkies, hippies selling the underground paper "The Seed," busking musicians with open velvet-lined guitar cases, Children of David weirdoes pushing printed pamphlets of philosophy as mad as a Dr. Bronner's soap label, amputees rotting in broken wheelchairs parked in the sun, schizophrenics raving on the street.

By sixteen, there was nothing to stop me from hitch-hiking to California to try to find Cora.

I asked farmers if I could sleep in their barns at night. Once one of the farm wives brought me a hot plate of meat and potatoes.

"What is it?" I'd asked politely and she said she'd tell me when I was done. Turned out to be moose. Kind of chewy but really just like pot roast. I appreciated her hospitality and deflected her worried looks by moving on before they awoke next day.

Culverts and bridges provided night protection from the elements and my down sleeping bag kept me toasty. I never let my Bowie knife leave my hand when I was sleeping. I prayed to the Universe for my safety. Nothing and no one ever touched me.

The Bowie knife I was sure to show everyone as a precursor to the ride. Strapped to my belt, it kept everyone on the up-and-up. Truckers, VW microbuses full of hippies, suburban mothers wanting to help, businessmen with evasive intentions all gave me rides and ended up laying money on me as I'd hop out, thanking them for the ride. By the time I hit Berkeley I had made over two hundred dollars simply by being a charming conversationalist. In the end, they'd all wished me well, pushing their addresses and phone numbers into my hand. They shared sandwiches, coffee, cigarettes, weed, clothing and one guy gave me a collapsing camping cup, a treasure of concentric rings I'd never before seen.

In a red phone booth in Berkeley I inserted a dime and put my trembling finger into the circular dial's little holes. A man answered on the fourth ring and said there was no Cora there, they'd moved a long time ago, he didn't know where.

"How old are you?" he'd asked warily, as tears clouded my throat.

"Seventeen," I was able to squeak, not sure why he wanted to know. Lying felt like the smart thing. I was on the defensive.

"Well, we're Sunshine," he'd told me. "You're welcome to crash here."

"Is he 'black' enough for you?"

Malcolm stretched both arms across the back of the wooden booth, swirling his toothpick on the side of his mouth.

I put my fork down, cocked my head and smiled. He didn't have to explain it.

"Oh, he could go all DMX on somebody if he had to. Simon's great in bed. He's a black Marine from Oakland, baby. I don't have to tell *you* how black that is."

Malcolm rubbed his fingers together.

"And," he said slyly, "is he 'white' enough?"

"Yup. That, too. Plenty of mainstream culture in the man. Simon's a brainiac, kinda nerdy, very endearing. He says really goofy stuff for a six-foot-some black man, like 'Super deal!' and 'Oopsie-daisy!' He religiously watches 'Battlestar Gallactica.' He won't dance, he can't play basketball, and he knows all the words to every fluffy song on the easy listening station. He likes James Taylor. He joined the Marines to truly help change the world, not in a naïve way like the commercials but in a genuine, heart-felt humanitarian way and to show kids coming up that you didn't have to be an asshole to be an officer. This from a guy who grew up, like you, at the height of the Panthers Black Power movement on their home turf. So yeah, he's 'white' and black enough. Thanks for knowing him so we could meet."

"Can't have me, so you pick my old friend from back in the day?"

"No, Malcolm, you sexy man, you and I had fun but this man is steady as hell. You are like expensive candy. He is everyday sunshine at the breakfast table. And besides, as you so strongly pointed out to me years ago, you are not available. We passed that point, you and I. Move on. Or are you jealous that your old buddy and I are getting along so well?"

"Of *course* I'm jealous! Remember what Mix said: 'Jealousy is every man's weakness,' and he's right. I'm an alpha dog, baby, so naturally I don't want anyone else having you. You mine, baby, marked territory. That's the way men see shit, don't matter what they say."

"I had a guy on route say something just like that last week," I remembered. "One of my customers. One guy in the office made some reference to asking me out, and the office manager stepped in and said, 'Hey, I saw her taking off her sweater in her truck the other day. She's *mine*.'"

Malcolm burst out laughing.

"See? Like the stripper making eye contact so the men think it's all about them. He saw you take off that FedEx sweater over your head and he claimed you, man. In his head, it was already a done deal."

"You men are really fucked up. You *look* at a woman so somehow she is yours?"

"Thas' right. And I'll bet since the office manager was the one who claimed you first, the other guy slunk away, right? The manager out-ranked him."

"He did! That's exactly what happened. Weird."

"Nothing strange about it. Men follow their dicks, baby."

Chapter Seven

The Sunshine family I'd crashed with was kind but I was a burden, I was sure. They were attempting their own re-structure in the demise of our common bond and they didn't need a Pony minor complicating things.

I took the amazing new underwater BART to San Francisco, heading for City Lights Book Store, sure the famed landmark's air itself would pulsate with knowledge and direction that I'd receive by osmosis. Just walking *into* the book store itself would change everything for me, I knew, as I'd entered the hallowed place with my knapsack and little down sleeping bag rolled on top.

I'd been right. The books spoke.

I wanted to be a writer.

Everything about them made my newborn mind latch on to their nipple. I spent a few hours curled up in a circular chair in the back, glowing with purpose, waiting for the next sign, when a man spoke softly.

"Hey, sweet thing," came his velvet voice from the book stacks.

An enormous, dazzling black man emerged, a black beret on top his tight afro, reflective sunglasses darkening his eyes. He stood wide-legged, his hands in the pockets of his black leather jacket. I stared, breathless, amazed at the Cosmos for putting exactly the right sign in front of me. The delicious apparition raised one eyebrow and spoke again.

"Wanna make some bread?"

LeRoi was a high-ranking Black Panther, busy returning power to the people by offing the pig and upping the revolution. He also had a high-paying side job moving kilos of cocaine and could afford to hide a white mistress in a studio off Jones and Eddy. White women made his dick hard but my skin color for him, politically, was something of a liability, needing subterfuge for satisfaction.

We struck a deal.

I took the apartment and spread my legs for LeRoi on demand, getting cash and a place to live with peace and quiet most of the time, free to pursue my new goal of writing. I needed a place to practice my craft off the street, something solid that would stick around for a while.

It seemed less like prostitution and more like an ideal situation to me. My every need was provided for. I got excellent, wild sex many times a week and then he'd leave me alone to create. I was doing my part to further the revolution and he was happy as hell I kept quiet and out of the way.

We were never seen in public together.

Despite having his own private prostitution elite, he had a Panther sense of fairness and equity that kept things balanced. Once LeRoi heard of my Sunshine past, he suggested gently that I could make serious money servicing his friends in kinky sexual trains. Every safety precaution would be taken, he assured me, and they would all pay handsomely for the privilege of secretly fucking white pussy.

Wide-eyed and learning as I went, I actually enjoyed the work. Bonus: my fuckable naiveté alone got me hundreds in the bank.

It seemed so *easy* to me, getting paid to fuck gorgeous men in their very prime, my wrists held tight while they spread my pussy and pressed deep into me. None of them would dare hurt me knowing LeRoi would slit their throats if I whispered one word of difficulty.

The women's movement had spread to the Panthers and LeRoi had been the first to side with the ladies, my working for him always my choice, my power. He told me I could opt out anytime I wanted to be free but worshipped me for my detachment, sex separate from emotion.

After the men would leave he would run me a hot bath, rub my back and feet, tell me how gorgeous I was, what an incredible woman, how he wanted to marry me and give me children, we'd move away to the country.

I knew he could never reconcile marrying an ofay with his political stance.

"Let's wait on that part," I'd smile into his long-lashed brown eyes as we would cuddle on the waterbed. "I want to see the world."

But I didn't, really.

I just wanted to find Cora.

LeRoi died at the business end of a gun.

I was devastated and had to leave the apartment in a hot hurry. The Panthers were infiltrated, charged with federal offenses and dissolved. Asian gang wars broke out in the Tenderloin. I wasn't really safe alone. I had no money or skills, save for prostitution, which looked mighty unappealing without LeRoi as a buffer. I had no clues to find Cora and now no money or place to crash.

I caught a Greyhound for Vegas, not knowing what else to do. On my 21st birthday, I bet everything I'd saved working for LeRoi and woke up next day with twenty bucks to my name.

What could I do? I went home.

Back in Chicago, I knuckled down with my birth family, now in a four-bedroom in Rogers Park. I was put on the sun porch in the front of the brownstone and cried for ten days straight.

Joey brought me chamomile tea and rubbed my back in silence. Faustino and my mother listened to my raving disconnect, telling me it would all ease down in time, that time takes time. Summer and Rain amused me with stories about the alternative college they attended.

Ray-Ray came by with Chinese food, his apartment in Wrigleyville off Addison twenty minutes away on the Howard L. He told me about His N' Hers, the gay bar under the L tracks owned by a cigarette-voiced wise crone who told him about the old days, when police raids and ruined careers shadowed gay life. Ray-Ray had discovered Halsted Street's Boys Town and felt comfortable there.

I raved and ranted about Black Panthers, diamond bracelets, my quiet room, the multi-colored pillows I'd sewn to re-create the Fawn Camp. Everything I'd made was gone. Everything I owned was in three bags at my feet.

Someone produced a thirty-pound black Royal Manual typewriter, leaving it outside the bedroom's French doors. A bottle of White-Out and a scarlet-ribbon-wrapped ream of crisp new paper glowed white next to the machine.

A desk space was immediately cleared of my knapsack and spare change, everything swept to the floor to make way for this perfect new machine. I pushed the clothes off the room's chair, dragging it to the newly created office.

Shiny keys each cupped to perfectly fit my fingers. Holding the smile-shaped edge of the hole on top I lifted the typewriter's metal lid to see curved metal prongs topped with upper and lower-case backwards letters. The smell of the horizontally striped red-and-black ribbon hit my serotonin receptors, making me high with hope.

I stopped crying and began to write.

I was 25 when Cora walked into The Heartland Café on the arm of a brooding, protective butch.

My heart double-filled with a lifetime's joy then burst the next moment. The partner clearly wasn't gonna let me anywhere near her Cora.

"Cora?" I whispered, leaning into her shoulder as I walked past her table, drawn without thinking, my need more urgent than anything before or since.

"Annalee!" she yelped, leaping to her feet and throwing her arms around me.

This increased the dark-haired butch's scowl and forever sealed me as her enemy. Cora did not introduce me.

"When can I see you?" I howled, meaning, of course, *alone,* and at this the butch got to her feet.

"Cor, let's go," she demanded, hands on hips, legs wide apart, ready for a gunfight at the Not-Okay Corral.

I didn't have room for this kind of energy in my life. I wasn't a fighter but my need to see Cora was greater than anything alive.

"Edgewater 4-4291," I whispered quickly as I kissed her cheek goodbye, heart pounding up into my throat. I then kissed her other cheek, repeating the number of my place on Castlewood in her other ear. I made a mental note to never leave home ever again in case she called.

Cora held me at arm's length as if drinking me in with her eyes, blinking a lot. I wondered if there was a hint of something else---domestic violence, maybe? Was she signaling something to me I couldn't read? Cora leaned forward and hugged me close, whispering "Mohawk 3-9110. Sherry's gone until suppertime. I love you."

I'd tried to rescue Cora but I used a little too much force. I wanted her free so badly I planned a middle-of-the-night escape, ready to take her to California, Madagasgar, wherever she wanted, just away from there. It took months of furtive phone calls to convince her it was the right thing, then more months to plan the getaway to the Left Coast.

The night of our rendezvous, Sherry came home unexpectedly early.

Words got hot, fists connected.

The cops got involved. There was blood evidence. Polaroids were taken of the bruises, the black eyes.

Cora chose to bail out the assailant, who had beaten her. Sherry threatened me with a knife and began a campaign of terror, repeatedly flattening my tires, stealing my license plates, calling and hanging up a hundred times a day and stalking me.

I finally took out a restraining order against Sherry. I didn't need more signs from the Universe. I gave Cora and the situation up for lost.

The next week I met Joe and a year later I was a mother.

Amanda had been my Pony-sister, one of the few with whom I'd managed to keep in touch. Her family had settled in Chicago, too, after the Ziller zenith and they had done their best to maintain relations with as many Sunshine as they could. Their door was always open, the coffee percolator always popping, hoping for company.

When Amanda had married, she and her husband had stayed in loose touch with me, sending solstice cards, party invitations, birth announcements from people I knew. I stayed more connected to Amanda than my own family. Chicago was a big town and my family moved a lot. They drifted away.

But if Amanda hadn't been a resource, Dew would have ended up at Cook County Psych Ward after a rough bout with the Chicago police, kept in custody longer because of the holiday weekend.

The Universe had protected my child through my unusual tribal connection, something others could not experience. I had to do something tangible to give back in my own world, just between me and the Spirit.

I built a temporary altar in my living room, placing a photograph of a double rainbow over Maui at the apex. Photos of Amanda and one of Ziller and Fernfeather were off to one side, a picture of Dew, Peanut and me on the other. Burning black boysenberry incense beneath Birds of Paradise and humanely-harvested peacock feathers in tall blue vases, I knelt on a purple silk cushion in silence, grateful to be alive and given so many gifts.

I wanted to Universe to know.

Drake's recovery was slow and painstaking. The facial stitches healed but itched unbearably. If Drake scratched at them, they would scar. The broken bones weren't setting as fast as the doctor liked and talk of metal pins for stability began to surface in the doctor's vocabulary. Drake didn't have disability and his savings were getting depleted just trying to take time to heal. The anxiety in his voice rose higher every time we talked.

"I'm going to end up under a bridge!" he would wail, and I'd spend a few minutes talking him out of such a scenario. Things will shift, I'd say, everything will be fine, you'll see.

"The sun will come out tomorrow…" I sang into the phone, doing my best Annie.

"Easy for you to say. You're healthy and well employed."

"Easy?" I snorted. I was pissed white hot in a second. "I have just lived through the evisceration of my child's entire brain and you think my life's easy?"

"Back off, Bob-a-Lou-ie. Don't be a Quickdraw McGraw. We are on the same side here," Drake tut-tut-ed.

"Sorry. I'll take it down a notch. Dew's been gone a few days now, back in Chicago for school but I haven't quite recovered."

"You will eventually, darling. Mothers always do. They smile through it all, weeping inside, remember?"

"I'm no martyr."

"No, you're not. That's *my* job. Hello? Back to me, please."

"Back to you, then. Where were we? You can come live with me and I'll take care of you forever, a lap robe thrown over your useless legs, Fluffy and Tiger joining you in your wheelchair while I ply you with goodies to keep you alive."

"I can be 'Heidi'!"

"With braids sticking out in a U-shape on either side of your head like Pippy Longstocking."

"I'll have little petticoats and pantaloons under my Swiss skirt and all the boys in nothing but leather lederhosen will carry me up to the top of the mountain where after an afternoon orgy I'll miraculously walk again."

"Sounds like you're going to be okay."

"Thanks to you, Grandfather, and the Swiss air. It's a miracle!"

"Seriously, when do you get your casts off?"

"In six more weeks. They're being cautious. The wrist isn't healing at all and the leg has two spots that still don't look good in the X-rays. I'm on my second cast with the arm and we're trying to avoid inserting pins in the leg."

"Wanna go see a movie or something?"

"I'm so sick of movies. It's all I can do in this fucking little apartment."

"Suggest something."

With Drake there was usually an agenda. He was a master at steering the conversation where he wanted it to go. It was easier to just cut to the chase and let him direct.

"The Timberline. I want to watch the country boys line-dancing. Did you know that line-dancing caught on for queers because of the old dance laws?"

"Tell me."

I knew this, but it was important for him to tell this story again. There were a few Gay History stories he repeated in a wide loop, pulled out for party entertainment or in a conversation's lull. The running shoe craze came from a summer on Fire Island. "Don't wear green on Thursdays or you're queer" originating with the Faerie People and their weekly woodland ritual orgies. Pinkie rings, the reason the color lavender was important, he could go on. Most of his knowledge came from Judy Grahn's 'Another Mother Tongue,' her detailed investigation leaving no sparkly gay stone un-turned.

"In the thirties it was illegal for men and women to single-sex dance, and they'd get arrested if they tried. So at least one woman had to be present at a men's bar or vice versa to make it look legit. Conga dancing in lines became the acceptable way for the same sexes to touch---they'd just stick an opposite sex person at the head of the line."

"Is that true?"

I asked this every time, too. It was a ritual now. I suddenly had a vision of us as very old people, still going through this charade in senility five or six times a day.

"I swear on the grave of Agnes Moorehead."

"Then the Timberline it is."

"See if Simon wants to go. Bring the whole gang. Malcolm and his Bubblehead Barbie wife. Gitta and Dick Van Dyke, too."

"He does look kind of like him. You're right. I'll ask 'em. Malcolm's wife isn't healed herself yet. I think she's still at home on a catheter. How's next Saturday?"

"How's Jerry?" I asked Gitta over Fair scones and Frappucinos. We met downtown for coffee at her secretarial job in a building with not one but two Starbucks. We often wondered what the exact plural of Starbucks was---Starbi? Starbuckses?

"Fun, nice, warm. He makes me laugh. No sex yet. I'm too chicken. How's Simon?"

"Fun, nice, warm," I smiled. "He makes me laugh. Sex on the first date. I needed to know and so did he. It was just…the right thing to do. We about got engaged from the moment we met so we had better know if the sex would work."

"And?"

"Oh, it works," I grinned. "He can fuck as good as any man and as good as any woman, too, which is a high compliment. He's not afraid to…how do I put it…use his hands and mouth as well as his dick."

"Right on. Good for you."

Gitta slurped her drink through her bright orange straw, hitting the cup's bottom.

"I'm too scared. What if Jerry's all show and it's awful once we settle down? I can't go through the divorce thing twice, Al."

"You hear the AA story on worrying about that?"

"No."

"This lesbian was at a party of a friend of hers, lots of women there, everything cool, and the host says, I've got someone here I want you to meet, she's from Brazil. The host takes the lesbian by the hand and pulls her along toward this woman she's supposed to meet and suddenly the lesbian pulls her hand away and says out loud, 'But I don't *want* to move to Brazil!'"

"In other words," Gitta summed up, a veteran of meetings now, "the lesbian had futured an entire relationship in the first ten seconds before she even met the woman."

"Right-o."

"Okay, I'll loosen up with Jerry. Things are going to be fine, right?"

"Yes, they are. You trust the Universe to send you someone good, don't you? Didn't you say you were making a list ala Malcolm, too, after you heard me doing it?"

"Yes. But…"

"But nothing. Stop at yes. Just say yes. Remember those trust games in the seventies, where you'd have to stand with your back to a bunch of people and fall backward so they'd catch you?"

"I hated those."

"Me, too. But I never fell on my ass. Someone always caught me."

"Okay, okay."

"Hey, whatchu guys doing Saturday? Drake wants to go to the Timberline. Malcolm says he's in, and Simon's game as long as I don't make him dance."

"The macho Marine at a gay bar?"

"He loves the idea of going to a gay bar. He said in California he was part of the Hash House Harriers and the most fun run was through the gay neighborhood during the Red Dress Run."

"Serious? Did he wear a red dress?"

"Swear to God, I have seen the photo of my new Marine Corps boyfriend, secure enough in his hetero masculinity to wear a red tu-tu over his running shorts, hoisting a beer after with other Red Dress men and women."

"You sure he's straight?"

"Loves titties and pussy. Good thing for me he likes big tits and curvaceous white women. He just likes everyone, is all. He thinks gay bars are wonderfully fun."

My writing was going nowhere.

Flooded with first exhaustion over Dew for weeks, then relief and joy with Simon, I couldn't put fingers to keyboard. Everything felt too raw, too close to the bone. I was no longer an authority on anything, smacked down by the Universe over my son's collapse then lifted by the warm kisses of this damn-near-perfect new man. I felt like clay, pounded down flat then molded back up to human, re-formed with new inside parts I couldn't explain. The words sat behind my skull, a silent pool.

I cleaned the house instead, playing loud music at night, sipping on herb tea. The curtains looked dusty so those came down, revealing mildewed windowsills and cobwebs in every corner. One project led to another long into the night, my feverish sleep unable to keep me going during my FedEx workday. Naps after lunch sustained me until I fell out on my evening couch in front of the news, only to wake at nine p.m. and start doing home chores.

Simon would email short notes or call once in a while, playing it cool. It felt like we already had the future locked up so why hurry it along? We had obligations to our respective households for a while---my mortgage, his lease. It felt like long foreplay to stretch things lazily out.

He wanted to give me breathing room, he said, let me write in peace.

I had never had a supportive partner who thought I had the Right Stuff, that my creative ability might weigh in heavy someday. I doubted my own flow sometimes, but I'd ended relationships over my art. No reading my shit was allowed, a rule that drove jealous partners to test it, ending trust. Simon couldn't have cared less what I wrote, he was never going to snoop at it. Reading was a chore to him, something they'd made him do at school, something with which he struggled. His support was completely altruistic, then and all the more pure.

I tried children's stories, re-working George and Beezy and Cheepie-Weepie, making up new Babushka the Mouse, Aphrodite the Giraffe and Feluga the Beluga stories. The unimaginative twists seemed structured and flat, just like the children's stuff I'd hated as a kid, insulting my intelligence.

Porn might make a quick buck, I thought suddenly one day, and who can't write porn? Cracking my knuckles, I put fresh sheets sandwiched around purple carbon paper into my IBM Correcting Selectric, hoping for raunchy gold that refused to appear. My own fantasies were full of color and depth but words felt awkward and stilted, like I was trying too hard. The repetitive nature of the work was actually very difficult to keep interesting. How many synonyms were there for dick and pussy? I couldn't find the plot vs. action balance.

Narrative, maybe, I wondered, thinking Sunshine stories would have a nostalgic feel, maybe qualify as family drama or cultural exchange. Maybe I could point a piece at a quarterly, or an upscale magazine. But opening the Sunshine Tribe to such scrutiny felt like prostituting my own family. I couldn't hang them out there to dry in the sterile, cruel Real World for a quick buck and fame flash.

Waiting under its plastic bubble cover, my typewriter looked like an old bonnet-style hairdryer, gathering dust.

As it turned out, Simon owned not one but two pairs of cowboy boots. He was late picking me up because he'd had trouble choosing between the two. Since one pair was black shiny leather and the other creamy buff ostrich skin, he'd had to tailor the entire outfit to the boots.

I had learned that though he looked awesome in casual shirts and jeans, Simon loved to dress well. He owned his own tuxedo, had five pairs of cufflinks, a bigger closet than mine stuffed with dress clothes and his seven pairs of shoes included white bucks. He wore shirt tail garters attached to his socks. The man always looked impeccable.

He said it was something he picked up as a teen, that others dressed too sloppily and he wanted to look like the men in the magazines. He intuited that it drew women, watching them go crazy for a sharp-dressed man.

For this reason Simon had skipped shop in high school, already well-versed in mechanics from working in his father's gas stations. He'd squeegeed enough windshields back in the full-service days to see a lot of good cleavage and wanted more of that. He joined Four-H and took all the ladies' classes, entered the baking and jam-making contests, and took Home Ec at school, surrounded by pretty girls who all wanted to "help" the lone man in their midst. Smart man that he was, Simon had found his bliss, women fawning over him from every angle.

He had more pussy than he could ever handle and took six dates to the Berkeley High Senior Prom, three on each side. Instantly crowned Prom King and all his beauties Queens, the roar of the crowd at his audacity was one of his highest moments. They rode in a stretch red Cadillac to His Lordship down on the Bay for their post-prom dinner, afterward partying in the park until dawn in his best clothes.

Simon had chosen the ostrich-skin boots and gone with a wheat-colored Western yoked shirt. His jeans over his incredibly long legs were heaven. I wanted immediately to stay home, and pushed him onto the couch, my legs straddling his lap.

We kissed a few times and he said softly, "C'mon, now, the others are waiting. We'll take care of that later."

His hand swept under my skirt, over my pussy.

I could get used to this man.

Malcolm pushed Drake's wheelchair up the ramp to the Timberline, with Gitta and Jerry close behind.

"You two make the cutest couple," Simon wisecracked as Malcolm turned the chair around the ramp's corner.

"Oh, Malcolm is *much* too good for the likes of me," Drake assured us, waving his hand. "His wife Brigette Bardot waits at home in a Merry Widow, ready to service him the moment he walks in the door like J, The Sensual Woman."

Malcolm stopped the wheelchair and looked at Drake, then burst out laughing.

"She *does* do that shit," Malcolm said. "She's always taking those Cosmo quizzes: How To Tell If Your Man Is Satisfied, How To Give Great Head In Three Easy Steps; How To Leave Him Begging For More. I hate that shit. It's like she's experimenting on me, doing secret reconnaissance. We'll get done and she'll say 'Well, how *was* it?' and then I realize I am supposed to critique some recycled Butterfly technique or some shit she read about. Jesus, I hate that. My dick won't even get hard for her anymore."

The silence in the group was stunning. An identical-looking lesbian couple pushed laughing past us while the greatest vulnerability a hetero man could speak hung there in mid-air.

"Darling, we *all* have our moments," Drake chimed in, reaching up to cup Malcolm's cheek affectionately. "Why, I couldn't even get Queen Mary to blow her smokestack by *myself* the other day, she just stayed limp in the harbor no matter what I tried. Don't let it bother you, you gorgeous creature. You are about to be worshipped as God Incarnate with that body of yours tonight. Why, these queens are going to think you're straight out of that gay Hootie Burger King commercial. Let 'em buy you drinks and fawn all over you. No need to worry about your dick. Just absorb the good energy and go home and jack off in the bathroom like the rest of us."

"Hootie it is," Malcolm smiled, put completely at ease, and he pushed Drake up to the door.

Simon and Jerry visibly relaxed, the fragile man-moment handled with enormous diplomacy by the least macho of them all.

We swept into the Timberline, the back of our hands stamped with a day-glo horseshoe and nestled up close to the rail as George Strait wailed "You Know Me Better Than That." Couples swirled on the peanut-shell polished oak floor, the colored gels spotlighting the better dancers. Pearl, the tiny ageless Asian regular, was wearing her pink petticoat dress tonight, a huge Minnie-Mouse bow in her beehive, and she was on the whippet-thin drama dancer's arm. All was right with the world.

I heard a slight buzz to our left and saw we were being stared at. The crowd of couples and groups around the elbow-high leaning tables were all watching us, with some rumbling underfoot.

A small lesbian came toward us in an Australian outback cowboy hat, its sides curled in and pointing down to the ground for and aft. Our eyes were adjusting to the dark as she approached.

"Excuse me," she spoke, looking down at Drake in the wheelchair and removing her hat out of respect. "Aren't you Drake Astor?"

"Yes," he preened, sitting up straighter. "And you, Precious, are…?"

"I'm Petey, and my friends and I would be honored if you and your posse could join us at our tables over yonder."

She pointed with her hat to the little crowd, who all suddenly smiled sheepishly then waved little hellos.

"Why, we would be delighted, wouldn't we, oh my Posse On Broadway?"

Once we were comfortably ensconced with Petey and her friends, drinks appeared for which we did not pay. The Seattle Gay News photographer and his little pocket camera flashed blinding Magicube shots of Drake Astor, new Poster Boy for International Peace. No fewer than fifteen dancers came up and shook his hand as if touching the hem of his garment.

Then came the kicker.

"Mr. Astor?" said a tall older woman I recognized from the Pride Parade.

Greta Cammermeyer had shaken my little Dew's hand at the Pride Parade a week after he'd wiped out on his foot-scooter, making half his face hamburger. High-ranking military status aside, she was a nurse first, expressing concern for my child when she'd stopped to greet us. Her lover had asked Dew if the bike was alright. When Dew grinned and said yes, she'd told him gruffly "Good man."

"Yes, I'm Drake Astor," he'd said, looking up into the eyes of this military wonder.

"Thank you for making noise," Greta said, shaking his hand.

"Thank you for your service," Drake choked out, his mouth left hanging open.

The waters parted as she moved away, Drake left speechless for once.

"Flies gonna come in you don't shut your lower jaw," Simon laughed, raising his Guinness with the other hand. "Hell, straight or gay, I know a military higher up when I see one. She's been in the press. Good for her. Here's to Greta."

Simon was a most unlikely military man, embracing the concept of aid all over the world but rejecting the war aspect. He himself had participated in two war actions and seventeen humanitarian missions, saving countless lives. He knew how many sacks of grain, pallets of material, jeeps or medical clinic set-ups it took to fill a ship or plane or any size, calculated down to the square foot, organizing more freight into the cargo hold than any of his predecessors. That had been his specialty, affording him his double-entendre Marine Corps nickname: "Squeezebox."

Jerry and Gitta danced around the outside edge in the wide beginner's circle. I hit the dance floor with a blond butch who asked politely, nodding first to all the men and butches, unsure who was my partner and so covering all the bases. Simon and Drake, surrounded by well-wishers, watched as I was twirled and spun, my body directed by another's grip and pure centrifugal force.

As Drake's muscle, Malcolm was the man literally behind the hero, holding the chair grips. The boisterous gay men recalled Malcolm's television debut at Shelly's funeral and soon dubbed him Secret Agent 007. Malcolm was plied with drinks all night as the worshippers tried to pry intimate truth from his lips. Reveling in his 007 role, he remained mysterious and aloof, enjoying himself immensely.

Drake was bookended between lesbian twins and shouted to me about Romulus and Remus. An SGN reporter yelled questions to Drake over the country twang, and Drake did his best to be witty at a high decibel level. The camera man with his Pocket Instamatic loved the twins framing his shot for next Thursday's write-up.

"Mary, Kate and Ashley, fame is exhausting!" Drake shouted in my ear when the Tush Push was announced and his new entourage all took to the floor. "When, oh when will the paparazzi leave me alone?" he grinned, squeezing my wrist with his good hand.

I thought of Whoopi Goldberg taking Sally Field to the mall in "Soapdish," creating an adoring mob of fans.

"You were great out there," Simon whispered in my ear as I sat on his lap to rest. His hands circled my waist as he held me tightly. "Go dance some more so I can watch. It's foreplay for me. Go on," he smiled wickedly. "It'll pay off for you handsomely later."

"Really?"

"Really."

"Jerry, wanna dance?" I asked just as he and Gitta were sitting down.

"Sure," he grinned at me. "You're probably gonna have to back-lead, though. I'm new at the two-step thing. Let's hope for a waltz, while we're at it, and then I promise you, I'll take you on in a more manly way."

Gitta waved us onto the floor and Jerry assumed the lead position.

"You'll do fine. Slow, slow, quick, quick, slow, slow, quick, quick. Relax."

Jerry held my hand tentatively but got stronger as he began to get the hang of it. I gently steered the action from my follow position, thinking of the feminist quote about Ginger Rogers: She'd done everything Fred Astaire had, only backwards and in high heels.

"You're quite good," Jerry commented, finally able to talk and dance at the same time.

"Thank you," I said, limiting the conversation so he wouldn't falter.

"I love Birgitta, you know," he said all of a sudden, eyes on mine, his feet moving automatically, gracefully.

"That's…that's wonderful, Jerry."

"I intend to marry her."

"Holy shit. Does *she* know this?"

He grinned at me and whirled me in a fast turn-about, trying out his chops. I heard Gitta applaud from the corner and Simon whistled.

"Not yet. I have a ring in my pocket. I've had it there for a week, waiting for the right moment. I wanted to make sure it was…okay with you, with the group. You all seem to come as a package deal and I hope I am good enough to get in the Inner Circle."

"Oh, wow, Jerry, you get right to the point, don't you?"

"Years of therapy," he smiled, dipping me backward as we slowly ended the song. "I know it's soon and all but we aren't getting any younger. I'm closer to fifty than forty. I want her in my world."

He bowed and I curtseyed, then we held hands back to the table.

"Fine by me," I said, tightening my fingers on his hand and leaning up to kiss his cheek.

"Fine by you what?" asked Gitta, searching our eyes.

"The dance," Jerry said, kissing her. "She says I dance just fine."

"You were awesome, Annalee. I wish I had that grace. I'm the only black man on the planet who can't dance or play basketball. Like 'The Jerk' in reverse. But watching you…" he pulled my ear to his lips, "…makes my dick hard."

"I'll drink to that," I replied, slugging back my Cosmo.

"Excuse me," said a tall drag queen who appeared in front of Drake, her safety-orange wig piled as high as Marge Simpson's. Long red nails raked Drake's thick hair and the slit of her skirt stopped at exactly at Drake's eye level. "Aren't you that Poor Little Rich Boy from Spokane who was the victim of an international hate-crime incident not so long ago?"

"Why, yes, I am," Drake exclaimed, looking down to the five-inch platform shoes then straight at the top of the slit. His eyes eventually reached up at the towering specimen's face as the stranger waited.

"I'm Magic Wanda."

Drake simply looked blank.

"Aka Larry O'Toole."

This meant nothing to me or any of the rest of us but we watched as Drake went completely pale.

"Oh. My. Fucking. God."

Drake spat each word out separately, his eyes never leaving the drag queen's face.

Wanda bent down and kissed Drake full on the mouth. To our astonishment, Drake reached hungrily around the ruffled collar of the taffeta red dress, holding the kisser in a tight grip.

We all stared at each other, waiting, mystified, as this transpired. It took a moment for understanding to be imparted, their shared moment completely private.

We waited.

Kissing finally released with a loud thwock, they held each others' hands as if reunited post-Titanic.

"Where, Larry, have you *been* all my life? Darlings," Drake shakily announced to us all. "Meet Lawrence O'Toole the Third, my middle school crush and first closeted kiss."

Over fresh drinks, they explained. After being caught near-congress in Drake's family wine cellar, Larry had been immediately cloistered in a distant Catholic boarding school then sent to Europe for social refinement. Drake had been hastily enrolled in a private prep academy then pushed into the University of Washington in Seattle.

Contact had been severed, everyone barely escaping public shame. In each family, the other boy's name had never been mentioned again.

Malcolm's wife Bernadette was well enough to attend the goodbye party we threw for them before they went to Alaska. Bernie was kinda dim but really nice. Her fake boobs and cat-eye curlique black eye-liner were distracting. She tried hard to smile through the event and we tried to include her.

It was clear we had all bonded without her, though, and the stories weren't as funny to her, our escapades vaguely threatening, as if something untoward had happened while she had been laid up. Malcolm seemed to acquiesce, being less loud, less boisterous, looking caught in the middle of two worlds.

It felt a little forced, trying to be glad one of us was moving on. It made me think of Shelly and how the void she left still hurt me so much I couldn't talk about her. I put her out of my mind. I'd miss Malcolm but he'd be a phone call away. He wasn't dead. Life revolved, things changed, to everything there was a season.

Bernie was excited to be going to Alaska or rather, she seemed glad to be leaving Seattle. Maybe her fall had spooked her, or maybe there were things we didn't know about their marriage. We hoped for the best for them.

Tears took over my eyes when Bernie patted Malcolm's arm and nodded in the intimate marriage-language that meant she was ready to go. When he hugged me close, Malcolm whispered "It's been a blast, hasn't it? Now take care of Simon, Al," and then they were gone.

Dew stayed quiet, no word from Chicago. I was so exhausted from his brutal illness and slow recovery that I guiltily welcomed the silence, following his lead.

He was a grown-ass man. He'd be fine.

Peanut was happy Dew was back in her portion of the country so as soon as she could get time off work, she was going to head down to Chicago. She had to make some money first, she told me in a moment of candor, because she'd been busted for shoplifting and had to pay a four hundred dollar fine.

Like Dew's illness that howled I was the Only One Who'd Understand, I was glad she felt comfortable enough to tell me these things. But I was exhausted with the supportive role. I sighed and counted to five before responding, thinking over my words.

"Did you learn something, then?"

"Yup. Not doing that anymore."

"What did you steal?"

"A lighter."

"Was it worth four-hundred-dollars?"

"It is *now*."

I burst out laughing, my cub always able to crack me up with her stark truths.

I was relieved my choices weren't of the same nature anymore, my problems on a different scale, my choices more reasonable over the last decade. But I had done insane things in my youth. Who was I to frown and judge? I'd taken hella risks. We are all lucky to come through alive, not ending up incarcerated or removing ourselves from the planet with some idiotic Darwin Award move.

Gitta and I had long discussed this aspect of parenting, the wheel that goes around, unstoppable, turning through time the same for everyone, all of us repeating an endless loop of similar mistakes, the pattern repetitiously stamped in everyone's DNA. Children do not absorb the parent's lessons and move on from there, and every parent is amazed that the children won't input experienced advice. Imagine how evolved mankind would be if each of us took the previous generations truths and errors into account and started from there.

With her boys in Kuwait, Gitta had to learn letting-go harder than any of us. She dreaded the knock on the door, sure one or both of her babies would be maimed or dead before war's end. I assured her Kuwait was safer than the conflict zones but it wasn't much help. Half a world away was still too far to safely touch them.

Meanwhile, Gitta had a grandchild growing in a teenager's belly east-of-the-mountains and it made her recoil in horror. I knew she tried to think of ways to love this new life coming along but it was a nightmare for her. The mother-to-be had a Facebook page with pictures of her sprouting tummy, posed in front of a Confederate flag and two sharp-toothed Pitbull puppies. The baby shower announcement had Rhonda registered at Walmart.

Gitta FedEx-ed a silver-plate piggybank and a hundred-dollar savings bond. Hoping to hear no more until the birth, Gitta stayed busy with Jerry who, evidently, was still carrying the ring in his pocket.

I guessed the moment hadn't yet arrived.

Larry O'Toole the Third took over pushing Drake's wheelchair, the t wo of them completely glued together. Larry threw himself into Drake's care, swooping in and comforting the man in every way possible, romancing him with Pike Place flowers, hot crepes from the little place down Queen Anne Hill, international newspapers from Bulldog News, and the occasional Blueboy. Nights were spent at one or the other's place.

They had intense childhood history together and began referring to their blueblood upbringing as "back in the old country." Years of catching up poured from one to another and soon it was like they had been together all their lives.

Larry did drag shows for fun, but the Rainbow Foundation he'd begun was what he lived for. His wealthy Irish Catholic family *hadn't* disowned him and he was positively drowning in money he tried hard to spread around to every worthwhile gay charitable organization he could. Rainbow Foundation benefited children in AIDS families, providing clothing, school supplies, field trips, counseling, summer camp and after school tutoring.

It made perfectly righteous, karmic sense to him to support Drake, sharing the old wealthy privilege they'd known as children, embarrassing Drake's parents in the process.

"Fuck those people," he'd fume, insisting Drake move into his Capitol Hill blue and yellow Craftsman with the wrap-around porch. "Let them watch you enjoy your life, made wealthy again by the boy from down the street. They wanted to see you squirm and beg, now *they* can all squirm, pretending we aren't doing our homo thing together two hundred miles away. Both sets of parents still lunch at the Club every month. Fuck them. The best revenge is living well. I will call my attorney the moment you agree and have papers drawn up. Since you've been disowned by your family, I can legally adopt you, and that would make you my next of kin. You'll be cared for into perpetuity. Just say the word."

"Whaddya think, Princess?" Drake asked me, gnawing his insides out over the offer of new comfort and stability.

It had come from out of the blue. He felt hurried.

"How old are you?" I asked. "How many times is such a deal going to be laid at your feet again? Is he good enough for you?"

"Thank you for that, darling. Yes, he is, and yes, I am getting older and no, this shall not pass my way again."

"Do you love him?"

"Yes, wildly so."

"Do you know him?"

"Like my own soul."

"Then the problem is…?"

My parents were Sunshine before I was born so I knew no other way of life.

Naked and barefoot, laughing with the other children, I'd scream through a game of tag under the willow trees, napping in the arms of whatever grown-up was available. This was how I grew. It seemed simple to me and only got complicated when I met up with the outside world.

I wondered if Amish kids or polygamists' children felt the same easy bond, their world the small norm from which they looked out. But our lack of rigidity made Sunshine a comfy way of being brought up. There was no fear, no authority figure speaking from on high.

We had lived in a little cabin, my family expanding and contracting with the flow, my parents floating easily between partners. I had stayed mostly in the Fawn Camp with my friends, coming to my mother only when I needed extra comfort or a touchstone. I don't remember my father much, except he used to tell me stories sometimes and play Revelry on the trumpet to call us home from the woods, but then he disappeared altogether. Other grown-ups abounded so I felt no real loss. There were lots of Pony siblings, a few Yins. Everyone got along.

We were taught to get out there and make our mark, start our own tribe.

Drake saw Larry's lawyer to make it official. The only couple among us who couldn't marry committed themselves first.

Come September, Jerry found the moment in Gitta's basement, water overflowing from her washer pipes, a wrench in his right hand.

As Birgitta shrieked that her whole basement was ruined, Jerry waded into the water and tightened the gushing pipe to stop the leak. Gitta burst into tears, saying she was tired of the responsibility, being a single homeowner was too much, the weight was too crushing, she couldn't afford another repair bill on her own, she couldn't do this anymore.

"I've got the perfect solution," Jerry said, taking off his soaked shoes on the basement steps. Since he was on the step below her, their faces were even.

Jerry pulled the half-carat floating solitaire from his jeans pocket.

"Marry me."

Malcolm said Anchorage was beautiful, wide open yet cosmopolitan. He said the smell of the air was a tonic to Bernie and she was much better. They'd even had a little sex, he chuckled to me over the phone.

"And ya know what? It was a'ight."

He sounded surprised.

"How's the job?"

"Same restaurant, different city. Got some fine-ass white women up here far as the eye can see."

I could tell he was rubbing his fingers together.

"Well, be choosy with the dick, you hear me?" I said, with a sudden pang of jealousy.

"Roger that. How's Simon treating you, speaking of choosy dick."

"He's a gift from the gods themselves. Fine as you to look at, smart, easy-going, worships the air I breathe."

"Give you a ring yet?"

"Nope."

"Christmas is coming."

"Fuck off. I miss you."

"Ya know what? I miss you, too, Al."

"I've re-thought Greece," Drake sighed, picking at his salad. "The leg's still not healing right. And I'm just so…"

He leaned back in his chair and looked away to the side, giving me his brooding profile.

"Comfortable?"

"Exactly."

Drake's face changed completely, lighting up with unconcealed glee.

"I am so fucking happy, Annalee, I'm just going to stay here and bask in the warmth of my sugar daddy. Mama-mia, he'sa one-a spicy meat-a-ball," he accented, pinching his fingers together in an imitation Italian pleasure gesture.

"Then *stay,* goofy! No one said you have to go out in the world and make something of yourself."

"But then I *wasted* those classes on Teaching English to Poor Hairy-Chested Boys."

"You did not. As mothers in every social class but yours would say, you now have a skill to fall back on."

"Larry is wonderful, Al. I simply have to be myself and that is enough. I sleep until I wake up, I eat whenever I want, I read, we go to the Market every day and he wheels me through the crowd like I am King Tut's solid gold living progeny. Mommy, could I get used to being worshipped in my own *home*, especially surrounded by expensive upholstery for which, I might add, I didn't have to pay."

"Someday I'll get the fuck out of FedEx and have a life. Maybe someone will support me so I can write."

Jerry and Birgitta went to City Hall on their lunch hour in October and got married, calling us all from downtown to come join them for an impromptu happy hour celebration.

Peak season was starting and I was determined not to let it throw me.

It was something I had to go *through,* like a bad acid trip, see it out until the end. I didn't have to like it but resistance simply made it harder. I made sure I slept a lot, ate vegetables and protein, went to the gym on weekends and saw Simon every spare moment I could.

As an early birthday present, I gave Simon a key to my house, the most trust-filled gift I could think of.

Simon began crawling into my bed in the middle of the night, shushing me when I woke, snuggling up deeply against my body. Sometimes there was sex, crazy and wild and full, and sometimes we just slept, spooned together. In the morning he'd pull on his work clothes and scoot out after a cup of coffee, his toothbrush dripping on my sink, the goodbye kiss all business as he focused on the day ahead.

I tried to get to his apartment once in a while to appear balanced but he understood my killing seasonal workload. Often as not he'd take me to dinner or bring something over just to make sure I wasn't having a bowl of cereal before collapsing. My feet got rubbed, my car got new windshield wipers, my orgasms were guaranteed.

Not a cat person, he begrudgingly gave in and acknowledged that my cats adored him.

Over rotisserie chicken from Safeway I learned his Oakland upbringing was a little rough in the beginning, then more middle class as his father's gas stations beginning to prosper. After they moved, Simon pole-vaulted at Berkeley High and tried to catch up scholastically with his peers, astounded at what he hadn't learned in the Oakland school system. He'd driven a Microbus to Alaska, married a fellow fire-jumper and had two children, then joined the Marines. His lesbian half-Jewish ex-wife was now in upstate New York, their children finishing college.

Simon was fascinated by Sunshine culture and loved to hear any story relating to my upbringing. He understood why Peanut wished I had had her when I was a hippie.

"Where's my jet pack?" Drake wanted to know, popping gherkins in his mouth.

Our entrees sizzled and flamed directly in front of us as we twirled in oversize chairs at 13 Coins' counter. It was four a.m.

We were celebrating, he and I, since the second cast had come off his successfully healed arm. Our lovers were unavailable, and Gitta and Jerry were on their mini-honeymoon in Vegas. I needed to blow off steam, peak season making me insane with stress. The FedEx drivers who weren't religious drank to get through and I was one of them, after years of toughing it out AA style.

We'd had a few all over town, ending up at the swankiest pre-dawn breakfast in town. Drake continued on the futuristic theme of which we'd obviously been robbed.

"What about my lawn chair with rockets attacked? And why is it always lawn chairs?"

"I know," I tipsily replied. "We were supposed to be like The Jetsons already. I'm still driving to work in a *car*. I thought I'd have a personal jet bubble by now or at least some see-through transport tube."

"Remember 'Queen For A Day'?" Drake said wistfully, calling up the victimized woman's biggest dream contest ever. The worst hard luck story won the weeping lucky contestant new home appliances, a stocked freezer, a beauty salon up-do, an ermine cape and a glittery crown to wear on the air.

"We didn't watch that show much, except when I was sick and home from school. I do remember The Jetsons. We had cartoons."

"I forget sometimes you were raised by leprechauns. You seem so *normal.*"

"Thanks, I suppose. Or else you are simply as bent as I am."

"Possible. Did everyone on your kibbutz have those midi-length llama inside-out coats with the embroidery all over them? And aviator sunglasses like Gary Puckett? I'll bet you wore Earth Shoes, didn't you?"

"When I lived in the Tenderloin I had glitter platforms. I wanted one of those llama coats really badly until I sat on a bus next to a girl who'd come out of the pouring rain and that coat stunk to high heaven. Like the worst wet dog you can imagine."

"The Tenderloin always scared me. I stayed in The Castro, of course. Did you listen to music on AM radio?" Drake asked. "I had 45's of Smokey Robinson and The Archies."

"We had a good stereo in the dining hall and an okay one in Fawn Camp. We had red plastic records of Burl Ives singing 'Little White Duck' and 'Big Rock Candy Mountain.' My favorite was 'Puff, The Magic Dragon.' I'd stack them on the record player and watch them drop. The needle would go over and then the next record would drop, remember?"

"My mother thought that Puff song was about drugs so it wasn't allowed in our house."

"Are you going to eat that radish?" I asked, since I knew Drake loved them.

"Darling," Drake immediately leaned in, catching the waitress flying by between us and the line cooks, "Would you be a lamb and get us some more antipasto? Thanks, Precious." He sat back down in his big chair. "Yes. Now you can have the last radish." He winked at me. "Have you seen it on menus as anti-pasta? Jesus, that slays me, like the Anti-Christ. Matter and anti-matter. Pasta and anti-pasta."

"Last week I saw 'pouched eggs' on a breakfast menu. And liver with smother onions. Is your arm feeling okay, Drake?"

"Weak, a little. My leg is getting stronger in physical therapy or maybe it's the motivation of the cute PT guy. My PT Gunboat, I call him. Just *looking,* darling, no worries. Larry and I are solid.

"Good, good."

"How's Simon?"

"Dreamy," I smiled. "A perfect Sunday kind of love."

"No ring yet?"

"What is it with you guys? We may be fated to be together but why the push? Malcolm said the same damn thing."

"Christmas is coming."

"Fuck you *and* Malcolm."

I put my name on the list to work Christmas Day at FedEx. Officially, we were closed, but at every call center and station there were handsomely-paid personnel still scrambling to attach the badly addressed, label-torn, information-missing, misrouted packages to their rightful recipients.

We kept a running sheet of incredible address errors. This shit list was comprised of the mangled attempts of shippers, mostly catalog call center operators, to translate the gift buyer's recipient address information.

James Jones
17 South
Settle WA 98134
(No phone, no company name)

South *what?* From the zip, this was an industrial area with thousands of warehouses. And I loved the city name.

Ann
Customer Service
Washington Mutual
Seattle WA 98101
(No phone, no department)

WAMU had four 35-story buildings, two mailrooms, five locations that did one service only such as commercial real estate, and three different internal tracking systems and gatekeepers through which to go. Ann was never going to see this package.

The hands down winner was the box addressed, simply,

Mary

Seattle WA

(No zip, no phone, no company name)

We knew the couriers who had picked these bonehead shipments up had known it was going to end up a miss-sort but they were so time-pressured they had not been able to correct it on their end. The company policy was to ship it on and research it en route or better, on the receiving end, making it someone else's problem.

Three or four undeliverable attempts sent things to the cage for customer service scrutiny when anyone had a single moment of time. This was the strong province of those who couldn't go on road, like injured, pregnant or sick couriers. No one, absolutely no one, ever, for any reason, ever got out of working peak. Your immediate family had to die before you'd be excused. If your grandfather passed away, too bad. Fred Smith had no grandparents and neither, at peak, did we.

Simon said he'd meet me at my place, and he'd have dinner ready with the home fires burning while I made double-time and a half in the last twelve hour push.

Christmas Day at FedEx was cake. The phone rang only every five minutes instead of five seconds, the warehouse sat full of silent trucks, and the cage's pile grew smaller as customers made special trips to pick up their orphaned presents. We didn't send anyone out on road except in cases of medical emergency, a prescription, say, or a kidney on ice. We made customers come to us, saying, "Well, we're officially closed, but if you wanted to come *get* your package, we'll be here until five..." It was the one day a year we had the power to make them come to us.

Us couriers were happy peak would be over in a matter of hours and we'd survived another one, spending this relatively easy warm, dry day in the office helping out. The customers were thrilled to be united with their gifts. Everyone was in great cheery form, wearing Santa hats or bell earrings and the happy recipients sometimes brought candy, homemade fudge or cookies. If we were really lucky they'd bring fancy bath salts, flowers or Tully's gift cards.

Our backroom favorites were the undeliverable perishables.

The big food catalog houses always wanted their recipients, especially at Christmas, to have the freshest product possible. A two or three attempt perishable was a wasted gift and with one confirmation phone call to the shipping house, we'd get the answer we wanted: The shipper would re-send a fresh gift the next business day to the corrected address and we were to destroy the original shipment.

"Destroy shipment!" the agent would yell out immediately after the authorization. She'd enter all the right codes, scanning the package each time a comment was added, covering her ass before we'd rip into the box and argue over the fresh lobster, cream-center Godivas, Omaha steaks, smoked cheese trays, Hawaiian macadamia nut cookies, New Orleans jelly roll, hazelnut Yule logs or Harry and David pears.

Sometimes it was wine, sometimes flowers. Once it was even tropical fish, fifty green Tiger Barbs that one of the nerdy guys took home to his 100-gallon tank. He thought he'd died and gone to heaven.

I called Simon from work, finally done with Christmas.

"I'm not sure what you're making for dinner, but we broke a case of Pouilly-Fuisse so I'm bringing some home. And I have some French candy, too."

"Perfect. They'll go great with the roaring fire and Prime Rib. What's your ETA?"

"Eighteen hundred hours."

"Roger that. Love you."

"Love you, too."

Despite my irritation at the fellows, I *did* wonder about Christmas and a potential ring. Things seemed so…foregone. Simon and I agreed easily, effortlessly on nearly everything.

Our child-rearing philosophies were parallel, though all our kids were grown. We'd been frustrated non-custodial parents who'd placated the other parent while disagreeing with them. We'd done what was theoretically best for the children--- not best by being non-custodial, but best by not contesting it and tearing the children apart.

We liked the house kept at about the same level of clean. Simon knew how to cook a little bit but appreciated my stronger ability and comfort in the kitchen, leaving that to me while he tinkered with my car or mowed the grass. Both of us had gender-specific skills and they meshed with silken ease.

Even his anger management style synchronized with mine. I'd explode out what was irritating me and he'd yell back his angle, his point making just as much sense. By the next line of the fight, we each had seen the others' side and realized some kind of happy conflict resolution. Our disagreement was done long before the adrenalin angry-rush dissolved, happily frustrating my old pattern of circular non-resolution.

Simon said what he hated about his ex-wife was her haranguing endlessly on one point. Even after Simon had agreed and the fight was over; she always had to see it from 86 more sides, examining the wart over and over until he wanted to throttle her. Realizing I was imprinted with the same affliction, I aggressively un-learned that behavior, stifling the ten other arguments as to why the thing I had already stated was true. He'd already agreed. There was no need to browbeat. I had never known that about myself and was grateful he'd brought it up.

We wished we'd have met in our teens when I was in the Tenderloin and wondered how differently things would have turned out. I wished we'd have had children together.

We spoke of fostering needy children.

Truth was, we were both too fucking old to start *that* shit over. We'd pass cute kids and ahhhhh over them, how darling they were, tell a bit about ours when they were that age, get briefly wistful, but moments later express how grateful we were that ours were grown. We could have a few decades of peace and quiet together.

Simon had my house steamy and warm with pretty little spinach appetizers, baked potatoes and rare red meat.

"Weren't nothin', ma'am," Simon grinned, pointing at the Trader Joe's frozen appetizer box in the recycle. "Stick some nails in the potatoes like back in my Marine Corps days, put the appetizers on a cookie sheet….you need new cookie sheets, by the way…and singe the meat in butter like my mama used to."

"And my Jewish gramma," I said, popping a little spinach quiche into my mouth. "My dad's mother. We visited her once in Philadelphia before my dad split. I ate for three days. Her cubed steaks in butter were my favorite. And black cows."

"What's that?"

"Root beer and vanilla ice cream. An ice cream float, I guess other people call it. You eat things my dad's family ate. Are you sure you're not Jewish? You put salt on your watermelon like my dad did, too."

"It brings out the flavor."

"And you hate vinegar, like he did. My dad would shudder if he smelled it."

"Maybe that's why I hate Tabasco sauce."

"You *sure* you're black?"

I hugged him as he turned the meat over in the sizzling butter.

"I'm gonna take a shower and wash away peak season. I'm finally fucking done with FedEx nightmare until next year."

"Enjoy."

My dusty navy uniform was thrown in the basket and I flipped on the bathroom light, ready for my shower. Instead, the bathtub was filled with bubbles and hot water, awaiting me. Grateful for this dream man I'd kinetically imaged from my list of ideal qualities, I sank into the hot tub.

"Take your time," Simon hollered from the kitchen. "Everything's on warm in the oven. I'm going out to get whipped cream at 7-11. Be right back."

He filled my eclectic inventory for my perfect man. I had told the Universe everything I wanted, daring to ask this time, refusing to "settle." The paper had been on my fridge for celibate months, entries in different color ink added sporadically over time:

Good-looking black man
Strong
Built thick
Long legs
Tall
Kind
Funny
Good sense of humor
Peacenik

Must hate televised sports
Loves children and tolerates cats
Has his own career path
Must have interesting dreams
Good in bed, nothing flashy, no s/m: emphasis on steady, frequent sex
Affectionate, must be a hand-holder
Must have boy skill set, fix cars and repair houses, have his own power tools
Must love girl skill set and admire it
Has to want what I want for the future: peaceful co-existence, holding hands
through everyday life, rare fighting
Has to know how to argue with no threat of abandonment underneath
Must not have the money angst I do and be good with money
Must know computers and how to fix computer problems
Has to smell good
Must like bigger women---no weight issues
Have decent running car
Good job with good benefits
Must want to retire early, build something, create something
Must have a sense of spiritual quest and connection but not to a Jesus-type God
Can't be too emotional, has to be able to "man up"
Can't be too hard

Simon came back, bringing a cool breeze swirling into the bathroom with him, his clothes smelling like the chilly outdoors.

"Got whipped cream for the pumpkin pie. I wanted sweet potato pie but no one makes it."

"You mean like Safeway doesn't make it? What do you mean by no one?"

"Yeah, like the store."

"*I'll* make you one, beautiful man. Sometime. Not today."

"My mom makes 'em the best."

"I'll call her, then. It has to be just like making pumpkin pie."

He looked horrified.

"It's *nothing* like pumpkin pie."

"Well, I'll make you one."

"Really?"

"Really."

"C'mon and get out now and eat my Christmas supper. I have a present for you."

My heart flipped over.

RKelly's "Marry Me" began screaming inside my head.

Maybe he would have a ring after all, a tiny jewel box tucked under my napkin, or inside the potholder mitten. He'd light a sparkler and stick it in the pie, the ring wedged between them. On bended knee while he joked about stiff joints and old age, how we weren't getting any younger, would I please be his next of kin? He'd pull the little box out of his pocket in a flourish at just the right moment like Jerry did for Gitta. Maybe it would be inside a big box to fool me, the huge parcel unwrapped to reveal the small box inside.

It was a Sony laptop, waiting at my place at the table.

"Merry Christmas, honey. Now you can write on something more modern than that clunky old typewriter. You can sit in *bed* and write if you want."

"Show me everything!" I smiled, kissing him, amazed that this man would drop a chunk of change for something so personal, so *mine*. He really did pay attention to what mattered to me.

I let my little disappointment go, my chest still stinging a little. If he spent this much dough on my shiny new machine with all the boy doo-dads he was eagerly explaining to me, there was no ring possible. Maybe he liked things just the way they were, living a few miles apart, our lives parallel.

Would that be so bad, anyway? Why did I want a little piece of metal and stone to have visible proof of his feelings and commitment? All those Sunshine years and I still longed to live a Diamonds Are Forever ad. The champagne glass would have a ring at the bottom. After many golden years, he would fly me to Rome to present our anniversary band in a crowded piazza, saying he'd marry me all over again.

But not this Christmas.

Simon excitedly turned the machine on, going into technical detail while describing the whiz-bang factors. I never understood boy toys, even though I had been trained across the board in basic life skills. Boy or girl, in Sunshine world everyone learned to change a tire, bake a loaf of bread, chop wood, cuddle a baby. But I'd had no feel for the manlier tools and activities. They frightened me, frankly, though it wasn't Sunshine to admit it. I had wanted to have a lot of babies and stay home, loving and being loved. That made complete sense to me, unlike the wow-power Simon was showing me, opening window upon multiple window, numerous programs running, set-ups taking place, passwords being chosen.

I knew when he went home I'd gingerly, timidly open the laptop, holding my breath, turning it on as if pushing The Button to blow us all to hell. Electronics were the ultimate boy frontier and they scared hell out of me. I understood their capabilities in a vague, general way. I got it that they were the wave of the future and I said good riddance to typewriter ribbons, carbon paper, White-Out, correcting tape, hand editing the same page over and over again. I loved the *idea* of writing and storing information inside an electronic Etch-A-Sketch, arranging the document, cutting, pasting, editing and printing it out later. It was having to learn *how* to do all that overwhelmed me.

"Let me get your present," I said, extricating myself from the cords and wires.

Simon was glued to the screen, his glasses reflecting the blue light. He was so goddamn handsome and he didn't know how lovely he was. He carried himself with dignity and strength but not a shred of conceit. When I'd tell him he was handsome, he'd laugh and say "Yeah, right. Whatchu been smokin', woman?"

It made him uneasy. It was charming. I hoped to be able to reassure him of his masculine charms until the day we died. I was fucking crazy about this man.

In the bedroom closet inside my cowboy boot was the beribboned box I'd gotten on my mid-week route down at Pike Place Market. The little jeweler on 1ˢᵗ had a lovely dyke working behind the glass cases who had pointed out their stunning cufflink collection. The green iridescent shell settings were perfect for Simon's wardrobe of earth tones and Jerry Garcia ties.

"Love you, Simon. I'm glad you came along."

I kissed the top of his head where his tight curls faded to the promise of a future bald spot.

He squinted into the screen, concentrating.

I set the white box on the keyboard and his face lit up, breaking away from his manly duty of setting up my computer.

"Woo-hoo! Sweet!" he whistled, taking out the shiny silver and green abalone man-jewelry. "Great taste, babe."

"I learned it all from you, darling. Can we eat yet?"

"I forgot the supper!" he yelled, scooting his chair out and rushing to the oven.

"Let's eat in front of the t.v. and let the computer boot up or whatever you call it," I suggested. I was afraid to bump the table, afraid I'd break it.

"We can watch the *game!*" he laughed, since we both hated t.v. sports except in short muted bursts from a bar stool. We were bar people, talking and drinking, spending money, feeling a little tipsy. He drank whiskey sours, no cherry.

Simon clicked on the Sci-Fi channel, his personal favorite, then Comedy Central for me. We settled on "Five Easy Pieces."

"Merry Christmas, darling," I snuggled into Simon's muscular arm, finishing my plate and setting it on the coffee table.

"I love you, Annalee."

Chapter Eight

"It's a girl," Gitta said. "I'm someone's grandmother now."

She was totally miserable. This wasn't how grand-parenting was supposed to sound to me.

"Well, what's her name? How much did she weigh? Is she perfect? Have you seen her?"

"Her name's Ariel and she was C-Section. The water broke and labor didn't start. I think she was somewhere around seven pounds."

"You sound so disconnected from this, Gitta. This is your flesh and blood, your son's child."

"I know, right?" she snorted. "I *am* disconnected. It's not my life over there on the East Side where everyone saves up for rims and ape-hanger handlebars. I can't believe my kids chose that life, and now it's permanent since this Ariel has been born. *Fuck.* You want *good* things for your children, ya know?"

Birgitta started to cry.

"You can't control their lives, Gitta. They make choices. This little one came into the world and she didn't ask to be born so give her a little space, okay? Her mama is happy, thrilled to have her, right? How could that possibly go wrong? It's not your agenda, not your optimal outcome but there's lots of joy there."

"Maybe it's because I don't feel well. I got some sort of flu or food poisoning the last day we were in Vegas and it's lingering, kind of low-grade. We had a blast, though. Jerry won two grand on a slot machine and we bet half of it back. It was great spending money we hadn't worked for."

"Go see that baby when you feel better. How're the boys?"

"Still in Kuwait. Still alive. Sam didn't even get to come home for the baby being born. Rhonda talked to him on videophone, though and showed him his daughter. How's Dew?"

"All quiet from Chicago. I hope that's good news. Peanut's working. Everything seems to be going okay. Dew once told me that kids tell their parents about an eighth of what's really going on and that's probably true. I don't want to know it all, I don't think."

"Larry wants to have a New Year's Day brunch. We aren't big on the party the night before but breakfast the day after is just our speed. You guys available? Gitta and Jerry are a green light."

Drake was watching "Absolutely Fabulous" as he talked to me. I could hear it.

Simon and I lounged naked in bed, the nights between Christmas and New Year's Eve a slow, marvelous comfort. We still had to work but it was much lighter. Time slowed down.

"I'll ask the boss. Hang on."

I covered the phone with my hand and asked Simon if we might want to brunch with the gang on New Year's Day. Reaching from behind me around my torso, he squeezed my heavy breast and kissed my shoulder.

"Sure," Simon whispered.

"We're in. What am I bringing?"

"Your cheesecake, please."

"What's Gitta making?"

"Breakfast casserole."

"What are *you* making?"

"Fresh squeezed orange juice, champagne, and Larry's homemade sticky pecan cinnamon rolls."

"Holy shit. We are *so* there."

Simon kissed my lower back. I giggled.

"Are you guys having sex?"

"Right now? No. Ten minutes ago, yes."

"Remember when I said most gay men want to have a lover to have the *appearance* of having sex? So they can show him off with friends and family? It's not like that with Larry. He actually wants me practically all the time. It's *exhausting.*"

"Lucky you."

"Indeed. A*nd* he pays the bills. See you on New Year's. How's eleven sound?"

Dew and Peanut got together at her place in Madison a day after Christmas and called me late, putting me on speaker phone. Chad was practicing guitar in the next room, strumming the same three chords over and over, while Dew and Peanut threw popcorn piece by piece to their dog as they talked.

"Nothing, Mom. Christmas just doesn't mean that much. It means no school."

They both laughed, their grueling college classes in a lull.

Dew sounded back to his old self.

I wondered if he would do harder drugs again or if he'd gone around the wheel enough for one lifetime. Pot was different than any other drug, so in my book, pot was soft. You never heard about anyone robbing a convenience store high on pot or hurting themselves or others after smoking a joint. I hoped he was thinking along those lines.

"Yeah, well, it just means peak season to me. I haven't enjoyed Christmas since Drake wore a cape."

"That was *Drake?*" Peanut ribbed me. "For real? I thought that was the *real* Santa Claus and all the other Santas had just misplaced their fashion accessories."

I laughed.

"Did you get the books I sent?"

They both chorused yes, like good children, and rushed to thank me for "As Nature Made Him" and "A Walk In The Woods."

"Well, I liked the donation to Heifer International very much," I said. "It was thoughtful of you."

"We know you like them. We figured you didn't need another sweater."

The New Year came in with fireworks outside and in, my hands gripping the massive Mediterranean headboard as Simon moved under me, holding my hips. Our voices beamed in the eternal echolalia of love, rising in unison. Flooded with slippery sea-salt union, our skin slid in ecstatic chiaroscuro.

That day I'd begun my latest essay, aiming for the high-minded literary mags that paid poorly but gave good street cred. I was at the doors of wordsmith fame, banging the kick plate hoping someone got tired of me and gave me a chance. I needed to make my own luck. This idea felt like a possible in.

It would be a break-through narrative, exposing progressives who blurted out the most insane things when asking about Simon and me. The constant references to his dick size seemed rather odd, something not inferred with a white boyfriend. Some Seattle liberals still had bewildering beliefs under all that socially aware Gore-Tex.

Revealing their un-evolved ideas, I'd be a star of the NPR circuit, signing inside covers at a little table at Powell's and Elliot Bay, flying to New York to spend three minutes at 0500 hours on Good Morning America. I'd see my book displayed in stores, be recognized on the street.

Mixed couples would thank me for speaking the truth.

With my inner fame virtually sealed and Simon's dick hitting just the right spot, fireworks exploded in purple and emerald green throughout my aura. It was gonna be a good new year.

"We brought some little brioche from that nice bakery in Ballard," Gitta said, setting down her quilt-wrapped glass casserole dish. Jerry unloaded a cloth grocery bag from Whole Foods with a bouquet of forced spring daffodils in purple paper sticking out the top.

"Nice to see you!"

Jerry and Simon did the manly straight guy hug: shaking hands while pulling in tight to touch opposite shoulders and slapping the other man's back.

"Hey, Gitta, you look great!" Simon said, kissing her cheek. "Something's different. The hair? The makeup?"

Simon always tried to notice the niceties about the ladies, which had always kept him popular. And Gitta *did* look different. I couldn't place it but Simon was right. She looked great, with high color. We hugged hello and I kissed Jerry.

"It's the cool weather. Suits my Norsk side."

She shot a look at Jerry and he smiled gently.

Jerry and Gitta cheek-kissed Larry and Drake.

We all admired the hosts' vintage aprons over their rugged 501's that Larry had gotten a decade before at Ruby Montana's funky Second Avenue store. Drake's was black with martini glasses printed in red and green, while Larry's was white with cherries, olives, citrus slices and paper umbrellas. Larry wore Christmas-bell house shoes that tinkled when he walked.

"I'm a Christmas Fairy!" Larry twirled. "I wore these shoes for the Children's Benefit Show as Fey the Christmas Tinkerbell. It was SRO. Made more than the goal for the Foundation and I had a blast."

The house looked effortlessly perfect, holiday touches everywhere. A stained-glass window mosaic threw a multi-colored slant into the corner of the great-room, the dining and living area combined. Larry and Drake's table had grown by a leaf and was covered in lacy mauve silk. A Barbie-sized feathered replica of the 'Angels In America' angel was their centerpiece, a little holiday wreath around his head. His wings spread over a bowl of speckled Rainer cherries and unbearably cute tiny pink and green Lady apples.

Hot cider with cinnamon sticks sat in a silver warming carafe, the handle wrapped in a gingham red-check napkin. Off to the side of the teak island counter sat the one-handled orange juice squeezer, a ceramic Italian bowl underneath to catch the rinds. A pitcher of juice was three-quarters full on the butcher block.

My cheesecake with raspberry sauce had turned out beautifully. The cake sat on a crystal pedestal, dripping deep red icicles down its edges. A bright circle of mint leaves I'd added off-center gave it a complete holiday feel.

Heavenly aromas wafted from the oven where warm cinnamon rolls rose, sticky with pecans and raisins, slick white icing waiting at the ready.

Drake popped the Dom Perignon, spilling a few drops on the carpet while we applauded.

"Happy New Year, darlings!" Drake cried, as he held the bottle over the sink. "Here's to all of us!"

Filling the champagne flutes with o.j. and bubbly, he handed them out.

Gitta set her drink down and got a serving spoon for her breakfast casserole.

Larry brought out a silver tray lined with romaine, on which sat paper-thin sliced lox, tomato wheels, onions and Swiss cheese, toasted onion bagels and a block of cream cheese.

"Drake says you're half a Jewess so I thought I'd make you feel at home."

I was stunned, touched at his offerings, and immediately smeared cream cheese on a mini-bagel, piling on onions, cheese and lox. The taste sensation in my mouth was wonderful, filling my brain with images of my grandmother in Philadelphia on Rittenhouse Square.

"Awesome! Thanks, Larry," I mumbled, my mouth too full to talk.

"Something I can do to help?" Jerry asked Drake, rubbing his hands together. Straight men felt useless without a project, I was starting to notice. Simon was poking through Larry's CD collection and had pulled out Harry Belafonte's Christmas Album. He then studied the CD player.

My eye caught the art-deco green Lenox "Autumn" china on the sideboard, festooned with tiny baskets of fruit hand-painted in dots and rimmed in real gold paint. I had never seen anything so exquisite in my life.

"Larry, where did this china *come* from? Lenox still makes this pattern but now it's white. They haven't made this style in decades."

"Isn't it incredible? It was my great-grandmother's, passed down to each first-born. If I'd have had an older sibling, swear to God I'd have killed 'em just to get the 'Autumn.' I *love* it that you know your hope-chest name brands. Since you have such a nose for finery, missy, come see the silver with my family crest. I even have the little salt dishes with the tiny spoons. We used those in big piles of coke once upon a time."

Larry swept his hand across the china hutch filled with incredible antique silver. "What's the middle initial for?"

"Lawrence Horatio O'Toole the third."

"La-HOT triple X, I call him, darling," Drake said, sweeping in. "SSSSSSSSSSS," he hissed, licking his thumb and pressing it to Larry's hip. "Hot as hell, this one. Grrrrrr," Drake growled, turning to go check the cinnamon rolls.

Larry blew Drake a kiss.

"It's all gorgeous, Larry," I told him, hooking his arm to admire his lovely things.

"Where did you learn about such things living under a mushroom in the forest?" Jerry asked me. He pushed his horn rims up on his nose, reaching for his Mimosa.

Hundreds of Christmas cards on a gold string wreathed the mantel behind Jerry, lending a homey air to the masculine wood and leather room. Framed by the fireplace, Jerry looked comfortable, like the quintessential white man posing for his holiday portrait with a libation in hand, leather patches on the elbows of his sweater. All he needed was a pipe.

"That Jewish grandmother again," I replied. "A few days in Philadelphia with her crammed a lifetime of girl education into my head. She liked Noritake over Lenox, though, and showed me all the patterns from a bridal magazine. I'd never seen such feminine excess before in my life and lusted after it all immediately. Naturally, I couldn't tell anyone about it back on the land. It wasn't Sunshine to want expensive, elitist things. But man, I drank in that bridal magazine like it was porno. I learned about thread counts, silver, crystal, china, how to pour tea, which colors went with which seasons and fabrics, how to check for good seed beadwork on a wedding gown, how to write a proper thank-you note. I wanted all of it. Still do"

Simon looked at me from across the room, his head cocked sideways, a little smile on his face.

"What?" I asked him.

"Well," he said. "This would be the perfect time, then."

We all stared at him. He set his drink on the sideboard and cleared his throat.

"Drake, stop messing in the kitchen and c'mere. I got something to say. Jerry, turn that music down just a touch, will ya?"

We all got quieter, stopping to listen.

"I got something to say to my girl. Annalee, I loved you the minute I saw you on television. Everything fits about you. You smile at me like I matter. I love the way you grab hold of something and won't let go, shaking it like a dog with a tug rope."

I heard the radiator kick on in the old house. The fireplace crackled. A bus went by on 15th, the shhh of the tires telling me it was raining again. My heart pounded in my chest as the others looked from Simon to me. He continued.

"My kids are grown. I've got a good job and a military pension. I don't have a big ring or anything, no box with a red ribbon. But with our friends as witnesses, I'm asking you to marry me."

My hand reached up and clutched my neck as I sucked in my breath. I was stunned.

The grandfather clock ticked somewhere down the hall.

Gitta cleared her throat.

"Jesus, girl, *answer* the poor man! I've got cinnamon buns to check!" Larry fussed, the suspense killing him.

"Holy shit. Yes, Simon. Yes! Of course I'll marry you!" I laughed and ran to hug him close.

"I'm thinking King Day," he said, immediately practical. Clearly he'd thought this out. "It's a three day weekend. I *always* take off Martin Luther King Day. We could go to Victoria on a sea-plane afterward or stay in town and have a big party. Either way you get a new dress and we'll get gold-braided wedding bands at that nice Pike Place jeweler you like. Someday we'll get Lenox china, too, I promise. Party or Canada?"

"Dealer's choice," I smiled, kissing his chest. My mouth was level with his nipples, his broad, smooth chest right under the Italian dress shirt.

Acres and acres and it's all mine, I thought. I wished Shelly could be here.

"Well, knock me over with a feather, sister, aren't we all just as cozy as little bugs snug in a rug?" Drake exclaimed. "If this hasn't been the most domesticated year *ever.* Is there something in the water that bit us all? Everyone all coupled up. We might as well live in little boxes made of ticky-tacky, we all look just the goddamn same. We could start playing weekly Canasta."

"Bridge," smiled Jerry.

"Euchre," Larry.

"Mah-Jongg," I murmured, still hugging my new fiancé. Who needed a diamond?

"Hearts," said Gitta, clearing her throat again. "And I have something to say, here, too, as long as we're having a bonding experience."

Jerry stiffened slightly, pushing up his glasses and setting down his drink. Gitta went and stood next to him, twirling her diamond nervously with her thumb.

"We wanted to wait until we had all the tests and everything to make sure it was alright, and I guess it is, because everything came back negative so I guess we worried for nothing and anyway…we know it's going to be hard but it's like it was meant to be so…"

Jerry patted Birgitta's shoulder, letting her take her time.

"We're…uh…I'm pregnant."

"Omigod!" I yelled without even thinking then slapped my hand over my mouth before I said anything else. Gitta wasn't much younger than me. I was stunned.

"Wow, man, good deal! Congratulations, you stud, you," Simon jumped in, pumping Jerry's hand.

"I'm going to *cry*," Larry choked, dabbing at his eyes. "An engagement *and* the pitter patter of little feet, all happening at our house. Imagine, Drake, at our age! We get to buy those expensive Natural Wonder toys down at the market and those darling little fur-lined moccasins!"

"Now we don't need to get a *dog!"* Drake laughed. "We can pour our cuteness attacks into a tiny boopsie-kins and spoil her rotten. Kids, this is *wonderful* news!"

"Gitta, are you feeling alright?" I recovered myself enough to ask, calculating her age and the risk factors.

"Oh, good Lord," Larry cried, swinging into action, "of course, what am I *thinking?* Omigod, I feel like Dick Van Dyke all of a sudden. Gitta, sit down, sit down, put your feet up, let me get you an ottoman, no, take this chair, it's much better, better back support. And no booze for you, young lady."

Drake took Gitta's untouched Mimosa and replaced it with fresh juice.

"I feel fine. I'm on all the pre-natal vitamins, and the morning sickness is almost gone, too. The specialist says I should be fine but there's a lot of extra precautions anyway. We've looked into the whole thing. The amnio says the baby's fine. We're gonna sell my house and get a place together, start the marriage with this new life. I feel so…honored to be given another chance, to do it over again. We certainly didn't *ask* for this or plan it but this baby must want very badly to be born."

"Why do you say that?" I wondered, thinking people get pregnant all the time.

"Jerry had a vasectomy years ago. He didn't want to procreate with his unbalanced wife."

Jerry nodded his head and shrugged his shoulders, smiling proudly despite himself.

"You'll be….how old when the kid graduates from high school?"

"Just…old. No matter. Life put this in our path so we're going with it. If my age makes me lose the baby, then so be it. But we'll protect it as fiercely as we can."

"What a wonderful story," Larry sniffed.

"You can order from Hanna Anderson again!" I laughed. "Her boys had *the* most stylish baby clothes of anyone I'd ever seen."

"They're Scandinavian clothes, bright colors, really practical, all cotton." Gitta smiled.

"I hope it's a girl," I said, wishing for a Gitta mini-me.

"Birgitte," Simon said, smiling a bit. "This means you have a granddaughter who will be older than your own child."

"Yup. Ariel's great-aunt or uncle will be younger than her."

"Well, we'll sort all that out as we go along," Jerry said, squeezing Birgitta's shoulders.

Her *tits* looked bigger, now that I thought about it. That's why she looked different. No wonder Simon noticed.

Jerry changed the attention back to us.

"So, Simon, how long have you been planning this wedding?"

"I meant it when I said I saw Annalee on t.v. and I *knew.*"

"Me, too. I saw Gitta and I had to have her."

Jerry kissed the top of Gitta's silky head.

Simon squeezed my hand.

"I was thinking instead of a big-ass ring, we could buy another house, Al. I have the GI Bill, which means I get a good loan. You want real estate or a ring?"

Simon grinned at me. He knew what I'd say. We *loved* to look at the real estate ads, and sometimes dropped in on Sunday open houses for fun.

"I'll take the house, for sure. Can we rent mine out? I want to keep it for the kids. They grew up there. So did I, really. We can get a gold band. And let's go to Victoria. That sounds nice."

"Cinnamon rolls are ready, everyone." Larry clapped his hands and ordered us to grab a plate. We were going to lounge all around the comfy living room furniture instead of formally dining at table. Everything was spread buffet style, and it all looked marvelous.

"Wait!" Drake yelled suddenly as we headed toward the gorgeous translucent green china plates. I wondered for a split second if he was going to pray.

We all stood still, waiting as he ran to the other room and came back, fiddling with a camera.

"Seconds away, hold on," he said. "Now stand back there by the table, Jerry, you and Simon in back since you're taller, and Larry, take off your apron and stand between the girls. Leave a slot for me to crouch below, hang on, I'm setting the timer and…go!" he said, tearing off his apron and rushing to get into the picture before the timer went off, all of us frozen in place.

"Say Farrah Fawcett-Majors!" Larry sang as the flash went off and the house phone rang.

Picture done, Drake answered the phone.

"Well, what excellent timing," he said into the phone, then held it up in the air. "Hey, everybody, it's Malcolm!"

My seniority got me five days off for our MLK Day wedding.

The honors were done at Larry's lovely home by a mail-order Universal Life minister, perfectly legal in Washington. Simon wore a white Nehru jacket with engraved brass buttons going all Ben-Casey down one side. My street-length black velvet wedding dress had an open back and a lot of leg show and the black ostrich feather comb in my hair lent an exotic air.

Gitta was my witness, her baby bump starting to show on her tiny frame.

Malcolm the best man flew in alone to sign off on our marriage license as a witness, kiss the bride and slap Simon on the back.

Jerry, Larry and Drake stood nearby, everyone dressed to the nines.

Simon's two children Will and Suzette, as well as my own two, had cheerily wished us well by phone. None of them could get the time off. Someday we would all be in the same room, a sudden family-by-marriage.

.

The Blue Canoe catered our little party at Larry's so no one would have to cook and we even got an employee discount on account of Malcolm. He regaled us with wild Alaskan tales all starting with "Swear to God, this really happened…"

Malcolm's wife Bernie was enjoying braving the elements with two big Malamutes and being out in the toolies, he said, as long as they had high-speed internet and UPS deliveries. She had to shop, no matter where she lived. I imagined Alaska required a whole new wardrobe, which had probably made her really happy.

"She really wanted to come," Malcolm said and we all nodded, but we knew it wasn't true. She hadn't fit well into the group, coming in too late, Malcolm's role carved out without her. Frankly, we were relieved to see him alone, brash and ribald, the man he was when she wasn't around, telling exaggerated stories of the last frontier.

It was also nice to see Malcolm from my wonderful new vantage point as his old friend's newly-minted wife. I took his hand across the table.

"Thanks for introducing us, Malcolm," I told him. "You got me a husband, just like you said you would. Made an honest woman out of me."

"And a captain of industry at that, mama. Man, you gonna take care of this little lady in the style in which she'd like to become accustomed?" Malcolm wise-cracked, taking his hand away from me and slapping Simon on the arm.

"She can have it any way she wants it, long as she keeps cookin' for me. Jesus, have you tasted her cookies? Or her cheesecake?"

"Why, yes I have," Malcolm slyly said, his mouth moving a toothpick to one side and avoiding my gaze so hard I could feel it.

The two men locked eyes.

A pissing contest could start, if they wanted to get into it, depending on everyone's attitude. We'd all had a few drinks.

I waited without moving, the two alpha males staring each other down over a food allegory.

Simon leaned forward, looking Malcolm in the eye.

"And its *fine,* ain't it brother?" he smiled, his eyes sparkling. They stared a second longer. "Too bad you already married or you'd have kept her sweet ass for your own!"

Both men burst out laughing and shook hands across the table.

"You a'ight, man, I don't care what ever'body say," Malcolm teased him.

"Yeah, I gotcha, brother. I'll help pull you up outta that mess you call a life. What the fuck you doin' in Alaska anyway? Only brother for five hundred miles, I'll bet."

" 'Member how you took Home Ec to be around all the girls? Well, my friend, it's a black man's wet dream up there. White women every-fucking-where and how many brothers? My dick thinks it died and went to *heaven.* Looking only. But heaven, man."

The braided gold wedding band was just the right weight on my finger. It felt so new that it distracted me when I held a steering wheel and when I wrote, my fingers hitting the wrong keys. Covered with dish suds it practically twinkled at me. My thumb kept twirling it around and around.

I loved being married.

Suddenly I was Mrs. CWO4 Ret. Simon Battles and it was wonderful. It felt weighty, a title legally connecting me to a man of means.

I was exactly the same person but as a lesbian I hadn't had the same right. It angered me that Larry and Drake couldn't have what we had: next of kin spousal status. Because we were allowed an ecclesiastical pronouncement and a signed register at City Hall, The Defense of Marriage Act accorded Simon and me any or all of the

"...total of 1,138 federal statutory provisions classified to the United States Code in   which marital status is a factor in determining or receiving benefits, rights, and privileges..."

I had also married a retired military man, giving me even *more* benefits and privileges.

If Simon dropped dead, I had his benefits and pension for the rest of my natural life.

The world felt easier as a married woman, buffered by a strong support. My brain rested in his butch skill-set, comfortable knowing that no electrical malfunction, roof leak or car breakdown was too big for him to repair, no gizmo at Home Depot too hard to find. Sunday mornings would be full of sex and afterward, pajamas in the living room to read the paper. We'd confidently push forward together, a united front, socially stroked for being part of the mainstream.

Everything felt…lighter.

"She's doing somersaults in the middle of the night and waking me up. And her kicks are like clockwork, four a.m. I haven't had a night's sleep all the way through in two months. It's like she's making sure I know she's coming."

Gitta was rubbing her basketball of a belly, her long blond hair resting on her swollen breasts. She couldn't drink coffee so we were having hot cider. The chilly spring rains were pouring downtown.

Two more months to go before the rest of us could meet Inga but Gitta seemed to know her well already.

"Jerry can't wait. She'll be his first child."

"His ex-wife was kinda off the deep end, wasn't she?"

"Yup. Fortunately he learned a lot about dysfunction in the first marriage so he came pre-therapized."

"Simon, too. Requires very little tuning. Isn't it nice?"

"It's nice to be so happy. Our kitchen cabinets are getting put into the new house this weekend and Jerry's painting the nursery a warm yellow with duckies everywhere. It's so sweet. I love the tiny baby clothes! And the maternity clothes now are actually attractive. Remember the smocked blouses with the Peter-Pan white collars we had to wear? It's way different than when we were having kids back in the day. How's your house hunt?"

Simon had moved into my place when we married, leaving most of his stuff in boxes in Peanut's old room until we found a place of our own.

"Not bad. Lots down south where we're comfortable, but the prices are climbing. We haven't got that big a down payment, just our tax returns, but I think we'll find something soon. He wants to live near the water and that's out of range. I want more bedrooms so I can have an office. It's hard to write now with someone else in the house. I've lived alone for a long time. That's the only thing that's hard about being married. He never goes home."

"I have hardly any time to think about it. Between work, doctor appointments and trying to get enough rest, I barely have a minute to remember what it was like to be un-pregnant and un-married. Sometimes I want to take the pregnancy off for a minute, set it aside and go do a few things. It feels like an alien eating me alive from the inside."

"Everything okay, though? No problems so far?"

"Nope. Gonna be fine."

"How's the boys? How's Ariel?"

"The boys are still stuck in the war machine. I am afraid to read the paper. They're freaked out at having a little half-sister but they'll get over it. Ariel's got a new tooth, from what the group email said, and the picture was cute in a Kmart kind of way. I'll get used to being a grandmother, I guess. How's Dew?"

"Like nothing ever happened."

"And Peanut?"

"Loves the gardening gig. She's cut back on school, going part time now. I think she wants to drag it out, make it last."

"Nothing wrong with that."

"When's Inga due again?"

"End of April."

"You'll do fine."

"I better. I'm too old to screw this up. Larry is hiring me to work at the Foundation as his Girl Friday. I can draw a salary while I am lounging around in my pajamas, answering the phone for him and opening mail. I left my "real" job and now I'll be able to bring the baby to work. He's just trying to shield my pride, since he has offered to support me completely and I'd feel so useless that way, so he proposed I have a title and a position, though it really means very little. It just preserves my working dignity, is all. And I like the idea of being a Girl Friday."

"So you quit your job to stay home and work part-time for Larry?"

"Yes ma'am. Careful what you wish for."

"I'm envious. I hate FedEx and working outside. I get so tired all the time and I want to have time to create. I know I can make a go of writing for money if I had the time. Working is wearing me out."

"It'll happen, darling."

"I make a mean cheesecake, too, so I may get a little bakery thing going on in the meantime. Try to bring down real money doing something I like. I can rent commercial kitchen space. Already wrote the business plan."

"And it will be called…?"

"Baked In Seattle."

"Love the double entendre! Sounds perfect."

"I just wanna grow tomatoes," Peanut exhaled into the phone.

"Please think about finishing college. Remember your mother? How she works 12 hours a day at a manual labor job because she never went to college?"

"You make good money at FedEx, Mommy. I make okay money growing tomatoes and I'm happy. Weren't you happy working for FedEx?"

Happy humping sixty-pound boxes in the freezing rain up a loading dock ramp or three flights of Pioneer Square stairs? Not unhappy, really, since I could eat whatever I wanted and not fluctuate in weight. I stayed strong. I worked alone in my own head, no boss shouting in my ear once I left the building in the morning. My flight benefits had given me visitation when the children were small that I never would have been able to swing.

But had I had a degree? Shit, I'd have taught school so as to be on the childrens' school schedule. Or I'd have gone into journalism, writing for a living. Or a million other things that open easily when you can say yes, you are a college graduate.

A high school diploma got me locked into a grueling profession that ate every muscle and bone in the body. Running on adrenalin, Starbucks, road rage and impossible deadlines, my job demanded functioning at a crisis level, making sudden adjustments for weather, late freight, or traffic impediments. On my right hip was my FedEx scanner, clipboard and my pager, my corporate ID was on a lanyard around my neck and in my pockets were pens, door tags, a two-inch thick Service Reference Guide, mints, lipstick, dog treats, my driver's license and Fitness For Duty state medical examiner ID. I carried a huge FedEx blue bag filled with my purse, enough food and drink for the 12-hour day, my FedEx sweater and raincoat, a spare pair of dry socks, a spare inhaler, two rolls of Astra printer labels, and my lunchtime novel. My office was a 1992 Grumman with a diamond-plate floor, every surface covered in thick, oily dust. I made seven dollars less an hour than unionized UPS drivers.

"Please think about finishing college, Peanut."

"I'ma take a break, Mom. Everything's gonna be fine. I have my own health insurance now that I'm an assistant manager. You found your way. I will, too, okay? Stop worrying."

"You talked to your brother lately?"

"Yes, last night. He's coming up next weekend to visit the dog. We share custody."

Peanut giggled.

"Well, it's important you put your differences aside and do what's best for the dog," I said dryly.

She laughed out loud.

"Long as Dew doesn't go crazy again and give him mushrooms like last time. What are you writing these days, Mommy?"

"Nothing much. Still adjusting to the new marriage. I don't have a room or an alone-space to write so nothing's coming to me. It goes underground. We're looking for a new house. It'll happen."

Time gently passed. Drake's wounds finally healed. Inga couldn't wait to be born, making The Seattle Times since she was delivered by Jerry and a doctor in the next car while the Ballard Bridge was up. Malcolm kept promising to visit.

We decided to stay at the little house.

I'd gotten the place over a decade before, full of cobwebs and broken glass and had worked hard to make it a showplace, down to the antique lace curtains I'd bought once upon a time. It was absolutely as charming as the first time I'd walked in the front door and I hoped that Simon liked living here with me. I figured he'd claim it more as his own once he swung a sledgehammer through a wall or two to build his long-awaited addition. Bring it on, I said to myself. He would only improve the place.

And hadn't I gone full-circle, wanting a handsome man at the hardware store to share my little dream house, and poof, here we were?

"Happy?" Simon asked, as he gathered an armload of firewood to warm the place up. It was raining buckets and staying home sounded great.

"What do you want to do about dinner? And yes, very happy," I said, looking out the front window at the property, blurred by rain and grey skies.

"I want it to magically appear. Let's call out for pizza," he kissed my head.

My phone rang.

"Al, it's Gitta. You guys busy tomorrow for brunch? Drake and Larry want us all over there. Inga has a new tooth and she sorta crawls now, if you help her."

"How's the cats?"

Both kids wanted to know, swapping out custody of the dog and calling me together on speaker phone.

"Great. I think they're happy. They're getting their winter coats."

"I'm going back to school, Mom," Peanut said. "Winter quarter."

"Honey, that's wonderful."

"I'm still gonna be part-time at the garden center."

"Do what you have to."

"I'm gonna go to grad school, Mom, I decided," Dew chimed in.

"Man, is it the water back there or what? I think this is great."

"Well, I thought maybe I'd just prolong paying back my loans as long as possible."

"Then you can get a PhD after that!"

"I could conceivably go to school forever, then, right?"

"Entirely possible."

"Well, I'm gonna stick with one degree."

Peanut didn't want to keep going.

"Either way. You guys know what's best for your own selves."

"I'ma be down there in two weeks, Al. I want to see you and shake that motherfucker's hand. He got a good job, sounds like."

Simon had a new gig at Fort Lewis, a civilian logistics job. "Now you can kick back and write a little bit. I hope you told FedEx to suck your dick."

"Malcolm, that company did me a lot of good over the years. I don't know why you diss them all the time."

"They liked you better when you were dykey. And they worked you to the bone and paid you shit."

"Well….I got along okay. But yes, I did tell them goodbye after all those years. Simon can support the show for a while and I'll see if I can write something worth a damn while I start the little cheesecake business."

"You can smoke paca-lolo now that you're no longer employee number 54526, is that right?"

I could hear the smile in his voice.

"Why, yes I can," I grinned into the phone. "Looking forward to seeing you, babe."

"I'll bring you a little sumpum-sumpum. Love the bakery name."

Larry's Capitol Hill home had never looked lovelier. In fact, everything about Seattle seemed to glisten and sparkle, washed in the morning rains. Fall morning sweater weather gave way to four o'clock short-sleeved sunshine, leaves alive in red and gold.

Drake ran to the foyer as we rang the front porch bell, his bare feet slapping on the radiant-heat wood floors. Flinging the door open, he threw his arms around both Simon and me, howling with joy.

"How are you, darling? You're absolutely skeletal, very Kate Hepburn. And Simon, you're hunky as ever. Lemme hug that barrel chest one more time!"

"How are you, Drake," Simon grinned. "And how's that partner of yours? Still doing good deeds with old family money?"

"He is giving it away as fast as he can, helping everyone he can get his hands on. Senior services for the gay community is his new thing. Ask him about it over the smoked whitefish he got especially for Miss Thing here."

"Smoked fish? Really?"

My eyes lit up. I hoped there were bagels and thinly sliced onions. I heard a little voice cooing behind me, soft and baby-like.

"Look at that child! She's a perfect angel!" I shrieked as Gitta and Jerry came up the walk, a blond vision in Jerry's arms. Inga was Gitta's little mini-me in tights, and her matching hat and muff in red velvet made her achingly cute.

Gitta and I hugged as the fellows all pumped hands and patted backs. Inga reached her arms out for Simon, deciding he was worthy of her princess attention and there she would stay for the course of the afternoon, never leaving his side.

"Why are you all still out here on the porch? Am I heating all of outdoors? Goodness gracious, Drake, let the people come inside!" Larry scolded, wiping his hands on a lime-green full-body apron as he came to the front door. "Ladies and gentlemen and princess Inga, please come in the house and try my hot highly-mulled cider." He kissed the baby on both her red cheeks. "I have hot, well, *warm* chocolate for *you*, Buttercup, I don't care what your parents say about it, it's a special occasion. Oh, it's so good to see you, Al. Now, Inga, my little lamb, you need to unlock your arms from around Simon's neck for just a weensy little moment-o and come see my new puppy Cuppy. He's about as big as a teacup and he will lick your little nose. Drake, be a lamb and take the coats into the music room, please."

Larry carried Inga to the kitchen with a wink.

"Something smells awesome," Jerry said, cuddling Gitta in what looked like a rare moment without their daughter between them.

"I think it's ham," I said, sniffing the air and looking around in wonder at my friends all in one room.

"Okay, cocktails, everyone," Drake clapped his hands, pointing at the bar in the corner. We all bellied up, our arms around each other's waists, happy to see one another again. Gitta pressed her hand into mine.

"Yes, cheers," Larry sang, his hand on Inga's head as she sat in front of him holding a blue rhinestone-covered leash. The tiniest dog I had ever seen was happily bouncing around in front of the blond baby girl. It's little toenails tink-a-tinka-ed on the hard wood, sounding like Huckleberry Hound on tip-toe. A pink bow blossoming around the neck dwarfed the little pooch's head.

"This, everyone, is our newest arrival, Candy Coated Streamlined Baby Cupcake a la'Orange, aka Cupcake, aka Cuppy. Isn't she the sweetest? Drake got her for my birthday and I could not have been more surprised!"

"You *said* you wanted exercise equipment."

"And she's just the thing, Drake, darling. I will burn calories as I shop for all her newest accoutrements. Now, let's eat, shall we? The ham is finally ready, and I have that smoked chubb for you, Annalee, with some bagel minis and onions and swiss cheese. Inga, let's put Cuppy in her little bed, right over there by the fireplace, that's a girl. Isn't it sweet? Pink satin, just like her bow. I have a high chair, Gitta, to make it easier for you to enjoy your meal with Miss Angel-food Herself. She is about the prettiest child I have ever seen. The dimples are amazing, very Campbell's Soup Kid. Does Inga eat smoked fish? She better, she's Scandinavian. Simon, can you press play on the CD player? I have Lani Hall all cranked up and ready. Good Lord, we have missed you seeing you all in one room!"

"Cheers," Simon said, raising his glass. "To good friends and long journeys."

"It's about a group of people like us."

"Like us? What us?"

We were smoking grass as we walked along Zenith Point. The tide was rolling out and there was at least half a mile of exposed sea-bottom, the seagulls yanking anemones out of the ground and dropping shells to crack them open. A brisk breeze blew in off the water, making the rocky shore ours alone. Malcolm passed me the joint and stared off into the horizon. He'd brought some killer smoke from Anchorage.

Enjoying the fullness in my lungs, I suddenly flashed on being 75 and still scoring pot, probably from some neighborhood kid in a furtive night-time deal. I answered slowly.

"Us like…you and me and our friends. Our partners. Our adventures. I think other people would want to read about it. We're interesting, aren't we?"

"Interesting, sure, but read-able? Maybe. Women'd read it." Malcolm smiled. "White women."

"I don't care who reads it long as someone buys it. I want to get published and bought."

"Why? What's your motive?"

Simon had said take the leap off the cliff. Staying in the little house made it possible for me to stop working. Simon had said What the fuck, if not now, then when? We can live on what I make. Say yes. He'd made me promise.

"My motive? I want to make money in my pajamas."

Malcolm choked with laughter, the smoke bursting out of his lungs. He pounded his chest as he recovered from the laughing, coughing fit.

"I know, I know," I smiled, watching him wipe tears from his eyes as the laughter subsided. "I know what image came to *your* mind. You follow your dick through life. I'm too fucking old to turn tricks. I want money to come right to my mailbox. Words can do that. I'm gonna give it a try."

"With people like us?"

I took the elbow of his Navy pea coat as we crunched out to the tidepools.

"Yes. About good friends. With people like us. I love you, motherfucker. Without you I never would have met my husband."

"Without you…lessee….I never would have gotten to watch you transform from a mullet-headed hippie to a long-neck swan. And I got to fuck a dyke. Wouldna had *that* without you."

There was a long pause as we walked along the slippery rocks. I knew he was gonna ask so I waited. He was a hetero man, he couldn't help it.

"He as good as me?"

I laughed. Malcolm himself had taught me there was only one right answer here. "Almost, babe."

"Alright, just checkin.' You happy for real?"

"You shittin' me? I'm solid, Malcolm. Seriously, thanks to you. That man is my perfect match. Good thing you weren't available."

"Fuck you."

"Fuck you, too, man."

Malcolm pulled me under his arm, side-hugging me as we walked along.

www.ingramcontent.com/pod-product-compliance
Lightning Source LLC
Chambersburg PA
CBHW021432110726
47901CB00008B/2390